A ROYAL ELOPEMENT

The Young Royals Book 5

EMMA LEA

Cover design by Michelle Birrell
Book design and production by Michelle Birrell
Cover photograph by tomertu
Licensed by Adobe Stock

❀ Created with Vellum

OTHER BOOKS BY EMMA LEA

This is Emma Lea's complete book library at time of publication, but more books are coming out all the time. Find out every time Emma releases something by going to her website (www.emmaleaauthor.com) and signing up for her New Release Alerts.

SWEET ROMANCES

These are romantic tales without the bedroom scenes and the swearing, but that doesn't mean they're boring!

The Young Royals

A Royal Engagement

Lord Darkly

A Royal Entanglement

A Royal Entrapment

A Royal Expectation

A Royal Elopement

Bookish Book Club Novellas

Meeting Prince Charming

Broken Arrow Trilogy

Broken

Cursed

Eternal

SWEET & SEXY ROMANCES

In my Sweet & Sexy Romances I turn up the heat with a little bit of sexy. No swearing, or very minimal swearing, and brief, tasteful and not too graphic bedroom scenes.

Love, Money & Shoes Series

Walk of Shame

Strictly Business

Skin Deep

In The Money

All At Sea

Love, Money & Shoes Novellas

The Five Year Plan

Summer Fling

Standalone Novels

Amnesia

HOT & SEXY ROMANCES

Hot & Spicy Romances turn the heat way up. They contain swearing and sexy scenes and the characters get hot under the collar.

Recommended for 18+ readers

TGIF Series

Girl Friday

Black Friday

Good Friday

Twelve Days

Twelve Days of Christmas - Her Side of the Story

Twelve Days of Christmas - His Side of the Story

ABOUT THIS BOOK

Lady Meredith Bingham thought that she had her life sorted. She was a member of the royal guard - an elite security team tasked with protecting the queen of Merveille. She was also close personal friends with the queen and part of her inner circle - the ladies in waiting. But then her mother had to go and ruin it all. Lady Caroline Bingham was sick of her daughter fooling around and playing soldier. She thought it was high time her daughter got serious about her future and found herself a suitable husband. With the duke pulling double duty as the country's prime minister, it was only right that his daughter start acting like a proper daughter of nobility. Much to Meredith's chagrin, the queen agrees that Meredith must step down from her post.

Prince Christophe Kostopolous was a prince in exile. For the last ten years he had been living under the pseudonym of Jamie Kosta, and for the last seven years he has been part of the royal guard. Very few people knew his true identity, but that was all about to change. The people he had been hiding from all these years have found him and he may finally have his chance to reclaim his rightful place on the throne of his small island nation of Kalopsia. The only problem is, he has fallen for a certain duke's daughter and she has no idea who he really is.

AUTHOR'S NOTE

The Young Royals takes place in a country that doesn't really exist. If it were to exist it would sit on the eastern edge of France bordered by Switzerland and Italy, quite close to Geneva. The country of Merveille (pronounced Mer-VAY) is a quiet, wealthy place ruled by a constitutional monarchy. It's capital city is Calanais which is situated on the shores of a beautiful lake called Lac Merveilleux and is where the palace, named Château de Conte de Fées, sits.

DEDICATION

To the faithful readers who contacted me at the end of 'A Royal
Expectation' demanding the next book...here 'tis.

PREVIOUSLY

Meredith

"Jamie? What are you doing?"

"Come on," he said, tugging my hand as we escaped from the palace and snuck into a dark part of the gardens.

It was thrilling, this secret liaison between us, and we had been lucky so far that we hadn't been caught. As the daughter of the prime minister and a duke, my dalliance with a security guard would probably not go down well. Jamie was more than just a security guard though, we both were. As part of the queen's personal security team, we were highly trained bodyguards who were prepared to step in front of a bullet to save the life of our sovereign. This was a fact that my mother hated with a passion.

It took a minute for my eyes to adjust to the darkness after the bright lights of the palace, but the soft lapping of the water gave me some indication of where we were. There was a small dock in the shadow of the castle where the stone walls sunk into the lake. I felt the wooden boards under my feet as we walked out onto the short pier, the sky a dome of midnight blue velvet above us. I took a deep breath of the cool, fresh air and smiled as Jamie trailed a hand over my cheek and down my neck.

He kissed me then and I sighed into him. We saw each other every day, almost every hour of every day, but it was so very rare for us to be completely alone. It had started out as some harmless flirting and then one day when we had been sparring together he kissed me. I was ashamed to admit that it was my first kiss. As the queen's companion and bodyguard, I hadn't had all that much time to date and men found me intimidating anyway. Maybe it was the fact that I knew forty-seven different ways to kill a man without using a weapon that scared them off. Or maybe it was the fact that I could bench press more than them. Not everyone appreciated the muscles that I had spent time cultivating, but fortunately Jamie did.

He lifted his head and looked down at me with a crooked smile on his face. The man was gorgeous. He had the real boy-next-door look going on and with his sense of humour and love of life, it was hard not to be attracted to him. It was a pity that it would never work out in the long run. I had mostly escaped the trappings of being a duke's daughter by first becoming Alyssa's companion when we were children, and then convincing my father to let me train at the academy to be one of her bodyguards. At the time it had seemed like a logical thing to do, to have one of Alyssa's friends also double as a guard, and thankfully my father had seen the sense in it despite my mother's protests. I was grateful for his foresight because I loved my job and I didn't want it to be taken away from me, although inevitably it would be.

I would eventually have to take a husband and I would be expected to marry well. My parents had not been so draconian as to try and find a husband for me but I knew that Jamie would not fit the bill. He was not nobility and therefore unsuitable for a duke's daughter. I thought the whole thing was a bunch of poppycock, but I didn't exactly have a say in the matter. Besides, Jamie and I were just having fun - neither of us had made a commitment to one another. With our jobs being the most important thing in our lives, I doubted either of us was prepared to give it up for the sake of a relationship. That would be what would have to happen. One of us would have to step down from the security detail and I knew neither one of us wanted to do that.

"Are you looking forward to our little field trip next week?' Jamie asked as he wrapped his arms around me and pulled me close.

"A month on a yacht visiting the tropical islands? Nah, it's not really my scene."

His laugh rumbled through his chest and made me tingle. "Yeah, me either," he said.

The queen and prince were starting their tour in a week's time. We would be away from the palace for a month and would be traveling by yacht, visiting the islands dotted around the Mediterranean. We would travel to Monaco first for a royal visit with the Prince of Monaco. We would then board the yacht, or fleet of yachts as the case may be, and travel to a small island owned by Merveille. We would spend a few nights there and then begin the tour of the islands off the coast of Spain and the Balearic Sea.

"I am looking forward to having some down time on Le Beau."

"I never understood why they named an island 'beautiful man'," Jamie said.

I chuckled. "It's because of the natives on the island. Apparently they're beautiful."

"It's still a stupid name." He was silent for a moment. "Are you going to hit the casinos?"

"I thought I might," I replied. "Are you?"

"Maybe... maybe we could go together."

"I'd like that," I whispered.

The island of Le Beau was kind of like the Las Vegas of Merveille. It was a popular destination for bachelor parties and girls' weekends. I had never been and I was really looking forward to seeing what all the fuss was about.

A giggle floated down to us from the garden terraces above and we both stiffened and lifted our heads to listen.

"We should get out of here before we're seen," I whispered.

Jamie pulled me hard up against his chest and kissed me fiercely, fogging my brain and making me breathless. And then he was gone, melting into the darkness and leaving me alone on the pier, stunned by the force of emotions that had swept over me with his kiss. I couldn't be falling for him, I just couldn't.

Jamie

I HAD BEEN IGNORING THE MESSAGE ON MY PHONE FOR THE PAST half an hour, but I couldn't ignore it anymore. I wanted to see Meredith one last time, just in case the meeting I was about to go into had the expected outcome. I had always known that it would happen one day, I just hadn't thought it would be so soon. Not that ten years in exile was exactly soon. Maybe it was more the fact that now that I had initiated a relationship with Meredith, I wasn't ready for it to be over.

I took a deep breath and tapped on the door. At the spoken command from inside, I entered.

"Benjamin," I said, acknowledging my immediate superior. "Von Bartham."

Both men nodded to me. "Prince Christophe." Von Bartham returned and I sighed audibly.

"Has it happened then?" I asked.

Benjamin sat forward in his chair and leaned his elbows on his desk. "No," he said. "Your father is still imprisoned, but there has been chatter."

"They know where I am," I said feeling the familiar frustration. I had been avoiding the traitorous insurgents for ten years. They had taken my father hostage and had murdered my mother and sisters. I had been lucky enough to escape and I had been biding my time in the hope of finally being able to reclaim the throne of my country.

"Yes," Benjamin said.

"I told Freddie not to include me in his wedding party," I said with a growl of frustration.

I had been so careful and Freddie was one of the very few people who knew who I really was. We had become close friends, not that anyone would know about it. I assumed Alex would know the truth now. Freddie had warned me he wouldn't be keeping any secrets from her. I had only asked that he waited until they were married. The last thing I wanted was for the entire palace to know my secret. Now it seemed it wouldn't matter. The cat, as they say, was out of the bag.

"So what do you want me to do?" I asked, resigned to fleeing in the middle of the night before anyone could drag me back to stand trial in what would be a farce of the judicial system.

The rebels who had attacked the palace on the small island that was my home were more corrupt than they accused my family of being. I hated to think what had become of the island paradise that I had once called home. My heart bled for the people I had left behind, but my hands were tied. I couldn't reclaim what was mine until we found a weakness in their forces and so far none had become evident. Many had branded me a coward for running away, and perhaps they were right. My father had urged me to run and I had only been a mere boy of fifteen at the time. He had promised me that by running, I would live to fight another day. Alyssa's father, King Edward, had been friends with my father and had offered me sanctuary. I had been secreted out of my country and sequestered in the castle of Merveille until the immediate danger had passed. When Von Bartham suggested I join the royal guard, I jumped at the chance. Spending time in America while Alyssa attended Harvard had further distanced me from the troubles at home. No one knew what had happened to me and many speculated that I was dead, a fact that the rebels touted to be the truth and to be at their hands.

"I want you to stick with the plan," Benjamin said. "Go on tour with Alyssa. Get lost on Le Beau for a while. Keep your head down. Von Bartham will monitor the situation from here and we will do what we can to remove any photos of you in the wedding party that might surface."

"And the rest of the guard? Are they to finally find out the truth about who I am?"

Benjamin studied me with his shrewd eyes before shaking his head with a sigh. "No. Not yet. This might all blow over and then we would have compromised your identity for nothing. We won't say anything for now."

"Does Alyssa know?" I hadn't thought to ask before. She hadn't treated me any differently, so I had just assumed the truth hadn't been revealed to her yet.

"Yes. So does Will. Alyssa was told in her security briefing after she took the crown. Will was told in his after he married her."

"And they are okay with me continuing on with the tour? Won't having me there increase the security risks?"

Von Bartham and Benjamin shared a look. "We don't think so. We will keep your duties out of the spotlight. You won't be visible at any of their public appearances and..."

"And what?"

Benjamin sighed. "We want you and Meredith to pose as decoys for Alyssa and Will."

I scoffed. "Meredith has bright red hair and looks nothing like the queen."

"A wig, some dark glasses. They are of a similar height and build. It was always part of the plan, and it is something that she has been trained for."

"And me? A wig and dark glasses?"

Benjamin nodded. "And some decent clothes." He smiled trying to lighten the situation. I wasn't known for my stylish dressing, something that had become a bit of a joke around the palace.

"Okay," I said, drawing in all the frustration and residual anger that seemed to be my constant companion.

I didn't think this would end well, but maybe I would finally be able to do something to help my people. Maybe this whole ordeal was finally going to come to a head.

CHAPTER 1

Meredith

I grunted with the impact of hitting the floor. It was not in the least bit romantic or lady-like. I didn't care.

Before he could get a good hold on me, I rolled to the side and sprung to my feet. I bounced a few times as I watched him move out of my reach. The smile on my face was wide. My heart beat strongly in my chest from the exertion and my lungs bellowed as I sucked in air. I felt good. I felt alive. This was what I was born to do and I was amongst the lucky few who actually had the opportunity to live their dream.

"Had enough?" I asked as Jamie got to his feet.

The training room was empty except for the two of us. This had become a ritual of sorts. A way to wind down at the end of the day with the added bonus of spending some uninterrupted alone-time together. There was also the fact that nobody would think it suspicious. No one would suspect that the two of us were seeing each other even though we spent every night together in the training room after our shifts had ended.

Jamie grinned slowly at me and I had to suppress a shiver. The man was far too cute for his own good. He had height and reach on me, strength too, but he wasn't overly large and muscle-bound like some of the guys. That's not to say he wasn't built. Like seriously built. His dark blonde hair was cropped short and he had a well-trimmed beard. It was his eyes though that got me. Every. Single. Time. They were grey and when he was smiling like he was right now, they were almost silver. I'd seen them turn dark and stormy and I might have to admit that that's when I liked them best. It might be because they turned that dark colour just before he kissed me - which was infrequently.

"Just letting you regroup, *agapoúla mou*," he said as he prowled toward me.

I knew that Jamie had Greek heritage, but we didn't talk much about his family - or mine for that matter. We joined the royal guard at the same time and had been training together for as long as I could remember, although it was only recently that our relationship had changed. We had always been friends, now we had slipped into something more. Something I wasn't yet willing to analyse. Something we weren't prepared to make public. We could both lose our jobs if the current state of our relationship became known.

"You know I'm winning, right?" I said as we circled each other.

Jamie may be bigger and stronger than me, but I was nimble and quick. Oh, and flexible which came in handy when we were wrestling. I couldn't help the grin that stretched my lips wide. I used to train with Alyssa, before she became queen, and we were fairly evenly matched. Since both Benjamin and Von Bartham had put a stop to our full-body-contact sparring, I had been training with the guys - Jamie more often than not. It's probably why our relationship changed. Couples that wrestled together, stayed together.

"What have I told you about counting your chickens?" Jamie said.

Before the words had even registered in my brain, he was on me. I barely had time to realise what was happening before I was lying on the ground with his body weight holding me down. I flopped about like a fish trying to dislodge his bulk, but it was to no avail. He flipped me over and locked his leg around my waist, pulling me toward his chest and then securing my arms by banding his around me. The body-triangle. My nemesis.

"Now," he breathed in my ear, "what was that you were saying about winning?"

I struggled vainly against the hold, but he had me locked up tight. We were both breathing hard. His hot breath was on my neck and it was only my pride that stopped me from melting against him. We were both sweaty and no doubt smelly and still I was having the best time. Well, apart from the fact that he had beaten me again. He knew my weakness. He knew I couldn't get out of this hold and he employed it whenever he thought I needed to be taken down a peg.

I struggled again, trying to roll us over, but he wouldn't budge. There was something about the way he moved that was deceptive and it got me every time. He lumbered, like he was slow and heavy, but it was all an act. The fact was that he moved with grace and agility that defied his size. I'd gotten cocky and miscalculated his speed - something I did far too often. You would think that all the time we spent sparring would mean that I would learn never to underestimate him and yet here I was, locked in a hold that I couldn't get out of. Again. It seemed that our after-hours training sessions always ended up with us in this exact position.

I relaxed my body, going limp in his arms. He and I both knew that he had won and that our bout was over. His hold loosened but he didn't let go of me. We sat like that on the floor, our bodies pressed close, my back to his chest, his breath in my ear. I closed my eyes. There was a war inside me. I liked this feeling of being wrapped up in him - even if we were both sweaty and smelling like a week old gym bag - but I was also annoyed. I was cranky at myself for falling for his deceptive movement and I was cranky at him for not only knowing my weakness but using it against me.

Annoyance won out.

I broke out of his hold and rolled away from him. I stood and smoothed out the body suit I wore while training. He leaned back on his arms and looked up at me, but I refused to look into those eyes that would see far more than I wanted them to.

"Meredith," he said as I walked away from him. "*Agapoúla mou,*" he said softly when I didn't answer him.

I didn't turn around to face him. I struggled to get my own

emotions under control. I felt him, rather than heard him, as he stood close behind me. His body heat seared me through the thin biometric fabric of my bodysuit. His hands landed gently on my shoulders and then slipped down my arms before tightening in a gentle grip. He spun me around so that I was facing him and tucked a finger under my chin so that I had to look up at him and into those eyes that had gone the stormy colour that I loved.

He dipped his head and brushed his lips across mine in the barest of touches. It was risky. Being together like this. Anyone could walk in and catch us. He did it again, increasing the pressure slightly and I couldn't resist. It didn't matter that I was mad at him, the way he kissed me broke through all my resistance. I kissed him back and his hands went into my hair, pulling it out of its ponytail so that it fell down in a tumble of red curls over my shoulders. I don't know why I didn't cut it all off. It would be definitely easier to manage. Jamie threaded his fingers through it as he kissed me deeper and I had my answer. He loved my hair and I loved the way he played with it.

An annoying and insistent beep sounded from the watch he wore on his wrist and he groaned as he pulled away. He pressed his forehead to mine and took a deep breath.

"I have to go," he said.

"Hot date?" I breathed, trying for levity but instead coming across as insecure and clingy.

He brushed a kiss on my forehead and sighed. "Meeting with Benjamin and Von Bartham."

"Oh?" I tilted my head back and looked up at him. "About the tour?"

Jamie shrugged as we separated and he ran his hand through his own hair making it stick up in all directions.

"Just some last minute details, I think."

"They don't want me there?" I asked. If it had to do with the tour that Alyssa and Will were about to begin then I felt I should be there.

"I think it has something to do with me impersonating Will," Jamie said, but he didn't look at me while he spoke. Instead he walked over to where his gym bag was and grabbed a towel, swiping it over his head and face.

"Oh," I replied, walking toward my own gear. "Okay well, I suppose I'll see you tomorrow then."

This bit was always awkward. When we were together we were in our own little world and things felt good, right. But when it came time to go back to the real world, things between us got awkward. I hated it. I hated that we had to keep our relationship a secret but at the same time I loved the intimacy it created. Besides, I wasn't ready to leave the guard and wouldn't ever leave it if I had the choice. There was no way our relationship could become public and both of us retain our positions. The fact was that if I wanted to be with Jamie, it would have to be in secret, grabbing stolen moments together whenever we could. It was this or nothing and right now, I was willing to make this enough.

I took a step towards the door and he reached out, taking my arm and pulling me into his body. I tilted my face up to his and he searched my eyes for a moment before lowering his head and kissing me. I closed my eyes and let the sensations flow over me, savouring them, memorising them. With a sigh, I broke the kiss and smiled up at him.

"See you tomorrow," I said and then turned and walked away, not looking back.

I WALKED INTO THE TRAINING ROOM THE NEXT DAY AND SILENCE fell. I tried not to let it worry me but it was happening more and more often. I had been part of this team from its inception. Alyssa and I were playing together as toddlers so it was only natural that I would be part of her security team. Lately, though, I felt like I was being pushed out. I'd tried to keep the fact that I was related to a duke on the down low but it was the worst kept secret in the palace. Everybody knew that I was the Duke of Monterey's daughter and ever since my dear old dad became prime minister, the guys in the team had been looking at me differently. I'd tried to ignore it. I just wanted to do my job and that meant I needed to blend into the background. That had become harder and harder to do but I'd never expected it to make the guys in the team treat me differently.

"Who drew the short straw today?" I asked as I dumped my gear bag on one of the benches that ran along the side of the room.

"Uh?" Aiden looked at me with puzzled eyebrows. He was pretty and a darn good guard but a Rhodes Scholar he was not.

"Who's up first to spar with me?" I asked, spelling it out for him.

Aiden rolled his eyes and turned back to the huddle where Cody and Scott were whispering about something. Carlos and Daniel were on duty - they had just relieved Jamie and me - and I had no idea where Benjamin was. He was the team leader and was usually present at every training session.

I shrugged and unzipped my bag. If the guys didn't want to talk to me then I wasn't going to push the issue. We had all been working together for a long time, there was no reason for me to feel insecure around them. The only new additions were Daniel and Carlos and that hadn't been until after the king and prince were killed. Carlos and Daniel were both part of the security team for the crown prince, but nobody could find fault with the way they executed their duty. What happened to the king and the prince was unprecedented and security had definitely changed since then. No one ever expected someone so close to the royal family to assassinate them. It was not something any of us were likely to forget.

The door opened and Jamie walked in, his hair still wet from his shower. I tried really hard not to ogle him. Being around him when the rest of the team was present was an exercise in discipline. Luckily I was a disciplinary master...er...a master of discipline? Whatever. The fact was that I knew how to compartmentalise. I had no trouble assigning Jamie to the compartment of team member when we were working together.

He grinned at me and my lips tipped up in an answering smile before I turned away so the others couldn't see my blush. Yep. Master of discipline, that was me.

"Where's Benjamin?" Jamie asked as he dropped his bag on the bench next to mine.

"No clue," I replied as I pulled out my water bottle. I took a mouthful before speaking again. "What's going on over there?" I indicated the huddle with a nudge of my head.

Jamie lifted his eyes to take in the three team members and his eyebrows came down in a puzzled vee between his eyes. "No idea," he said.

I stayed where I was as he lumbered over to join the huddle. I watched with my peripheral vision as I pretended to be completely engrossed in my gear. Jamie spoke to guys for a moment and then looked up and caught my eye. His face was inscrutable. I had a bad feeling that whatever was being discussed had something to do with me.

Was it paranoia to think that there was a conspiracy brewing? Or was I just narcissistic? I turned my back on the gossip huddle and tried to push the nagging feeling out of my mind. It didn't mean anything. Maybe one of them had a crush on some poor unsuspecting girl, maybe even one of the ladies in waiting. I had a foot in both camps so they definitely wouldn't want me knowing anything like that. It was an interesting thought though. I snuck a look over my shoulder and looked at the four boys who I had practically lived with for the past seven years. It went without saying that I thought Jamie was attractive, but I had never really looked at the others in that way. I suppose, if I was being objective, Aiden, Cody and Scott were good looking men. But of the unattached ladies in waiting, I didn't think any of them had a chance. Savannah was like a French poodle who would look down on them like they were gutter trash. Don't get me wrong, I loved Savannah, but I often wondered why she didn't get a crick in her neck from the way she held her nose in the air all the time. The only other unattached LIW was Margaret. Margaret the mouse. These guys would send her running for the hills if any one of them showed any interest in her.

Before I could puzzle it out any further, the training door opened and Benjamin stepped into the room. He wasn't alone.

"Listen up," Benjamin said, drawing everyone's attention. "I want to introduce you to a new member of the team."

We were all too well trained to gasp in surprise - out loud anyway. I definitely gasped internally and I have no doubt the others did too. My eyes went to the interloper and narrowed. Those feelings of paranoia rose sharp and fierce. The newcomer was a woman.

"I'd like you all to meet Danika Lazos. She will be joining the team for a probationary period after which we will decide whether she will become a permanent member."

"I didn't know we were looking for a new team member," I said. It may have come out as a little...petulant.

"I didn't realise we had to pass all our management decision by you first," Benjamin replied.

"Maybe not," I said, not backing down. "But a new team member is a big step. Especially with the tour coming up and that we don't know this chick from Adam."

Benjamin stared me down. We had a good working relationship. He was tough but fair and we had been through a lot together. When Daniel and Carlos joined the team we were all consulted. I didn't like that he was bringing in a newcomer without even mentioning it to us.

"Would you like to perform some sort of hazing ritual on me?" Danika asked. She had an odd accent that I couldn't place. "Would that make you feel better?"

"Actually yes," I replied, taking a step forward. "I don't know you. In fact I've never seen your face before, so forgive me for being a little suspicious that some unknown person is joining our team."

"Meredith—" Benjamin's voice held a warning but I didn't heed it.

"Alyssa is not only my queen but she is my best friend. I think it only right that I vet the new girl before we turn her loose on our monarchs."

Benjamin rolled his eyes but the other guys seemed to grin with anticipation.

"So what do you think would be fair?" Danika asked. "Pistols at dawn?"

I grinned...well, I bared my teeth at her. "How about a quick bout here and now unless..."

Danika shrugged off her jacket and pushed up her sleeves. "Here and now," she said, "sounds good to me."

"Unarmed," Benjamin said, catching my eye.

I gave him a sharp nod and pulled out the weapon I had holstered under my arm. I removed my shoulder holster and sheathed knife I had strapped around my thigh. Similarly, Danika removed her own holstered weapons. We circled each other on the mats.

"All of them Meredith," Benjamin called, crossing his arms across his chest.

With a harrumph, I removed the other various weaponry hidden on my person. I was good at hand to hand combat but it paid to be prepared. I made a small pile of my hardware and felt decidedly naked without it on. Benjamin gave me a nod and I turned my focus back to the new girl. Danika.

We began circling each other once more. I watched the way her body moved. She was slick with long-limbed grace. She was perhaps a little taller than me, but I definitely had more muscle mass. I wasn't bulky as in, say, Olympic weightlifting proportions, but I wasn't skin and bone either. She went to move, but I pre-empted her and got the upper hand quickly. She gave a good fight, but I had her down and pinned swiftly. I was a ninja like that. I had to be when I regularly sparred with the other men on my team. If I couldn't be as powerful or as intimidating as they were then I needed to be resourceful. Some might call it sneaky, but I liked to think of it more as being smart.

Danika tapped out of the hold and I stood, proud of myself. Benjamin smirked at me.

"Are you done?" he asked.

"For now," I replied.

"Great. So can we please get on with the rest of the training session?"

CHAPTER 2

Meredith

I was running late - an unforgivable sin - but was it more unforgivable than turning up in my training gear? I couldn't help that the training session went long. Okay, maybe it was my fault that the training session went long, but it was my job and the queen and prince's lives depended on us doing our job right. Plus, there was the new girl. I still didn't trust her. I didn't like the way she looked at Jamie - like he was dessert. I beat her in the initial sparring bout we'd had, but as I watched her through the rest of the session I wondered whether she had held back with me. The woman had skills and it kind of annoyed me. Not to mention the other guys fawned all over her. Okay, maybe fawned was the wrong word. My guys didn't fawn. But they didn't give her crap like they gave me and I know Cody went easy on her in their grappling session.

I slid into the back of the BMW that was waiting for me at the entrance to the palace. Once the door was closed and the car began to move, I took a deep breath and tipped my head back against the seat. I closed my eyes and tried to stop the raging thoughts that kept circling my brain. I was so discombobulated. Not a great way to be when I was supposed to be leaving in a couple of days on tour with the queen. We didn't expect any trouble. Well, we always expected trouble, but there had been no chatter that anything was afoot, so there were no major security concerns. But still. I needed to have my game face on. Not only would I be escorting the queen and prince on their visits, but I would also at times be impersonating her. It was something I had done when she was younger, not so much now. The whole idea was to give Alyssa and Will some moments of privacy from the press that was bound to follow them. Jamie and I would pretend to be them - not talk or do interviews - but just be seen around town enjoying the sights. That way the eyes of the world would be on us and Alyssa and Will could have some time out of the spotlight.

Which was all to say that this weird paranoid feeling that was making me jumpy needed to quit it. I couldn't afford to be distracted. This trip was too important. This was my career and I needed my head screwed on straight to make sure I did it properly.

The car came to a stop outside my parents' house and I sighed as the door was opened for me. Château de Monterey was a hulking beast of a castle complete with crenelations and murder holes. It was a fort, really. A throwback to times of war. Where the Château de Conté de Fees was a fairytale castle with whimsical turrets and fanciful stained glass windows, Château de Monterey was a battlement. It had been softened over the years with gorgeous gardens and subtle lighting. The moat had been drained and the drawbridge replaced by a regular bridge, but it was still unmistakably a battle fort that had played a pivotal role in our country's independence. But to me it was my childhood home. I had grown up here and knew its secrets. I loved its history and was proud that the Binghams had stood beside the St. Benéts for all these years. The first king had bestowed the honour of duke on my distant grand pappy and our two families had been tight ever since.

I took the stairs confidently and smiled at Norman as he opened the door for me. I didn't need an escort, I knew they would be waiting for me in Mother's favourite room. She would be sitting on her chair ready to give me the look of disapproval as soon as I entered. Not only was I late but I was wearing pants - almost as big of an unforgivable sin as being late. Two strikes to me and dinner hadn't even started yet. At least they weren't jeans, which I'd almost worn. She probably would have sent me to my rooms to change if that had been the case. It wasn't that I didn't like dresses - I wore them often - I just preferred to wear pants. There were many more places to hide weapons when you had pockets and a waist band. It was also easier to move in a well-tailored pair of pants and you didn't have to worry about flashing your unmentionables if you happen to have to do a roundhouse kick.

I heard the dulcet tones of my brother and stopped in surprise. He and Alex had only gotten married a couple of days ago, why were they here and not on their honeymoon?

"Come along Meredith," Mother called through the open door. "We are waiting for you."

"Drat," I hissed under my breath. My mother had ears like a bat. I forced a pleasant smile to my face and stepped into the room. "Good evening everyone," I said in my best duke's daughter's voice. "Please excuse my tardiness but I got caught up at work."

Mother hummed disapprovingly and I stepped up to brush her cheek with the obligatory kiss. My father pulled me into a tight hug and a smacking kiss on the top of my head and then I turned to my brother and his new wife.

"What are you two doing here? I thought you would be off on the great European adventure."

Freddie stood and pulled me into a hug. "I've got your back, sis," he whispered into my ear and then stepped back with a big grin on his face.

Alex stood too and hugged me, holding on a little longer than necessary. Why did I suddenly feel like I was going to the gallows?

"Dinner is served ma'am," a footman said from the door.

"And none too soon," Mother said as she stood. My father took her elbow and preceded the rest of us out the door.

"What's going on?" I whispered to Freddie as I walked behind him and Alex.

He looked over his shoulder at me and gave me a sad smile. "It's going to be okay Mer," he whispered back.

I swore silently in my head. I didn't like this. I didn't like it at all.

I took my assigned place at the table and the first course was served. It may only be the five of us for dinner but it was presented as if it were a banquet. Mother didn't believe in doing things by halves, not even a simple family dinner.

Once every one had tried a spoonful of the soup, my mother turned her eyes on me. "It's time, Meredith," she said.

I looked at her with a puzzled frown. "Time for what?"

She sighed and put down her spoon like I was being deliberately obtuse. She folded her hands on her lap and stared me down. "It's time for you to resign your position from the royal guard."

The spoonful of soup was halfway to my mouth when I froze. I took a beat to school my reaction - flinging the hot soup at my mother in a fit of pique would not do anything to further my cause - and slowly lowered my spoon back to the bowl.

"I'm sorry?"

My mother sighed again like the weight of the world was on her shoulders. "I have been patient. I have stood back and let this ridiculous display of rebellion go on against my better judgement. I allowed you to follow Alyssa overseas to America for four years. When she came back I thought that finally you would give up this notion that you are a body guard. But it has been nearly two years and here you are still, running around like a common enlisted soldier. It's time for it to stop."

"This is my career," I said turning to Freddie for help, but he returned my look with one of pity. I next looked to my father but there was no help to be found there either.

"No, Meredith. This was just a distraction. You are the daughter of a duke and it's high time you started acting that way. Your father is now the prime minister. Can't you see how ridiculous it is that you continue to serve on the royal guard? There are expectations that need to be met and I am at the end of my patience waiting for you to do the responsible thing."

I stood to my feet and slammed the napkin that had been on my lap on the table. "Do the responsible thing?" I tempered my voice so I wasn't yelling. I really did want to yell, though. "You don't think I'm being responsible?"

"Sit down," Mother said with a resigned sigh. "There are other people who could do your job." She said the word job like it tasted bad. "But your father only has one daughter and there are responsibilities that come with your nobility."

"Name one thing that is more important than me doing my job," I said as I sat heavily in my chair. I felt betrayed. I thought at least Freddie would stick up for me or Alex even. But the two traitors sat silent, their eyes pitying me.

"Marriage," Mother said.

"Pardon?"

"Marriage is more important than you continuing on as a royal guard. You are a duke's daughter—"

"I really don't see how being daddy's little girl has anything to do with me getting married or not. And it has nothing to do with my job. A job I love by the way, not that anyone seems to care about that."

"Kitten," Daddy started but then was shushed by Mother.

"Don't mollycoddle her," Mother said. "She needs to understand the importance of her position and her role. We are in this position because you spoiled her for far too long." Mother took a breath and then turned to me. "Meredith, you were never meant to be in the guard for this long. I allowed it when you and Alyssa were young. I even allowed it when you traipsed across the ocean to go to university with her because I thought the education would be good for you. But you were always meant to come back here and take up your position as Lady Meredith. It is even more important now, what with your father's new position and the changes that are happening in Parliament. Alyssa has paved the way for something that many women among the peers have longed for and it gives you a very unique opportunity."

"I don't understand."

Mother sighed. "Because of the changes that Alyssa is spearheading you have the unique opportunity to take up a title of your own."

"Excuse me?"

Mother rolled her eyes. "Your father is The Duke of Monterey, your brother is The Earl of Avonlea and you, my dear, are The Countess of Bellemere."

"Grandmother's title?"

Mother nodded. Her own mother had been a countess before she married The Duke of Newbury - my grandfather.

"But I don't want to be a countess," I said, looking around the table. "I'm happy as I am. More than happy."

"If you refuse the title then it will go to your cousin Amelia," Mother said, grimacing.

"She can have it," I said. I didn't particularly like Amelia but she was still welcome to my unwanted title.

"Mer," Freddie said. "It's not that simple. There are other factors to take into account—"

"I don't see how there is anything else to discuss. I don't want the title. I just want to keep doing my job."

"The queen has already informed Von Bartham that you will be stepping down." This from my father.

"What!?" I jumped to my feet again. Betrayed by my closest friend.

"Sit down Meredith."

"No. I will not sit down. I'm leaving. I need to speak to the queen."

"Meredith," Alex said, her soft voice cutting through the rising din in my mind. "You have an appointment with her tomorrow. I will be there too. There truly are things you need to know before you make your decision. Please, just take a moment and hear all the arguments before you make a choice that you can't change."

I sat back down and looked at the food on my plate. My soup had been taken away while we argued and now I stared down at a delicious looking pasta dish except that I no longer had any appetite. The past few days and the whispered conversations that stopped when I walked in the room suddenly began to make more sense. Everyone else had known that I would be axed from the guard. That's why they had been shutting me out. They knew what was about to happen and no one had felt to inform me. So much for loyalty.

I DIDN'T SLEEP MUCH AFTER THE DISASTER OF FAMILY DINNER. I dismissed my maids when I got back to the palace and drowned my sorrows in a carton of salted caramel ice cream that I pilfered from the kitchen. The rest of the night I spent planning my arguments against my forced resignation. I was royally vexed that my closest friend in the entire world had betrayed me this way. And betrayal it was. How could she make this decision without even discussing it with me? Why let my mother break the news to me? It went entirely against the friend code and I was not going to leave our meeting until I had vented all that built up anger.

I let my maids dress me the next morning. My head was too full of words and arguments to think about clothes and hair and makeup. Tamara and Chantel had been with me since I came back to Merveille and after a few false starts they had learned what I liked. I wasn't as fussy and feminine as the others in Alyssa's entourage, a fact that I'm sure my maids complained about to the other maids, but I really didn't care. This was who I was and everybody just had to live with it.

I walked toward the queen's office like I was walking to the gallows. My job was important to me. I wanted to keep it. I didn't understand why Alyssa was insisting I step down. It was out of character for her. She was all about women doing the jobs that they wanted to do. It was her whole platform in Parliament and for her to turn around and make me resign just seemed...odd.

I ignored Aiden and Cody who stood outside the door to the queen's office and stepped inside. Priscilla smiled at me from the desk outside Alyssa's door.

"She's waiting for you," Priscilla said and I nodded.

Did Priscilla know what was going on too? Of course she did, she was the queen's personal assistant. Priscilla would know more than even Alyssa knew.

I took a deep breath and then knocked lightly on the door. At Alyssa's called permission to enter, I pushed the door open and stepped inside. The office was already full of people, no doubt they had been having a powwow before I arrived on the best way to tackle the sticky situation of Meredith and her absurd notions of wanting to be independent.

"Thanks for coming," Alyssa said, all business. That let me know what the tone of the meeting would be. All business. "Have a seat."

Everyone was seated in the plush couches that took up one corner of Alyssa's large office. Von Bartham and Benjamin were present, as were Freddie and Alex.

"I understand that you know what this meeting is about?" Alyssa began.

I nodded. "My mother so kindly informed me last night that I will be resigning from the guard."

Alyssa grimaced. "I'm sorry about that," she said, her voice and her eyes softening.

"*Et tu Brute?*" I whispered before clearing my throat. "Are you?" I asked. I felt comfortable challenging Alyssa because we had been friends for so long. She was a good boss but a better friend and that was why this whole thing irked me so much. Why didn't she come to me first before making the decision?

"I wanted to talk to you before your mother did but I was over-ruled. The duke and duchess thought it better if it was to come from them."

"No," I said with a shake of my head. "It wasn't better. I'm still completely confused why you would do this. Have you lost confidence in me as one of you security team?"

"Oh god no," Alyssa said, looking to Benjamin for help.

"You're a security risk," Benjamin said, not mincing his words.

"What?"

He sighed and leant forward in his seat, resting his elbows on his knees and clasping his hands in front of him. "With your father's position as prime minister, you are now a target in your own right."

"There has been chatter," Von Bartham added. "Threats."

"Against the queen?" I asked, startled.

Benjamin shook his head.

"Against you," Freddie answered.

"What?"

"Meredith, honey," Alex said softly, "they see you as a way to get to your father."

"But that's ridiculous."

"Unfortunately it's not," Benjamin said tiredly. "I tried to find some way around this whole thing. You're a good operative, Meredith, one of my best. But I can't have you on the team if you are going to bring an added threat to the queen."

"So this has nothing to do with my mother's ridiculous idea that I get married and become a countess?"

Alyssa and Freddie shared a look. "That is the other side of this coin," Freddie said. "The title is real and we do want you to take it up. It has been neglected for too many years and it is the perfect opportunity for Alyssa to show that she is serious about the shift to a more equal-opportunity peerage. The whole marriage thing is neither here nor there."

"What about the tour?"

This time Von Bartham and Benjamin shared a look. "We want you to still go on tour with us. We will keep you out of the eye of the public as much as possible. The threats we intercepted do not seem to be any immediate danger but they did alert us to a future hazard if we didn't do something now."

"So I go on tour and then when we get back, what? I'm kicked off the team?"

"Mer," Freddie breathed, "you can't look at it like that. We all know and understand how you feel about being a guard and if there was any way around this whole thing, then don't you think we would be doing it? The fact is that you present a danger to Alyssa. Benjamin can't have the team's attention split between trying to protect you and Alyssa. You understand that don't you?"

I nodded. I understood it but it didn't make it any more palatable to swallow.

CHAPTER 3

Jamie

I t felt a little like déjà vu standing outside Benjamin's office. I tapped on the door and waited for the command to enter. Benjamin sat behind his desk, Von Bartham stood in the corner and the presence of the third person surprised me. Danika.

"Take a seat," Benjamin said.

I nodded and strode across the room to sit in the chair he indicated.

"You know Danika, of course," he said, "but what you don't know is that she is here because of her expertise."

I nodded again, unsure what to say or think.

"Danika is an expert in the tensions on Kalopsia," Von Bartham supplied helpfully.

I raised an eyebrow and turned to look at her. She was studying me intently, uncomfortably so. I shifted in my seat.

"Oh?" I asked. Did that mean she knew who I was?

She nodded once and then with a look at Benjamin for permission, she spoke.

"I have studied Kalopsia for many years," she said. "I worked for the Greek government. Intelligence."

I didn't let anything show on my face at the words she was saying. Greece had always had an interest in Kalopsia. We were brothers in a lot of ways, but most of the time Greece looked at us covetously. Our position within the Aegean Sea put us close to the Greek islands, but we had managed to keep our independence. They wanted to bring us under their flag, but we had resisted all attempts - both diplomatic and military.

"Things on Kalopsia are worse than we originally thought," Benjamin said. "There is civil unrest and talk of a rebellion."

I snorted. A rebellion to try and overthrow the first rebellion. It was kind of ironic.

"It's not what you think," Danika said. "The people want the king reinstated. The rebellion is working toward making that happen."

I took a long, slow breath. It was news I wanted to hear. It had always been my goal to return to Kalopsia and take my place beside my father. Not because I wanted to be a king with all the trappings, but because I knew that my father was a good ruler. The uprising had happened because of false rumours spread through the media and corrupt militia who were bribed to take the country by force. I had my suspicions as to who had initiated it, but had never spoken those suspicions aloud.

"Do you have news of the king?" I asked.

In ten years I hadn't heard a single thing about the man that I had idolised. He simply disappeared. The insurgents had bragged about having him locked up in the dungeons that still occupied the lower bowels of the castle where we had lived, but no one had seen him since the farce of a kangaroo court that they had paraded him to. The trumped up charges were a joke and the judge obviously corrupt but the people had believed it.

Danika shook her head. "No. I know there are people working on it."

"You have spies inside the castle?" I asked, surprised.

"Not exactly," she said, not giving anything else away.

I turned back to Benjamin and flicked my eyes over to Von

Bartham. "So what does this mean for me? And for the tour?"

Von Bartham and Benjamin shared a look.

"Nothing. For now," Von Bartham said.

"It's why we've brought Danika on. She is going to be the eyes and ears on you."

"Excuse me?"

Von Bartham sighed. "There has been some noise about you," he said.

Damn Freddie for putting me in his wedding party. He had pretty much outed me to whoever was looking for me. Even though I had aged ten years and grown quite a spectacular beard, I had no doubt that I had a striking resemblance to my father. If someone was looking for me, they would know who I was without too much trouble. My secret had remained so because I was never in the spotlight. No one took notice of the security detail that followed the queen because their eyes were all on the queen. Freddie had changed that by asking me to be a groomsman.

"Wouldn't it just be easier to pull me from the detail?" I asked with a sigh.

"It's too late to do that," Benjamin said. "You know the queen and the prince well and you have been on the team for seven years. We can't get someone to replace you or your experience this close to the tour. At this stage you're more of an asset than a risk."

"Do Alyssa and Will know?"

Von Bartham nodded. "They were updated this morning in their security briefing."

"And they are happy with it?"

Von Bartham nodded again. "Alyssa insisted. She said she wouldn't feel comfortable with a new team member, not on her first tour, anyway."

I took another deep breath and sighed. "Okay. So nothing changes. You don't want the team updated?"

Benjamin shook his head. "It's best if it's kept to just us for now. Danika's job will be to look for threats around you. The rest of the team will have their focus on the queen and prince. You just need to do your job and everything will be fine."

I didn't like keeping this from the rest of the team. I didn't like keeping this from Meredith.

"I don't like the secrecy," I said. "If I'm adding an extra layer of threat to this whole thing, then shouldn't they be made aware of that?"

Benjamin nodded slowly. "I understand what you're saying and I assure you I didn't make this decision lightly. There are other unrests within the team and I really didn't want them to lose their focus when we don't think there is a real threat at this stage. With Danika watching your back, there isn't any need to split the team's focus."

"What unrest?" I asked.

Benjamin shook his head. "I will tell you more, later. But for now just let it go. You have enough to worry about."

I dragged my hand down my face and exhaled roughly. I didn't know what to think of this latest news. I managed to keep the worry about my father locked away most of the time and after ten years it had gotten easier. But now that everything had been stirred up again, the old pang was back. I missed him. I missed them all. I had been able to mourn the loss of my mother and sisters, but not knowing whether my father was alive or dead was like an open wound that never seemed to heal. The whole prince-in-exile thing was a weight that I carried constantly. Some days it was light and I could almost believe that I was a normal person and then other times, like now, it felt unbearably heavy and weighed on me.

"Are we done?"

Benjamin nodded and I stood. I need out of the small space. I needed to run and to clear my head before I went on shift. I nodded to the two men and Danika and then strode out the door.

"I WHAT?"

Benjamin looked at me like I was daft. "You need to shave off your beard."

My hand instinctively went to my beard and stroked the whiskers that I had been cultivating since they had first sprouted out of my chin. It had taken ten years and a lot of ribbing from the rest of the team, but I finally had a beard I could be proud of and now they wanted me to shave it off.

"I don't understand," I said, too traumatised by the news for my brain to work through the look in Benjamin's eyes.

He sighed and rolled his eyes. "You will be impersonating the prince," he said slowly. "Will doesn't have a beard, ergo..."

I really hadn't thought this whole thing through. Of course it made sense now but when we had first talked about it they had told me a wig and dark glasses. Now, instead of a wig, I would be dying my hair and shaving my beard? I didn't mind the hair dye so much, it would wash out, but it hadn't even occurred to me that I would be sacrificing my beard for the country and the safety of the monarchy.

I fingered my beard again. Sadly. I heard a twitter of a giggle behind me and I turned to see the two maids that had been tasked with the job of shearing me. I had to get a haircut too. That, I didn't mind so much. But parting with my beard was a big step. I wasn't mentally prepared for it.

"Maybe Cody or Aiden would be a better body double for the prince," I said, still refusing to sit in the barber chair.

Benjamin took a moment to think over my suggestion. "I suppose," he said. "That would mean I would have to rotate one of them into Meredith's shift. They would need to get work closely with her for the next few days and then while we were on tour they would need to buddy up."

I clenched my fists at my sides and tried not to crack my molars with the tension in my jaw. I didn't want Cody or Aiden anywhere near Meredith. And there was no way I wanted them to hold her hand and get all lovey-dovey with her while pretending to be the queen and prince.

The strength and suddenness of the jealousy I felt surprised me. Meredith and I had been friends for a long time before anything happened between us. And what was happening now was so new that I didn't realise the depth of my feelings for her. Thinking about her with another man's hands on her - even if they were only acting - was like poking me with a red hot poker. I'd be damned if Aiden or Cody got to play house with her while I watched on from the sides.

"Fine," I gritted out. "Shave it."

I sat in the chair and closed my eyes. I couldn't watch. I would have to make sure Meredith knew the sacrifice I was making for her. She would owe me.

The thought made me smile. Then I frowned. Would she like the un-bearded Jamie? That thought led to other more concerning thoughts. Would she like the real Jamie? The Prince Christophe Jamie that she didn't even know about?

I knew it was against protocol, but there was an ache in my gut to come clean to her. We had been carrying on this little clandestine affair for months now. Before I'd even known what was happening, it had gotten a lot more serious than just having fun. My reaction to her working closely with Aiden and Cody had cemented that fact in my brain. It had started out with a bit of teasing and harmless flirting. We worked well together and trained together often. We were most often paired together on shift and the constant contact had built to something more than just teammates or even friends.

"Are you ready?" Benjamin asked.

I kept my eyes closed and nodded. I needed to distract myself from what was happening to my face.

I thought about Meredith. I thought about the first time I had kissed her. We had been sparring in the training room after hours. She used to train with Alyssa before Alyssa became queen. Since then, Meredith had almost seemed like she was at a loose end. I had offered to train with her. We had sparred before, and I knew she was good, but after a few weeks of training together, I realised just how good she was. Her speed and agility put me to shame - most of the time. As mixed sparring partners went, we were pretty well matched. Until I found her weakness. The body triangle. The first time I had used it on her, she had been furious. She was magnificent when she was angry. All that lovely long red hair flying around her face and those piercing blue eyes that snapped with cold fury. Even now, thinking about it, I had to control the shiver that threatened to wrack my body. I had kissed her. I didn't know what had come over me but I had gone with my instinct and I had kissed her. And she kissed me back.

I smiled at the memory. It had been like trying to hold on to a live wire. She snapped and crackled in my arms, her anger pulsing through her and into the kiss turning it hot and dangerous. I had lost myself in the taste of her and the feel of her. When I had lifted my head and looked down into those fierce blue eyes, they were no longer snapping with fury but burned with something else entirely.

"What was that," she had said, her voice a low growl.

"Something I have been wanting to do for a long time," I had replied. It was a surprisingly true statement that I hadn't realised was true until I had uttered the words.

"Do it again," she had said.

Not one to argue with a beautiful woman, I kissed her again. The fire and electricity burned hot between us, but it was no longer fuelled by her anger. Something else burned between us now.

"All done," one of the maids said and my eyes popped open.

The man staring back at me was a stranger. The eyes were familiar, but the clean shaven cheeks and strong jaw that I saw were foreign. It was a shock and it took me a few moments to find my voice.

"I look like I'm twelve years old," I growled.

Benjamin laughed. It was rusty and cracked from not being used very often. In fact I probably couldn't even remember the last time I'd heard him laugh.

"You look like that arrogant little kid that first joined the guard," he said.

"I wasn't arrogant," I said, reaching up to smooth my hand over the whisker-less skin. It was surprisingly soft.

"You were a little upstart," he said with a feral grin. "But we managed to tame you."

I didn't know how old Benjamin was. He didn't look all that much older than me, but in the ten years we had known each other he hadn't seemed to age at all.

"So I'll do?" I asked, looking up at him.

There was something in his eyes that I couldn't place.

He nodded once and then his eyes shuttered. "You'll do," he said gruffly before turning and striding from the room.

CHAPTER 4

Meredith

I walked into the training room and sighed. I still could not believe that I was being forced to give up the one thing I had trained my whole life for. What was I meant to do with my time? I had been too shocked and distraught over the news to ask the pertinent questions. What did being the Countess of Bellemere mean? There was no count, which meant I would hold the title independently, but were there responsibilities to go along with the title or was it in name only? As far as I knew, no one had held the title since my grandmother. There was a country estate called Bellemere in my family's holdings...was that part of the title? Would it become mine if I accepted?

Not that a country estate would make it any more palatable. As far as I was concerned, I was getting the raw end of the deal. I had worked hard to make it to where I was. Basic training had been brutal and then I'd had to go one step further to even be considered as a candidate for the royal guard. Much like the SEALs or SAS, soldiers had to go through more specific and advanced training, so did I with the guard. Then there was all the psychological and body language stuff we had to learn. I was a soldier who had bled to be part of the guard and now I was being tossed aside. It really sucked.

The door opened and I looked up and my breath caught.

The man who walked toward me looked like Jamie but decidedly not like Jamie. I would know his broad shoulders and confident stride anywhere, but his face...his face was...I had no words.

"Jamie?" I whispered.

He grinned at me and scooped me up, twirling me around before setting me back on my feet and kissing me thoroughly.

"Hey Mer," he said when he lifted his head. "What do you think? Can I pull off the clean shaven thing?"

I reached up and ran my hand along his smooth cheek. This skin was soft and a slightly lighter colour than the rest of his face. He had a strong jaw and his lips...wow. His lips were soft, I already knew that from kissing him, but I'd had no idea that they were as full and pillowy as they looked without the beard to obscure them. I bit by own lip as I dragged my thumb across their fullness.

"Mer?" Jamie growled and I looked up into his eyes which had gone stormy grey.

I shivered.

I dragged my hand down over his chin and felt the strong cords of his neck. He swallowed, his eyes not leaving mine.

I cleared my throat.

"It's different," I said. My voice was thick and cracked as I spoke.

He leaned down and rubbed his clean cheek over mine before nuzzling my neck. My eyes fluttered closed and I breathed in his scent. It was spicy and citrusy, an after shave balm maybe? Whatever it was, it was new and I liked it. A lot.

"Does this mean you want the beard to stay gone?" he asked, his voice gruff.

"I don't know," I said, leaning back to look him in the eyes. "It's going to take me a while to get used to seeing you like this."

He grimaced and untangled himself from me. He lifted a hand to rub his chin and shook his head. "I'm having a little trouble getting used to it myself," he said.

"Why? Um, I mean," I cleared my throat. "Why did you shave it off?"

"Because of the tour."

"Oh." I nodded. His job impersonating Will.

"I suggested that Will try and grow a beard in the next few days, but they weren't keen to suggest it to him."

I grinned. Will with a beard would be a sight to behold - all that thick dark hair.

"It wouldn't matter anyway," I said. "It still wouldn't look anything like yours."

Jamie grunted non-comittally.

I bit my lip as I watched Jamie go through a couple of stretches to warm up before we sparred. How would he take the news of me being forced out of the guard? What would it mean for us?

I cleared my throat and he looked at me questioningly.

"I-uh-I have news," I said, walking over to the bench and sitting down.

Jamie straightened from his lunge and waited for me to go on.

"I'm leaving the guard," I said in a rush.

His eyebrows popped up and his jaw worked as if he was trying to speak but unsure of what to say. I hadn't realised how much the beard had obscured his facial expressions.

"When?" His voice was low and gruff.

I took a big breath and let it out slowly. "When we get back from the tour."

He moved his gym bag and sat down beside me. He rested his elbows on his knees and his eyes looked at the floor between his feet.

"Why?" His voice was barely a whisper.

"Apparently I'm now a security risk for Alyssa."

His head turned sharply toward me. "What?"

"Because of my father. There have apparently been threats. Von Bartham and Benjamin are concerned that if someone were to target me, Alyssa might get caught in the cross-fire."

Jamie exhaled roughly, his nostrils flaring. I couldn't read what was going on behind his carefully shuttered eyes.

"You thought I was leaving because of us," I said. It wasn't a question.

I jumped to my feet and began to pace. Jamie and I had never really discussed what was happening between us. We had just let it happen organically without bothering to label it. Now he thought I was pushing for more. He thought that I was choosing to leave the guard so that there could be something more between us. And he wasn't happy about it.

I coughed out a rueful laugh. "You don't need to worry," I said, "I won't expect anything from you. I'm to be a countess. My grandmother's title. I'll probably be shipped off to the country to prop up an ailing estate or some such thing so there is nothing for you to worry about."

My back was to him so that I couldn't see the relief in his eyes. I could withstand just about anything but that.

A pair of strong arms wrapped around me and tossed me to the ground. I fought him, but he had taken me by surprise. We rolled on the mats until he finally had me trussed up in the body triangle hold and I was immobilised.

"Are you ready to listen to me now?" he asked in my ear as he held me tightly against his chest.

"What's there to say?" I asked, not willing to give him the satisfaction of seeing me upset.

"Obviously a lot if you think I want this thing between us to end."

I snuffed out the little flame of hope that tried to ignite inside me.

"It's okay, Jamie. I knew that this thing between us was just temporary."

Jamie swore softly and then flipped me over, holding my arms above my head and using his body to pin me to the mat. I looked up into his eyes and saw a fierceness there that made my body erupt in goosebumps.

"No one ever said that this was temporary," he growled in my ear.

"That's just it," I said, trying to flip him off me unsuccessfully. "We haven't said anything about what we're doing."

"Meredith," he said, his voice softening. He pressed his forehead to mine and nuzzled his nose along mine. "That doesn't mean that what we have has no value to me."

"What does that even mean, Jamie?" I asked, close to tears with frustration and hurt.

Jamie rolled off me and laid down on the mat beside me. He took my hand in his, weaving our fingers together.

"I don't know, Mer," he said, "except that I'm not ready for it to be over."

Jamie

I CLUNG TO MEREDITH'S HAND, LETTING THE FEEL OF HER SKIN against mine ground me. Things were moving too fast. For the last ten years, nothing had changed and now everything was changing.

She had looked so vulnerable as she told me that she was leaving the Guard. I knew how important it was to her and how hard she trained to make sure she wasn't a liability because of her size and gender. Everything she had known was being taken away from her and she thought that it would mean that I no longer wanted her either. My heart clenched at the thought that she didn't know how I felt about her. The fact was, I didn't even know how I really felt about her. I had never sat down and analysed it. All I knew was that whatever we had was not done.

But then, was the decision already being taken out of our hands?

Meredith knew nothing about who I really was and as much as I wanted to tell her, I couldn't. It had to remain a secret. What sort of relationship could we even have with such a thing? Would she even want to be with me if she knew the truth? A prince-in-exile wasn't exactly a catch, not for someone like Meredith. I was an alien living in her country at the pleasure of her queen, who could choose to deport me at any time. If I became a liability or a security risk, Alyssa would have no other choice.

"I'm not ready for it to be over either," Meredith said quietly beside me, "but I don't know how it's going to work once I'm no longer in the guard or even living in the palace."

"You'll still be a lady in waiting," I said.

Meredith snorted and I turned my head to see her roll her eyes. "It won't make sneaking off together any easier. Right now we have legitimate reason to hang out, once I'm out of the guard, I won't see you."

She turned her head and looked at me, her face a picture of sadness. I reached up to cup her cheek. "We'll work it out *agapoúla mou*," I whispered before brushing a soft kiss across her lips.

She sighed into me and I rolled over so that I was facing her. She did the same and I pulled her close, tucking her head under my chin. It wasn't very romantic. The training mats smelled like sweat and something else unidentifiable. We both wore the biometric suits that we trained in with only our hands and faces uncovered. The lights overhead were bright and harsh and there was a coolness to the big warehouse-like building. But there was nowhere else I'd rather be.

"So what was your meeting with Benjamin about?" she asked as she snuggled up under my chin. "Was it just to talk you into losing the beard?"

I chuckled and wove my hand through her hair, letting the red-gold strands slide through my fingers. "It did take some convincing, but no. The meeting was about Danika."

Meredith stiffened in my arms. "What about her?"

I shrugged awkwardly because of the way we were laying. "Benjamin wanted me to give her a run down on the tour."

"She's coming with us?" Meredith asked, rolling away from me and looking at me with narrowed eyes.

"She is," I said, sitting up and looking at her curiously. "You don't like her?"

"I don't know her," Meredith said, rolling up into a sitting position as well. "Which is exactly why I don't like the thought of her coming with us."

"She seems experienced—"

"That's not the point," Meredith said, her eyes flashing. She got to her feet and began to pace. "There is a palace full of guards that we could bring with us. It's goes against all our protocols to have a new and untrained member on the team for the tour."

I slowly stood, confused by Meredith's apparent instant dislike for Danika.

"Is this because she is to be your replacement?" I asked.

Meredith swung toward me, her eyes flashing and her hands planted firmly on her hips.

"She's my replacement?"

Whoa. Okay. How could I extricate myself from this minefield and keep all my body parts intact?

"I don't know?" I hedged. "I just assumed—"

"Yeah well you know what they say about assuming," she spat and then stalked away from me. "What on earth is Benjamin thinking?" she muttered to herself. She swung around to face me once again. "Does Alyssa know? Has Alyssa even met her?"

I opened my mouth to answer, but Meredith turned away from me again and resumed her angry pacing.

"It's just not right," she said under her breath.

I stood back and watched her. Was it wrong that I liked seeing this fierce side of her? I knew she was angry and probably hurt too, but I couldn't help but admire the fire that had ignited in her. Meredith in a pique was magnificent.

"Meredith," I said, trying to bring her attention back to what we were supposed to be doing.

She looked over her shoulder at me, her eyes sparking like blue fire. "What?"

"Let's train," I said.

I could see how tense she was and training was the only way I knew how to relax her. We were the same like that. The physical exertion would do us both good because I was just as tense as she was, if for a different reason.

"Fine," she said and shook herself as if she could physically shake off the irritation that plagued her.

We took our positions on the mat and circled each other. Meredith was focussed, her eyes darting over my body watching for the slightest hint that I was about to make a move. Meredith may have been smaller than me in both height and weight, but she was a skilled fighter and I would trust her with my life if it came down to it. I understood the reasoning behind her being removed from the team, but she would be missed. And that wasn't just my feelings for her talking.

She came at me fast and my mind was consumed by alternately defending myself and going on the offence. I felt the stress leech from my muscles as we grappled. Meredith was a smart fighter, using her head and physics to get the upper hand over an opponent that was bigger and stronger than her. I had to concentrate on her and not let the earlier conversation with Benjamin invade my brain. Compartmentalisation. It was lesson we learned early on. We had to in order to do our job effectively.

We were both breathing hard when Meredith caught me unawares. She had me on the ground and pinned before I realised what she was doing. I tried to lever her off, but she had me locked down tight. She grinned down at me, the mask of worry that had been on her face earlier was wiped away. If her beating me in a bout was what it took to do that, then I was willing to fall on my sword any time she needed me to. Not that she would appreciate me telling her that and not that I was in any way letting her win. She had pinned me fair and square, a fact that she was very well aware of.

The door to the training room opened and Meredith looked up. I couldn't see who walked in, but whoever it was made Meredith loosen her hold on me. I took advantage of the distraction to flip her over and under me. She grunted with the impact and I grinned down at her.

"Am I interrupting?" a female voice said from the door. I looked up and saw Danika smirking at us.

It was Meredith's turn to take advantage of the distraction. She didn't reverse the hold like I thought she would. Instead she wriggled out from under me and jumped to her feet, walking away from me and toward the bench where her bag sat.

"Just training," I said, getting up more slowly.

"Oh," Danika said, "sorry to interrupt. I was just wondering if we could go over—"

"It's okay," Meredith said, slinging her bag over her shoulder. "We're done here. He's all yours."

I gritted my teeth to stop my jaw from hitting the floor as

Meredith walked out of the room without looking back. What was that?

"I don't think she likes me," Danika said with a smirk as she watched Meredith leave.

Yeah. I didn't think she did either. I also didn't think that was the only thing going on with her.

Meredith

I WALKED INTO THE FAMILIAR STUDY AND BREATHED IN THE comforting scent. My father was bent over his desk, just the lamp on the table lighting the room. This place had so many memories for me - good memories. I had often sat on my father's lap as he worked. He would tell me about what he was doing and even though I didn't understand a word of what he was saying, the sound of his voice was a comforting balm for whatever had sent me scurrying into his office. Usually a disagreement with my mother.

"Hey daddy," I said quietly.

My father lifted his head and smiled at me. He looked tired but that didn't dispell the joy that I saw on his face when he saw me.

"Hello, kitten," he replied, leaning back in his chair and stretching his arms above his head. "What are you doing here?"

I shrugged and stepped closer, trailing my fingers along the leather bound tomes that lined his bookshelves.

"I just wanted to see you."

It was true. Whenever my life felt unsteady, visiting with my father always brought stability. Right now the very ground under my feet felt like it bucked and swayed like an earthquake and I needed something to ground me.

"Come and sit," he said, standing from his office chair and leading me over to the big leather chesterfields that were as familiar to me as he was. We sat next to each other and he put an arm around me, pulling me close. "Talk to me."

I didn't know where to start or what to say. With a sigh I laid my head on his should and looked up at the picture of our ancestor that hung above the fireplace and sighed.

"Why didn't Louis become king instead of Jacques?" I asked.

My father tilted his head to the painting of Louis, the first Duke of Monterey, and took a moment before replying. "I suspect it was the same reason I didn't claim the throne when Edward died."

When Alyssa's father and brother were killed in a hunting accident, my father was the next one in line for the throne - a little known fact at the time.

I turned to look at him. "And why was that?"

"Because I knew that even though I could be a good king, Alyssa would make a better queen." He sighed and I felt it rumble in his chest. "Edward and I discussed it before Jacob was born. If he died before he produced an heir, he wanted me to take the throne. But I knew that I couldn't do that to Alyssa. There may not have precedent for a female to take up the title and responsibility of head of state, but I knew if anyone could make it work, it would be Alyssa."

"So Louis?"

"Louis probably knew that Jacques would be a better ruler and so he threw his support behind Jacques' claim." He turned to look at me. "What's this about kitten?"

"I don't want to leave the guard," I said, truthfully. "I don't want to be a countess."

He exhaled slowly but I didn't feel any censure in it. "Remember when you first came to me and asked me if you could join the guard?"

I smiled. I remembered. I had my whole argument rehearsed for why I should be allowed to join the royal guard and I was prepared to argue for as long as it took for him to agree. "Yes," I said, "I explained to you why I was the best person to be by Alyssa's side."

He smiled gently at the memory. "I was so proud of you that day. Do you remember what I told you?"

"You said that I could join as long as I knew that one day I would have to take on the responsibilities of my own family," I said softly.

"I know you love the guard, kitten," he said, shifting so that I was looking into his eyes. "But both Alyssa and I need you for a greater calling."

"Being a countess is a greater calling?" I scoffed.

He nodded solemnly. "You know what the queen is trying to achieve in Parliament. She needs a bill to pass that will make it legal for an entailed title to pass to daughters and not just sons. We have a unique opportunity with your grandmother's title to prove her case. Up until now there has been no one to take the title and Bellemere has suffered for it. If you take it up and prove to the Parliament that this is a viable bill, it will go a long way to getting it passed."

I felt the responsibility of what my father was telling me settle on my shoulders like a physical weight. Up until now I had viewed the title as little more than a courtesy and a way for my mother to get her wishes. Now that Daddy had put it in perspective I understood that there was more going on than just what was happening in my own little world. I might not want the title but by taking it up, I would be paving a way for other women in my position who did want to take a title, to get their inheritance. How could I turn away from that?

I stretched my neck up and kissed my father's whiskery cheek.

"Okay Daddy," I said. "I'll do it."

"Thank you kitten," he said and beamed down at me. "I knew I could count on you."

CHAPTER 5

Jamie

For the next few days we were all consumed with the logistics of the queen's first international tour. Advance parties were sent to Monaco to prepare the hotel suites we would occupy and organise on-the-ground transport. We would only be in Monaco for a few days before boarding a small fleet of yachts to cruise the Mediterranean. I had seen Meredith in the course of our jobs but she had not come back to our regular after-hours training sessions. Stubborn redhead. I wished she would just talk to me. I understood that she felt threatened by Danika's presence but that was no reason to avoid me. We still hadn't really sorted out what was going on between us or what we wanted to be going on between us.

Maybe that was for the better.

I liked Meredith. A lot more than I was willing to admit even to myself, but that didn't negate the secrets I was keeping from her. Was it fair to engage in something with her when I knew there was no future for us? The simplest solution was to just tell her and let her decide whether she cared enough about me to see where this whole thing would go. But I couldn't do that. There was too much at risk.

Revealing my true identity to her would inevitably tip off whoever was hunting me. I couldn't do that and risk bringing the danger to the queen. Or Meredith. I couldn't risk her in all of this.

"Are you ready to go?"

I looked up from my luggage - luggage that was identical to Will's luggage - to see Cody leaning against the door of my suite.

I nodded. "Yeah. Let's do this."

Meredith and I would be flying to Monaco separately from the royal party. The whole body double ruse would be for naught if people saw the four of us together. It had been decided that Meredith and I would keep out of the public eye as much as possible unless we were impersonating Alyssa and Will.

I followed Cody out of the residential wing and toward the staff entrance of the palace. Freddie was waiting for me when we exited the doors into the pre-dawn light. We hugged briefly, slapping each other on the back as good friends did. He pulled me aside and Cody took my luggage to give us some privacy.

"I'm sorry," he said and I frowned at him.

"What for?"

He sighed and rubbed the back of his neck. "I should have listened to you about the whole groomsman thing."

I grinned and slapped a hand on his shoulder. "They found me because they were looking for me. I'm out with Alyssa enough that they eventually would have put it all together."

"I still feel bad about practically outing you."

"I was happy to do it. You have been a true friend to me Freddie, right from the start. I don't know how I would have lasted this long without having you in my corner. It was a privilege for me to stand up at your wedding and I won't stand for you apologising for it."

"Well, for what it's worth, I hope my actions haven't brought the house down on you."

I grinned at him. "Maybe I want the house to be brought down." I sobered as I searched his face. "Things are bad at home, you know? I desperately want to do something but as long as I am still in hiding my hands are tied."

It was Freddie's turn to slap a hand on my shoulder and squeeze encouragingly. "The day will come, Chris, when you will be free and when you are, I know you are going to do great things."

Hearing the diminutive of my name was a jolt. Nobody called me Christophe or Chris, but Freddie knew I needed to hear it. He had always been the kind of friend who knew just what would shake me out of a funk. The last few years had meant that we hadn't been as close as we could have been, but it hadn't lessened the strength of our bond.

"Thanks Freddie," I said, my voice rough with emotion.

Before he could say any more, Meredith walked out of the door and stopped, staring at the two of us. She had been weirded out by Freddie asking me to be in his wedding party. She obviously didn't remember those first few weeks that I spent hiding in her parents' castle or the fact that Freddie and I had become such good friends.

"Mer," Freddie said affectionately, scooping her up in a hug. I envied his easy and public affection for her. I wanted to pull her into my arms and hold her until she softened against me and spilled all her secrets. She had been standoffish and sullen around me since Danika had interrupted us and I was determined to get to the bottom of it.

"What are you doing here Freddie?" she asked when he put her down. "Why are you not on your honeymoon with your lovely wife?"

"Alex refused to leave until the queen was officially out of the country."

Meredith rolled her eyes. "Of course she did. Well I guess we know who wears the pants in your household."

"And I wouldn't have it any other way," Freddie said with a wide smile.

Meredith finally looked at me and something flashed in her eyes before she shuttered them. "Are you ready to do this?" she asked. Her voice was devoid of the usual friendly inflection and casual teasing that had become our norm.

"More than ready," I replied and I hoped she knew that I was talking about more than just our mission.

Meredith

THE FLIGHT TO NICE WAS UNEVENTFUL. I SAT AT THE BACK OF THE plane, away from Jamie. I knew I was being a coward but seeing Danika walk in on our training session brought it home to me that what we were doing had an end date. There was no way my parents would even entertain the idea of me dating someone like Jamie. I knew he and Freddie were friends - which I still found odd, by the way - but friends was a long way from romantic interest. The fact of the matter was, he was a body guard and I was soon to be a countess, not to mention that I was the daughter of a duke who also happened to be the prime minister. The press would have a field day if they ever found out that Jamie and I were more than just colleagues.

We landed in Nice and were hustled to the helipad for the second leg of the journey, which would bring us to Monaco. I couldn't hide from him in the smaller cabin space of the helicopter. He sat beside me and his thigh brushed mine. Just that incidental touch had me rethinking all of my carefully thought out reasons for ending what we had. The fact of the matter was that I was attracted to him - and not just his body. There was something about being with Jamie that made me happy. I don't mean a frivolous, bubbly, giggly happy. No. Being with him made my soul smile and my body relax. Stress and tension seemed to leak out of me whenever he was near. It was an addictive feeling - he was addictive. It was one of the reasons we needed to call the whole thing off. I was in far too deep for something that had started out as a bit of fun.

Before I even had time to enjoy the closeness of him, we were landing in Monaco. It was only a six or seven minute flight from Cote d'Azur airport to the heliport in Fontvieille. We exited the helicopter and rushed across the tarmac to the waiting limousine. Our arrival in Monaco was low-key. All the pomp and circumstance was being reserved for the arrival of the queen and prince. Right now we were just tourists, although in a few hours we would be slipping into our roles as the queen and her consort.

Jamie sat close to me in the back of the limousine as we travelled through the city to our hotel. He seemed to be in the same mind as me - the words we needed to say would have to wait until we were completely alone. The driver of the limousine was not one of ours and

Cody rode shot-gun. Anything we said now would be heard by all and sundry and ours was not a conversation that should have an audience.

Due to the fact that we would be impersonating the royal couple, we would be sharing a suite. Ours was the floor below Alyssa and Will's but still boasted incredible views and a private entrance. Of course we wouldn't be entirely alone. Just as Will and Alyssa would have a contingent of security, so would we. It was all to keep up appearances for the room attendants. They had to believe, if not that we were the royal couple then at least we were royalty of some description. What we didn't want them to know was that we were impersonators.

The suite was beautiful. It was a favourite of Winston Churchill and I could see why. The view was spectacular and the suite decked out with every luxury travelling nobility would need. I was not a stranger to the luxuries of royalty. I had grown up in a castle and worked and lived in a palace, but there was something different about staying in a hotel. Especially a hotel such as this that tried to emulate those very palaces.

I wandered through the suite, ostensibly taking everything in, but really I was avoiding the moment that Jamie and I would be alone. I knew what was going to happen and I didn't know whether I was strong enough to resist him. As I had tossed and turned in my bed over the last few nights, I had known, without a shadow of a doubt, that breaking things off with him was the right thing to do. But now, after spending just a few moments in his presence with the gentle brush of his arm or leg against mine as we travelled together, all those reason seemed insignificant.

I was not a woman who held a person's title in high esteem. Even the queen. I had known her all her life and my love and respect for her came not from the fact that she was my queen, but from spending time with her and knowing her motivations behind her decisions. Alyssa had earned my respect and love, it had not been automatic because of her title. I would literally die for her. I had signed up for the privilege because I believed in her and what she was doing. I had every confidence in her rule because of how I had seen her when no one else was watching. Which was all to say that if this thing between Jamie and me was just between the two of us, I wouldn't have any hesitation in wanting more with him. I didn't care that I was to be a countess and he was a body guard. The difference in our 'stations' or 'classes' was irrelevant to me. I thought it completely antiquated. But the fact was, our relationship had many more ramifications than just what would happen between us.

The door closed and I knew without turning around that Cody had left us. I stood at the window, looking out but not seeing the view. I heard the soft padding of his footsteps as he approached me and I held myself still. I wanted to run - to where, I didn't know. Part of me wanted to run to him, meet him half-way and throw myself into his arms. The other part of me wanted to run and hide in the bedroom and refuse to come out. Instead I made myself stay, rooted to the spot.

His scent enveloped me first and then I could feel the heat of his body as he came to stand behind me. I closed my eyes as his hands skimmed my shoulders and then down my arms before they came around my waist and pulled me back against his hard chest.

"Meredith," he whispered in my ear and I melted against him. I couldn't help giving in to the pull of him.

"Talk to me *agapoúla mou*," he whispered, placing a soft kiss on the side of my neck.

I stifled a soft moan and a shiver, fighting against the desire to just give in to him. Why did it have to feel so good to be wrapped in his arms? Why couldn't I be strong for both of us?

"We can't do this, Jamie," I forced out. My voice was rough.

"Because you're leaving?" he asked.

He hadn't loosened his hold on me like I thought he would and I was grateful for that.

I turned in his arms and looked up into his beautiful face. It still took me a minute to reconcile his shorn cheeks and I reached up to cup the smooth skin, running my thumb along his bottom lip. His eyes darkened to that delicious stormy grey and I sighed, resting my head on his chest.

"Yes," I said, "because I'm leaving. There are so many complications. This, what we have in this little cocoon, wouldn't survive out there in the real world."

I heard him grind his teeth and his arms tightened around me. "I'm not ready to let you go just yet," he said. "I'm not ready for this to be over."

I bit my lip and told myself not to cry. "I'm not either," I whispered.

He tipped my chin up and brushed a soft kiss over my lips. I opened my eyes and looked up at him, need and want warring inside me with responsibility.

"We have the next month," he said gruffly. "Can't we just have this time together and then decide what will happen when we get back?"

I searched his eyes and couldn't help myself. "Okay," I said softly, against my better judgement.

"That means we can't talk about it or think about it until we get back," he said.

"Okay," I said again, knowing even as I did that I was only going to cause myself heartbreak.

"Good," he said.

He lowered his lips to mine and kissed me. I had missed him so much over the last few days and it wasn't until I felt his lips against mine that I could finally take a deep breath without my chest aching. Whatever this was between us, I was helpless to stop it.

Jamie

"HEADS UP," CODY SAID COMING BACK INTO THE ROOM OVER AN hour later.

I turned from the window to find an entourage entering the room behind him.

"What's this?"

"Alyssa and Will have arrived," Cody said.

"O-kay," I said slowly as I watched two palace maids and a valet start setting up what looked like a portable beauty salon. "Are they coming here?"

"No," Cody said with a smirk. "This is all for you and Meredith."

"What is?" Meredith said as she stepped out of her room.

Meredith had escaped to her room, pleading a headache. She had looked a little peaked, now she looked like she had just woken up. Her hair was a tumbled mess of curls around her face and down her back and her eyes were a little sleepy still. I wanted to cross the room and take her in my arms, kiss her soft lips and breathe in her scent. But I couldn't. We had an audience.

"This," Cody said, indicating the industrious servants behind him.

"Andrea? Collette?" Meredith said. "What are you doing here?"

The maids stopped what they were doing and turned to curtsey to Meredith.

"I'm sorry Miss," one of them replied, I wasn't sure which was with. "Tanner told us we were to come."

"Tanner?" I asked, shooting a look at Cody. The palace was a big place and employed a lot of people. I would probably know this Tanner if I saw them, although I doubt I would know their name. I didn't even know if they were male or female. Cody shrugged.

"Tanner is in charge of the lady's maids," Meredith said absently before turning back to the two women. "Tanner told you to come? What was she thinking?"

"She was probably thinking that it was improper for a queen to travel without her maids," Alyssa said from the doorway.

The two maids curtsied and the valet bowed as the queen and the prince entered the room.

"I don't understand," Meredith said, but I was starting to.

We were to impersonate the queen and her consort and that meant we needed to have our own entourage. Which also meant that we would never be alone.

"You are going to need help getting ready for outings," Alyssa said patiently.

I was aware that because of Meredith's station - being the daughter of a duke and one of the queen's ladies in waiting - she had her own lady's maids. Case in point, the two women now unpacking an extraordinary amount of beauty products.

"Jamie," Will said, coming over to shake my hand. "This is Collins. He will be your valet."

"My valet?"

Will smirked. "Of course. No prince worth his salt would go anywhere without his valet to ensure he was properly attired."

I could tell by the humour in his eyes he was amused by this whole charade. Being that this was his and Alyssa's first ever tour, we had never had to have body doubles before. This was new to all of us.

"I don't think I'm going to need—"

"Meredith," Alyssa said, her voice a warning.

Meredith huffed out a breath. "Fine," she said and flopped down on a nearby couch.

"Excellent," Alyssa said with a grin. "So tonight you will be hitting the casino on our behalf."

"We are?" I asked. According to the itinerary, our first public appearance wouldn't be until tomorrow.

"There's been a change in plans," Benjamin said entering the room, closely followed by Danika.

"You don't mind do you?" Alyssa asked, looking down at Meredith.

"Of course not," Meredith said with a smile.

I had been witness to these two women as they had grown up together. They had a bond that even Alyssa's being crowned as queen couldn't break.

Will slapped me on the back. "Excellent news," he said, walking over to Alyssa and pulling her into his side. "Come along sweetheart. We have a whole evening of uninterrupted alone time to get to."

I couldn't help but grin as Will ushered his wife out of the suite. I couldn't imagine what it was like for them being constantly surrounded by maids and security and secretaries. I knew that their weekends and days off were routinely interrupted by some state business or such so I could understand their eagerness to carve out a little bit of solitary time for just the two of them.

"Cody and Danika will be your escorts tonight," Benjamin said looking down at the tablet in his hands. "We leave in two hours."

"So I have time for another nap," Meredith said.

"I'm afraid not, Miss," one of the maids said.

"Surely it's not going to take two hours to get me ready?" Meredith looked horrified at the thought and I had to stifle a grin.

"I'm afraid so, Miss," the maid replied.

"Fine," Meredith huffed out. "But I'm not going to do it with an audience. You need to take all that stuff and set up in the bedroom."

The maids hopped to and I couldn't help but grin.

"You think this is funny Kosta?" she asked stalking toward me.

"Not in the least," I said, but couldn't stop smiling.

"Ah, Mr. Jamie, sir?"

I turned to the valet who stood beside me.

"Collins was it?" He nodded. "What is it?"

"I need to start dressing you as well."

Meredith laughed loudly and gleefully.

"Pardon?" I asked.

Collins cleared his throat and blushed. He was so young. I was probably his first solo flight.

"The um, hair dye and..."

"Right," I said, taking pity on him. "Well, you should probably set up in my room too. Can I at least have a shower first?"

Collins nodded, seeming relieved at my easy acquiescence.

I turned back to Meredith. "I shall see you in two hours," I said.

She smirked and wiggled her fingers in a little wave as she flounced across the room to her door and disappeared.

"This way, sir," Collins said.

CHAPTER 6

Jamie

I stepped out of my room and adjusted my cuffs. The suit fit perfectly, as well it should. I had gone through a number of fittings with the tailor to get this result. Getting dressed with a valet was an experience. I hadn't had anyone to help me dress since I was a child. My memories of life on Kalopsia were vague. The last few years on my island nation were fraught with civil unrest and life in the palace had not been easy. My father had tried to keep us sheltered from it as much as possible, but I was a curious child and had found a way to sneak in to meetings unobserved. The things I heard were scary, but not scary enough to deter me. I knew that I would one day sit on the throne in my father's stead and it was important to me to know all that went on behind closed doors. I'm pretty sure my father knew that I was in those meetings but he never barred me from them. He too understood that it was important for me to know what was happening in my own country.

I shook off the melancholy that having a valet had inspired and looked up. Alyssa was standing with her back to me, looking out over the view. She looked beautiful, even though I could only see the back of her. Her dark hair was twisted up on top of her head leaving her long, elegant neck bare. The back of her dress dipped low, exposing soft skin and...I cleared my throat. I had seen Alyssa dressed in all manner of outfits and never once had I had this reaction to her.

"Your Grace?" I said, my voice sounding foreign to my own ears.

She turned around and at first glance I would have sworn that it was Alyssa, but the smirk gave her away.

"Meredith?"

"What do you think?" she asked.

I stepped closer to examine her. I had never realised just how alike Alyssa and Meredith were. She was wearing a dark wig and brown contacts to hide her ice blue eyes. The make-up she wore seemed contoured to create an illusion of Alyssa's features, but on closer inspection, I could see Meredith underneath it all. I now knew all about makeup contouring, having undergone the procedure myself.

"I'm a little shocked," I said, lifting my hand to cup her cheek, but dropping it before I could make contact.

"I'm a little shocked by you too," she said.

I was also wearing contacts, but no wig. My hair had been dyed to match Will's. "You think I will pass for the prince?" I asked.

She nodded. "And me?" her voice was soft and unsure.

I shook my head. "No way will you pass for the prince," I said and it took her a moment before she laughed.

"Dork," she said before giving herself a shake. "Okay. Let's do this."

I offered her my arm and she slipped her hand through my elbow. It was just a small touch, but I liked it. It had been too long since I had held her in my arms and there had been far too many people surrounding us. This small moment in time was a glass of water to my parched throat.

I opened the door to find Cody and Danika standing sentry. Meredith's hand on my arm tightened and I glanced at her to see her lips thin. I didn't know why she disliked Danika so much. I understood that she didn't like the thought of being replaced, but the other woman was only doing her job. I rested my hand over hers and gave it an encouraging squeeze. She looked up at me and searched my eyes before smiling a tight smile.

"So, blackjack, craps or the penny slots?" Cody asked as we walked toward the private exit.

"Can you see Alyssa playing the penny slots?' Meredith asked dryly.

Cody chuckled. "No. I suppose not."

"Roulette," I said.

"Not poker?" Meredith asked, looking up at me. "Like James Bond?"

I grinned. "Maybe later."

It was only a short stroll to the casino from the hotel. The nineteenth century building stood strong and proud in the evening twilight and I couldn't help but feel a little excitement at being in a place that had become synonymous with wealth and celebrity. I may be a prince in my own right, but I had been living anything but a royal life. Not that I was complaining. I was grateful to Merveille and the St. Benéts for taking me in when I needed it. They had given me an opportunity when other doors had been slammed in my face and I would always be in their debt.

"Wow," Meredith breathed quietly beside me.

I wasn't the only one impressed by the grandeur.

We were met at the door by the concierge and I let Cody deal with the man as I looked around. I tried not to look like a gawking tourist, but it was hard.

"Maybe we should just play the penny slots," Meredith whispered and I grinned.

"You are meant to be the queen," I whispered back. "Don't let all this fluff intimidate you."

She gripped my arm and straightened beside me. We were playing a role and we both needed to remember that.

We followed the concierge into the casino, getting swallowed up by the crowds. Cody and Danika stayed close to us, but I realised it was just as important for Meredith and I to keep our eyes open.

Meredith

SERIOUSLY. I SHOULDN'T BE SO IMPRESSED BY THE DECOR AROUND

me. Merveille was not a poor country. We were wealthy and our palace was beautiful and I was surrounded by history and elegance every day. Still...there was something about being in the Casino de Monte Carlo that was thrilling. Maybe it was the fact that it was famous or maybe it was just the energy of the casino patrons as they placed their bets at the tables. Or maybe it was Jamie. Being so close to him and being able to touch him in public. Maybe that was what was giving me the thrill.

I think I had been as shocked as he was when I turned around and saw him standing in the living room of the suite. At first glance I thought he was Will. That was the point, I suppose. I hadn't really thought it through - the whole impersonating the royal couple thing. It had just been another job, a mission that we had been assigned. Seeing him in that suit, his face looking so much like Will's and his hair dark... it was a surreal experience. I can honestly say that I had never been attracted to Will in all the time I had known him. But seeing Jamie dressed as Will was playing havoc with my insides. There was still something so very *Jamie* about him. Not that anybody else would probably notice. But I did. My body did. It was like my soul recognised his underneath the disguise. It seemed a weird thing to admit, but there it was. And maybe, if the way he had looked at me earlier was any indication, he had felt it too.

I didn't know what it meant for us...this connection. It was more than just being attracted to a pretty face or a nice body, although Jamie certainly had both. It ran deeper than that. So deep that even when he was dressed as the prince, my heart still knew him. I didn't want to examine it too closely because I knew if I did I would find it hard to walk away from him. And walk away I would need to do. A month from today when this tour was over and we returned to Merveille, I would have to walk out of his life and never look back. I should have been guarding my heart against it. I should have been pulling away from him in preparation of what was to come.

But I couldn't.

I knew that I would not come out of this unscathed and yet there was nothing I could do to prevent myself from falling. I had already fallen if I was truthful with myself. I couldn't let myself dwell on that. I couldn't acknowledge the depth of my feelings. It would only hurt more when we eventually went our separate ways. Our relationship had always been doomed to fail, and there was no happy ending for us in all of this. We had both known it from the start and yet here we were, playing with fire nonetheless.

Danika stepped up to Jamie and leaned in to whisper in his ear. I didn't like the way she was so familiar with him. I didn't like the way her hand rested on his chest and how close her lips were to his ear. It was inappropriate. It was unnecessary. And it just really ticked me off.

I didn't realise I was squeezing Jamie's arm so hard until he rested his hand over mine and gave it a squeeze. I looked up at him and he raised an eyebrow at me in question. I couldn't help the flush that bloomed in my cheeks and I looked away. He leaned down to whisper in my ear.

"Danika says they have a roulette table ready for us," he said.

I nodded and forced a smile on my face as I looked up at him. "Okay."

He searched my eyes for a minute until he was satisfied and then smiled down at me. We followed Danika and Cody through the gambling rooms until we reached a set of glass doors that led out onto the terrace. I stepped out and took in the spectacular view of the sun setting over the water and sighed. Merveille was a landlocked nation, with only Lac Merveilleux as the closest body of water. It was not the same as the sea.

"This way," Jamie said quietly and I looked up at him. His eyes were soft as he looked back down at me and my heart clenched. How could I say goodbye to this man? How could I possibly walk away from him when the time came?

I nodded and let him lead me over to a private table. The croupier nodded to us as we took our seats. The concierge placed a large stack of chips in front of each of us and I stared down at the hard plastic bricks in shock.

"A gift from the prince of Monaco," the concierge said with a bow.

I smiled up at him and nodded in response. Holy moly! There was a small fortune sitting in front of me. These were not the small discs that I was expecting, but large rectangle pieces in different colours.

It may seem strange to outsiders, but I very rarely handled money of any description. I didn't have a credit card or even a simple debit card. The palace paid for everything. If I wanted to buy clothes, I just had to sign a slip at the boutique - sometimes I didn't even have to do that. Even when we lived in America, all our needs were taken care of by the household staff. I couldn't even remember the last time I held actual cash in my own hand. Now I had several hundred thousand dollars in gambling chips in front of me and I didn't know where to start.

"When you are ready, Your Highness," the croupier said.

I looked up and him and nodded. He spun the wheel and dropped the ball, calling for bets. I picked up a chip, not looking at the number printed on it for fear of losing my nerve, and placed it on the red diamond. Jamie followed suit, choosing to play red as well. We were the only two players at the table and it felt weird. Jamie's hand snaked under the table and rested on my thigh. He squeezed gently in encouragement as we watched the ball spin around the wheel. The ball dropped into a black pocket and then skipped a couple of times before coming to rest in a red one. I breathed a sigh of relief. I didn't think I was cut out to be a gambler.

Jamie

I DIDN'T KNOW HOW MUCH WE WON OR LOST. THE ENTIRE NIGHT seemed to blend into one colourful montage. What I did know was that I was having the time of my life. There was something so incredibly freeing about wearing someone else's face. But it wasn't just stepping into Will's skin that made the night fun. It was the beautiful woman who sat beside me.

We had never been on a real date. There had only ever been stolen moments between us, but sitting beside her now and being able to freely touch her in front of all these people was a revelation. I couldn't get enough of her and I found any excuse I could to hold her hand, touch her arm or lean in and whisper in her ear. We were supposed to be behaving like the queen and her prince, and I had taken that to heart. I had seen how affectionate Alyssa and Will were. They loved each other and didn't mind letting the world know it. They were obviously more reserved when acting in an official capacity, but when they were just out together, there was obvious affection between them.

I took advantage of that.

Meredith had relaxed into the role as well. She looked up at me with a winning smile and a sparkle in her eyes that even the dark contacts she wore couldn't hide. Hesitant at first, she had taken to gambling after winning a few rounds of roulette. We had moved on to black jack and were now playing *trente et quarante*. Meredith was on a winning streak while I was sitting back indulgently and watching her play. To be honest, it was more fun to watch her than to play myself.

We had gathered a crowd. Lookie-loos who had been drawn over by Meredith's delighted laughter each time she won. I shifted closer to her, needing to let those around the table know that she was mine. It was possessive and caveman-ish, but I really didn't care. Meredith was a beautiful woman and when she was smiling and having fun like she was right now, she glowed. It was only natural that people would be drawn to her.

"I think we should go," Danika said, leaning in close.

I knew she was just doing her job, but I would have felt a whole lot more comfortable if it had been Cody whispering in my ear. Danika had taken her directive to watch me closely to heart. She hadn't been more than an arm's length from me all night. It felt a little claustrophobic and heavy handed. I had tried to subtly hint at Cody that they should swap places but he had either not picked up on my cues or he was ignoring me.

I nodded to acknowledge Danika without looking at her.

"Let's call it a night, *agapoúla mou*," I whispered in Meredith's ear.

She leaned her head toward me, resting it on my shoulder. "After this game," she whispered back.

She looked up at me and I would have promised her the world had she asked for it.

Somewhere along the way, her disguise had become invisible to me. To others she was as she had been made up to appear - the young queen of Merveille. But to me, she was Meredith. After the initial shock of seeing her in the suite, the fake hair, the contacts and the carefully contoured makeup had melted into the background and the Meredith I had come to know and love shone through.

I swallowed thickly. Love?

Had I really fallen in love with her?

I looked down at her, watching as she placed her final bet, and my heart sung. It was pathetic really. I was sure I heard some sappy Disney tune playing in my head. I breathed through it. No. I refused to believe I was in love. Sure, I loved her. We were friends, buds, mates, colleagues. I would die for her, literally. But 'in love?' That was another thing entirely.

The crowd gasped and then cried out as Meredith lifted her hands in a winning fist pump like a prize fighter. I couldn't help the affectionate grin that split my face. Cody and Danika worked at dispersing the crowd as the croupier slid Meredith's winnings across the table. There was a casino attendant at her side in moments to take the chips.

"I'll have the winnings transferred to your hotel," he said.

"Oh, no," Meredith replied, looking up at me with wide eyes. "I wouldn't feel right about taking them."

"Your Highness?" the man asked, puzzled.

Meredith looked around and then pleaded with me with her eyes.

"Is there a charity of some sort we could donate the winnings to?" I asked and the man smiled.

"Of course," he said with a bow. "I will take care of it."

I thanked the man and then helped Meredith down from the stool. She tucked her hand through my elbow and rested her head on my shoulder. I liked the feel of her pressed up against me. I liked even more that we didn't need to hide it from anyone.

"Did you have fun?" she asked and stifled a yawn.

"I did," I replied.

We walked slowly through the casino, following Danika and Cody. The crowds had thinned out and I felt like we were in our own little bubble.

"So did I," she said. "Once I forgot that I was playing with real money."

I chuckled. "I think that's part of the psychology behind using chips instead of actual cash," I said. "It's easier to forget the value."

"I nearly died when that man placed all those chips I front of me."

"I know. I saw the look on your face."

The evening air was cool as we stepped out of the casino. It was fully dark now and the hotel was lit from below with large floodlights. It looked amazing. I could almost pretend that Meredith and I were out on a date, well except for the two body guards who led the way.

We were quiet as we entered the hotel and then the suite. Danika and Cody checked the rooms before taking up their positions outside the door. I walked Meredith to the door of her bedroom and pulled her in for a hug. Her maids were waiting inside and no doubt Collins waited for me in my own bedroom, but I wanted to end the night like I had fantasised about ending a date were we ever to go on one.

I tipped Meredith's face up to mine and lowered my lips to hers. She sighed against me as she opened her lips and welcomed my kiss. I kept it gentle and light, even though I wanted to deepen it until we both forgot our own names. Before I could get lost in her, I lifted my head and kissed her temple.

"Good night *agapoúla mou.*"

"Good night Jamie," she whispered.

CHAPTER 7

Meredith

We spent a further two days in Monaco before we boarded the yacht that would take us to Le Beau. Alyssa and Will made a few public appearances and met with Prince Albert II. Jamie and I didn't go with them. Our positions as their body doubles superseded our positions as their security team. Not that anybody would see us and think we were them - my red hair would make sure of that - but Benjamin thought it would be prudent to limit the amount of time we were seen together with them.

I didn't mind so much. It meant I got to laze around the suite or by the pool. I even went to the beach a couple of times. I loved the water. I hadn't realised how much until I had spent the morning laying on a sun lounge in the sun with the soft shushing of the waves as they hit the shore. I could get used to a life like this.

It also meant that Jamie and I got to spend time together. Not that we were alone. Either Cody or Danika was always with us. I didn't mind so much, except that I did, I just couldn't let it show. I especially didn't like it when Danika was with us. I tended to hide in my room, which was counter-productive. What I should have been doing was making sure I didn't leave her and Jamie alone. I didn't like the way she looked at him. I didn't like the way she manoeuvred herself to always be close to him. Instead of staking my claim and telling her to back off, I ran away.

I was so confused. My feelings for Jamie grew day by day but I knew our time together was limited. As much as I wanted to imagine a world where we would be free to pursue a relationship together, real life just didn't happen like that. For Jamie and me to even consider being together as a couple, he would have to leave the guard. I would never ask that of him. He, like me, had trained for years to be in the guard and he loved it as much as I did. I was already mourning my imminent departure from it and there was no way I could ask him to leave just so we could be together. That wouldn't be fair.

A shadow fell across me and I looked up to see the man himself smiling down at me.

"I thought you might like a drink," he said.

I grinned up at him, banishing the depressing thoughts that had been swirling in my head.

"You thought right," I said.

He sat on the sun lounge beside me and handed me a cold glass full of some fruity drink - including brightly coloured umbrella. We sat in silence for a moment, looking out over the bow of the yacht to the endless water that surrounded us.

"We'll be on Le Beau tomorrow," Jamie said.

"Yeah," I said.

This was the first full day on the yacht. We had boarded yesterday afternoon in Monaco and we would dock on Le Beau tomorrow afternoon. To keep up the ruse of us as body doubles, we were on a separate - identical - yacht to the queen. We had our own entourage and whenever we were topside we were supposed to be in disguise. No need for all the makeup, but I did have to wear the wig and big dark glasses. I'd even added a big floppy hat for more than just sun protection.

"Let me rub some sunscreen on you," Jamie said. "We wouldn't want you getting burnt."

I sat forward and turned my back to him. I had been given a spray tan before we left Merveille. My skin was fairer than Alyssa's and I did have the tendency to burn. Having a fake tan wouldn't stop that, although it might hide the lobster red colour I would turn if I allowed myself to get too much sun.

The sunscreen was cold and I shivered. It had nothing to do with Jamie's hands on me. None whatsoever. He had to pull the sun bed he was sitting on closer and I could feel the heat of his body behind me. He pulled the long dark hair over my shoulder and placed a soft, sneaky kiss on the place where my shoulder and my neck met before smoothing sunscreen over the very same spot. It was risky, being this close, but we were supposed to be pretending to be the queen and her consort. It may seem like we were in the middle of the ocean where no one could see us, but neither of us were that naïve. The press were crafty and with technology these days I didn't think it was possible for us to ever be safe from prying eyes. Where there was a will, there was a way.

As if my thoughts conjured them, we heard the telltale sound of a low flying helicopter. We had no way of knowing if it was press or simply a joy-flight from nearby Spain, but it was better to think the worst. I turned to face Jamie and my eyes dropped to his lips. Why not take advantage of our anonymity? I leaned forward and brushed my lips over his. He growled low in his throat and his hands went into my hair to pull me closer. We hadn't had much cause - or opportunity - to kiss since we had been on the yacht, so I made the most of it. I drank him in, savouring the feel of his lips on mine. The spicy scent of him filled my nose and I lost myself to the moment, trying to imprint it on my memory so that I would have something to keep me company when we were apart.

He lifted his head and looked down at me. I couldn't see his eyes because they were covered by his dark glasses, but I imagined they had turned stormy grey.

"Well played *agapoúla mou,*" he murmured before brushing a soft, quick kiss across my lips.

He stood and walked back inside and I huffed out a breath as I turned back on the sun lounge and lay back down. I closed my eyes, holding on to the moment as long as I could. Part of me wished that this would never end. It was honestly the first time I had ever imagined a life outside of the guard. If Jamie was with me, I think I could even be happy.

Jamie

WE DOCKED ON LE BEAU IN A FLURRY OF ACTIVITY. ALYSSA AND Will had already arrived incognito and were ensconced in the hotel where we would all be staying. The Mayfield was a new hotel and casino and by all accounts it was worth every penny of the exorbitant prices they charged.

I took Meredith's hand as we crossed the gangplank to the dock and relished the small amount of contact.

"Your Highness," Benjamin said, sketching a bow.

I raised an eyebrow at him. He wasn't supposed to meet us on the dock. I knew we had a security briefing with him within the hour of our arrival, but seeing him here on the dock set off alarm bells in my head. Had something happened? I could feel Meredith stiffen beside me as the same thoughts were more than likely running through her head.

"I apologise for the interruption," Benjamin said as he fell into step beside us.

"Not at all," Meredith said. "Is there something we need to be made aware of?"

"I'm afraid I must steal the prince away for a few moments," Benjamin said. "The car will take you to your spa appointment. I will ensure that the prince is returned to you by the time you are finished."

Meredith's mouth pressed together in a thin line. "Of course," she said.

The fact that Benjamin wanted to see me alone kicked my heart rate up a few notches. It could only mean that there was trouble on Kalopsia, or that he had news at the very least. I brushed a kiss on Meredith's cheek and then helped her into the car. Benjamin escorted me to another waiting car and I slid into the cool interior surprised to see the queen waiting for me.

"Your Grace," I said, nodding my head in a bow of respect.

The door closed, sealing us inside together. Just the two of us.

"It's uncanny," she said after a moment of examining me.

I lifted a hand to my hair and pulled down the dark sunglasses I was wearing.

She seemed to shake herself and then take a deep breath. "I need to ask you a question," she said.

I inclined my head, indicating that she was free to ask me whatever it was she wanted.

"What are your plans?"

My eyes popped wide as I lifted my head to look at her. "Pardon?"

She sighed and turned to look out the window at the passing scenery. "You can't stay as part of my security team forever, Jamie. You and I both know that."

I let out a long, slow breath as I thought about what she was saying. Alyssa and I had never discussed who I really was or the implications of it if it were ever to be made public.

"I can honestly say that I didn't ever think the day would come where I would be in any position to *do* anything," I answered truthfully.

"And now?" She turned back to look at me and I tried not to squirm under her gaze.

Alyssa had changed so much since becoming queen - in good ways. She had become confident and assertive and from what I could see, authority sat well on her. She was a good ruler and a queen who had the best interests of her people at heart. It was the kind of ruler I would want to be if I ever had the chance.

"Now I still don't know what my future holds."

"But you do understand that your time in exile is coming to an end. One way or another, you will be exposed." She said it kindly. It wasn't a threat.

I rubbed my hands over my face. "I know," I said, resigned. "Of course I want to be able to step into the role I was born for. I just have no idea what that role will be now. I don't even know if my father is still alive. I don't know if my people even want me back."

Her features softened. If anyone could understand what I was going through, Alyssa would. She had faced a similar dilemma when her father and brother were killed. There had been no provision in the long history of Merveille for a female heir. She had had to fight for her birthright, much the same as I would be forced to if I wanted to be a prince-in-exile no longer.

"And what of Meredith?"

I managed to keep my face from betraying the surprise I felt. "What about her?" I asked carefully.

She picked up a newspaper that was sitting, unnoticed, on the seat beside her and handed it over to me. On the front page was a photograph of two people on a boat. They were kissing. If I wasn't mistaken, it was Meredith and me.

"Would you like to explain this?" she asked.

I cleared my throat. "We were just doing as we have been instructed to do," I said, stiffly.

"You knew this photo was being taken?"

"We weren't positive," I replied. "We heard the approach of the helicopter and took a guess."

She handed over another paper. This one was open to the society pages and had several photographs of Meredith and me at the casino. I took the paper and gazed down at the pictures. There was obvious affection showing on both our faces as we laughed at something. It was a great photo of us, except that we looked like the queen and Will.

"And these?"

I looked up at her, but there was nothing showing on her face to give away what she felt. I didn't know if she was upset or concerned.

"We were doing our job," I said.

"Meredith is my best friend," Alyssa said. "I care about her a great deal."

"I am aware," I said.

"I don't want her to get hurt."

"You think I would hurt her?"

"I don't think you would do it intentionally," she said and sighed. Her rigid posture relaxed a bit as she glanced away and then back at me. "She's leaving the guard."

"I know."

She looked surprised at that. "I didn't think Benjamin had announced it yet."

"He hasn't," I replied, "Meredith told me." I don't know why I told her that. I was trying to assure her that there was nothing going on between Meredith and me, and yet I was giving myself away with the words I spoke. "We work together a lot," I clarified. "She felt I should know."

Alyssa nodded slowly but I didn't think she believed me.

"And you will be leaving soon too."

It was a subtle warning. Not that she would be kicking me out of the country, but that the time was coming when I could no longer hide. I knew that too.

"Does Meredith know?"

I shook my head. "No," I said with a harsh exhale.

Alyssa's eyes softened. Did she understand how hard it was for me to keep something like this from the woman I was very quickly falling for? Did Alyssa have an inkling of the way I felt and was trying very hard to deny?

"The last thing I want to do is hurt Meredith," I said, looking her in the eyes. "I know the situation is...unfortunate. We will both be going our separate ways when we return to Merveille. Until then we are both just trying to do our jobs as best we can under the circumstances."

Alyssa didn't say anything for a long time. The car came to a stop and the door opened. I moved to get out but she leaned over and rested a hand on my arm. I looked into her eyes and saw a whole tumult of emotions before she locked them down.

"I care about both of you," she said. "And I only want the best for both of you."

"I know," I said and then stepped out of the car, sliding my sunglasses on.

I headed into the hotel, although the last thing I wanted was to be trapped in a room, no matter how luxurious it was. I needed to run, to move. I needed to get rid of this restless feeling that had come into my body after my talk with Alyssa. I knew that continuing this thing with Meredith was playing with fire, but every time I tried to retreat, I was pulled back in by her smile or a look. She was intoxicating and I couldn't seem to get enough of her. It couldn't last, we both knew that, but it didn't stop us continuing to crash together. I didn't know what the future held past this tour. For all I knew there would be nothing left of my country by the time I actually got to do anything about it. I couldn't ask Meredith to stand by my side while I tried to resurrect what had once been a great, if small, nation.

I smiled at myself. Meredith as my queen? Where had that thought even come from? We weren't headed down that path. We were just having fun and soon enough, that fun would be over.

CHAPTER 8

Meredith

I walked into the suite of The Mayfield and I was blissfully alone.
Three days in Monaco, two days on the yacht and it felt like I
hadn't had a minute to myself. I usually didn't mind having company,
but these last few days had felt crowded so the silence of the suite was
welcome.

I wandered around, taking everything in. The hotel in Monaco was
all nineteenth century beaux-arts architecture, but The Mayfield was
sleek and modern. Shiny, white tiles led to thick, plush, dark carpet.
White leather sofas and dark, chocolate wood furniture. Recessed
lighting was strategically placed to highlight the minimalist artwork
that took the form of sculptures and large canvases that hung on the
walls. The main area of the suite was dominated by an entire wall made
of glass that looked out over the ocean.

I walked over to the windows and stood for a moment taking in the
view. I didn't think I would ever get enough of seeing the ocean. I
opened the door and stepped out onto the balcony. There was a light
breeze and I closed my eyes and dragged in a breath of the fresh, salty
air. A couple of hours in the spa had ended with a glorious massage and

combined with a few moments of solitude, I felt myself relaxing. I hadn't realised the tension that had built up in me since the tour began. There was so much going on in my head, the least of which was whatever was happening with Jamie and me.

This entire tour was so out of my depth. I had known that part of the reason I was in Alyssa's security team was because there would be times I would need to impersonate her. I had been trained from a young age for that very thing. But the other times I'd had to do it had only been for short bursts. A quick walk from a car into a building to distract the press while Alyssa went in through another entrance. This whole 'living' like Alyssa had me a little on edge. I wasn't used to having to act like a lady all the time. I sighed. I supposed it was something that I would have to get used to since everything about my life was going to change once I returned home.

Countess Meredith. I rolled the words around in my head and grimaced. Despite having been raised in a ducal household, I had never aspired to hold a title myself. I was happy to be the nameless, faceless body guard that followed the queen around. The press generally left me alone - just the way I liked it. That was until daddy dearest took the role of prime minister. I gritted my teeth and then sighed, shaking my head to dispel the sudden tension that had returned to my shoulders. It wasn't fair of me to expect him to give up something that he was so obviously good at. Besides the fact that Alyssa needed him, my father was what our country needed to lead it through the changes that Alyssa spearheaded. I just hadn't expected the fallout to be me having to give up what I loved.

I turned my back on the view and walked back into the suite. I crossed the spacious living area and entered the bedroom where my luggage had already been unpacked. My laptop sat on the small desk and I took a seat in front of it. I told the girls back home that I would keep them updated on what was happening. So far I had done little but send them a quick text to say everything was going well.

I opened the lid of the laptop and clicked on the icon for my email account. The topmost email was from my mother. I hovered the mouse over the subject line that was written in all caps. I could simply delete it and pretend that it had gotten lost in the black hole of the internet, but she would only send it again and then I'd have to deal with her bad mood. I took a deep breath. No. It was better if I dealt with this head on.

Dear Meredith,
  I hope this missive finds you well.

Only my mother would start an email so formally. I couldn't restrain myself from rolling my eyes.

As per our previous discussion, I have attached a list of possible suitors.

Excuse me? Possible suitors? What discussion?

And a schedule of events that require your attendance when you are returned.

Okay, so maybe I should have just deleted this email after all.

Please read through the list and number them in order of preference so that I may begin making overtures toward them.

You have got to be kidding me. My mother wanted me to rank my potential suitors so that she could set up dates with them on my behalf? That seemed...clinical, even for her. And where did she even get this list? Were these men who had shown an interest in me? Or were they a list of men who she felt would make advantageous associations? I had never been close to my mother. We had such different philosophies on life that we had never seemed to bond. How would she even know what kind of man I was attracted to, or didn't that matter? Was my future husband to be chosen for me purely on his breeding and family tree? Would I have any say at all?

Well, of course I got to prioritise her list, so I suppose that was something.

With morbid fascination I clicked open the attachment helpfully named 'suitable and appropriate members of the peers.' I assumed by appropriate she meant single and within an acceptable age. Suitable had to indicate her idea of who would make the most advantageous match with our family. I wondered as I skimmed the list if she had ever emailed Freddie with a similar one. I couldn't imagine that Alex would have been my mother's first choice for her first born and heir to the Bingham line.

I had a weird floaty feeling, like I was high up and watching my life play out before me as if I were just a spectator. I suppose there was some part of me that had always known this day would come. Had I really expected my mother to let me stay in the guard indefinitely? Whether I acknowledged it or not, this had always been the inevitable outcome. I suppose I had hoped that when I married it would be because I had fallen in love. I wasn't a romantic and I didn't have daydreams about some prince riding up on his white horse to sweep me off my feet. I just thought that the whole love, marriage and starting a family thing would happen organically. That I would meet someone, have a courtship, fall in love and marry.

Images of Jamie flashed behind my eyes and I gasped. No. I had never once thought that what Jamie and I had would go any further. I had never once imagined him as my life partner. Until now. Until a list of potential mates was presented to me and none of them could stand up against the only man who had ever really held my interest. I skimmed the list again. I knew every single one of these men and none of them sparked even the slightest curiosity in me. Some of them I could cross off immediately. Others I liked well enough, but there was nothing about them that made me want to get to know them better.

I closed my eyes, shutting out the list of names that stared back at me accusingly. Spending this time with Jamie was a double-edged sword. Pretending to be a couple was messing with my head. Having him touch me, kiss me, hold my hand in public was giving me ideas of what it could be like if this thing between us was real. And I wanted it to be real. It took an effort to actually admit that to myself. I didn't care that he was a body guard or that he wasn't on the approved list that my mother had so kindly curated. I wanted Jamie and me to be together for real. He had hinted that it might be possible for us. That when we returned and I left the guard, there might be a chance for us to pursue this. I had turned him down, but what if...

THE DOOR TO THE SUITE OPENED AND I COULD HEAR VOICES AND laughter. It seemed my idyllic solitude had come to an end.

I shut my laptop and went to the ensuite to check that my personal revelations weren't written all over my face. I knew I needed to talk to Jamie, to see if he was serious about what he had proposed. The trick was bringing it up without asking him directly. I needed to get a feel for what he was thinking without actually revealing my own thoughts or feelings. No way was I going to put myself out there on the wire unless he was on the same page. I had learned never to show my vulnerability to my team. As the only female, I had been warned that showing any form of weakness would distract the rest of the team from their objective. It was a natural reaction for men to want to protect anyone they deemed weaker, so I had to show them that I was just as capable and in control as they were. If my teammates were worried about me, then they wouldn't be focused on Alyssa.

This same applied to having this discussion with Jamie. I needed him to be honest and if he was worried about offending me or hurting me, then he would simply tell me what he thought I wanted to hear. But I needed the truth. I needed to know what he was feeling and what he was thinking. How to find those things out without directly questioning him was the trick, and I had no idea how I was going to do it.

Happy that I looked normal and not like some love-sick puppy, I walked out into the main living area of the suite to see Jamie and Danika wrapped in each other's arms. I came to an abrupt halt, not quite sure where to look or what to say. My mouth went dry and I was pretty sure my heart literally stopped beating.

Jamie looked up and saw me standing there and broke the hold, grinning at me over Danika's shoulder.

"Hey Mer," he said, guilelessly.

Danika whipped around to look at me, a guilty expression crossing her face quickly before she smoothed it away with a cool smile. The same smile she always bestowed on me. The very same one that never seemed to reach her eyes. Eyes that held a calculating and distrustful look whenever they were turned in my direction.

Jamie walked over to the small kitchenette that had little more than a bar fridge, a sink and a fruit bowl. He opened the fridge and snagged a bottle of water, holding it out first to Danika and then to me in invitation. I shook my head, my heart pounding and my ears full of a rushing sound. I guess I had my answer. Jamie and I were over.

I turned to go back to my room, not prepared to sit in the same airspace as these two and watch as Jamie moved on. But I stopped when Jamie called my name.

"Meredith," he said.

I didn't turn around, but I did wait for him to continue.

"There is a pretty decent gym downstairs. We haven't trained for a couple of days, do you feel like a workout?"

"You didn't get enough when we were just down there?" Danika asked and any hope that I had that maybe I had misconstrued what I'd seen, fled.

"Hardly," Jamie said. "That was just a warm up."

"Maybe later," I murmured, moving toward my door once again.

Before I could escape, Jamie was behind me. I could feel the warmth of his body on my back even though he wasn't touching me. I could smell his aftershave. The scent would always be one of my favourites but now it would also be a reminder of what could have been.

"Mer," he whispered in my ear. "We need to talk."

I scrunched my eyes closed and clenched my jaw against the sob that wanted to break out of my chest. Nothing good ever came from those four words.

"Not now," I said. I needed to get away from him.

I tried to open my door but he hooked his arm through mine and spun me around to face him. My defensive reaction was automatic and my forearm came up to press across his throat while my other hand gripped his wrist. He didn't move but looked at me with a sardonic smile and a quirked eyebrow.

I took a breath and relaxed my stance, letting him go, but not before I saw Danika step up behind him as if she was going to intervene to protect him. Wouldn't he just love that? Two women fighting over him. Fighting for him.

I dropped my head and shook it slightly. No. He wasn't like that. Although it was possibly a fantasy that most men indulged in. Jamie wasn't the type of guy who would get off on it. We were genuinely friends and I had thought more.

"Maybe I will go to the gym," I said, lifting my eyes to his.

"Great. Let me just—"

"Alone," I said and turned around to go into my bedroom to change.

I closed the door behind me and leant against it for a moment. I could lay the blame of this whole debacle at the feet of my mother. If she hadn't sent me that list then I wouldn't have even entertained the idea of something more happening between Jamie and me. The thought of the two of us potentially being in a real and public relationship wouldn't have even entered my mind if I hadn't been forced to think about my future partner. Yep. This was all my mother's fault.

I strode over to the chest of drawers and pulled out some training gear. I changed quickly and grabbed my phone and earbuds, jamming them in my ears and hitting play on my playlist. 'Alter Bridge' blasted in my ears and I relished the heavy rock as I escaped my room and then the suite without making further eye contact with either Jamie or Danika. I needed to find my Zen so that I could get back to the place I was when I first arrived at the suite. The relaxed and calm Meredith that had been massaged into a boneless lump was long gone, and in her place was a twisted and bitter woman with her mad on. I needed to burn off this ugly feeling with a hard workout and maybe I would find sanity while I was at it.

Jamie

I STOOD FROM THE COUCH AS MEREDITH CAME OUT OF THE BEDROOM dressed for the gym. I went to speak, but she didn't even look at me and she had her earbuds in, so she wouldn't have heard me anyway. I was clueless to know why she was giving me the cold shoulder. I needed to talk to her about what Alyssa said to me. We needed to be on the same page if Alyssa took her aside and questioned her too. I would have gladly spilled everything to Alyssa if I knew that was what Meredith wanted, but something told me she wanted to keep what was happening with us under wraps for now.

"Can you show me that move again?" Danika said from behind me.

"Huh?" I turned around to face her.

"You know, that hold you just had me in. You were going to show me how to get out of it."

"Oh right," I said with a little shake of my head. I had seen Meredith and had completely lost my train of thought. I couldn't help the little grin that turned up the corners of my mouth. No one had ever had that effect on me. Seeing a beautiful woman had never been enough to distract me, but Meredith was a whole different matter. The woman had the ability to make me lose every rational thought that came into my head.

I pulled Danika back into my arms, holding her close, caging her in.

"You need to make sure you can get your hands under my arm, here. Do you see?"

Danika nodded as she wiggled her fingers between my arm and her chest.

"And then you need to able the right amount of pressure—"

"Oh whoa! Sorry man. I didn't mean to interrupt."

I looked up at Cody who had just walked into the suite, dropping my arms from around Danika.

"What's that supposed to mean?" I asked, puzzled by the slick grin on his face.

"You need to hang a sock on the door or something if you are going to go all co-ed on me."

I turned to look at Danika who grinned back at me and I suddenly realised what it must have looked like. Oh god. Meredith had seen the same thing. No wonder she had been so cold toward me. I was such an idiot.

"There's nothing going on," I said gruffly. "I was just showing Danika...Why am I even explaining this to you? I have to go." I needed to get to Meredith and explain what she had seen. I would get down on hands and knees and grovel if I needed to.

"You're not going anywhere," Cody said, all teasing gone from his voice. "Benjamin wants to see you in his suite."

I ran a frustrated hand through my hair. "What about Meredith?"

"What about her?" Cody asked. "Benjamin just said you and Danika."

I swore under my breath. If he wanted to see just the two of us then it had something to do with Kalopsia.

"Fine," I said. "Let's go." Meredith would have to wait. I just hoped that she was going to be in a more forgiving mood by the time she got back from the gym.

The suite where Benjamin and the rest of the team were staying was one floor down. The floor we were on was split into two penthouses - Alyssa and Will were in one and Meredith and I were in the other. There was a guard placed at the elevator doors as well as outside both rooms. The level below had four suites. One was set up as a communications room and the others were for the various personnel who had accompanied us - other guards and support staff.

I knocked on Benjamin's door and waited for it to be opened. Daniel nodded to me before stepping aside to let me in. He stepped out and closed the door behind him leaving Danika, Benjamin and me alone. The weird Skype alert sounded from Benjamin's computer before either of us could say anything and then Von Bartham was on the screen.

I tried not to show the tension that knotted me up inside. I was desperate for news from home. For ten years I had had little or no news and I had tried to forget that I was a prince in hiding, exiled by those I had been born to serve. Now, I was getting regular updates and each one was worse than the one before. I had been gone too long. I tried to reason with myself that this was what the people had wanted. That they had willingly and knowingly supported the coup that had destroyed my family and displaced me, leaving me without a home, without even a country. Now it seemed that most people hadn't even understood what was going on. My heart broke for the innocents who chafed against this new rule and bore the brunt of arrogant and narcissistic men who had no care for anyone but themselves and their own interests.

"Take a seat," Benjamin said and I realised I was still standing just inside the door.

I nodded once and moved across the suite to the large mahogany table where Benjamin sat. He angled the laptop so I could see Von Bartham and there was a spread of aerial photos on the table around the laptop. Arial photos that looked very like shots of the castle I had once called home.

"What's going on?" I asked.

CHAPTER 9

Meredith

The suite was quiet when I returned. The guard on the door nodded to me, but I didn't know him well enough to ask the questions I needed answers to, namely where was Jamie and did he leave with *her*?

Where the solitude of earlier had felt good, now it felt suffocating. I didn't know where things stood between Jamie and me and sitting around the suite waiting for him to return felt too passive. The workout at the gym helped but I still felt restless and unable to settle, like a cat on a hot tin roof. I showered and changed, my actions automatic as my brain revisited the snapshot of Jamie and Danika in an embrace. It felt so out of character for Jamie but I couldn't deny what I saw.

"Ugh!" I growled to myself. "Stop it!"

I paced around the bedroom. We had a 'night off.' It was probably just as well because I didn't think I would be very convincing as Alyssa right now. My laptop pinged with an incoming message and I shot daggers at it, wishing I had actual daggers to throw at the offending machine. My hand even went to my thigh where I had a knife strapped, but I clenched my fist, grabbing air instead of the knife and growled out a frustrated noise not unlike some wild animal. I couldn't stay here. I couldn't sit around and pretend I didn't see what I saw between Danika and Jamie. I couldn't sit around and let my mother's plans for me fester in my brain. I needed to get out and just forget about this nightmare that my life had become.

I pulled on my shoulder holster and then a light jacket to cover it. I left my long hair down and only put on the barest hint of makeup. I was not pretending to be Alyssa tonight. This was just me and I wanted to feel like the real me for a change. Since this tour started I had been pulled in so many directions and I hadn't been able to just let my hair down and be Meredith. I was either playing Alyssa or I was acting like a wealthy, anonymous celebrity. Tonight I was neither. I was just me.

I walked out of the suite, nodding to the guard on the door, but not engaging in conversation. The guard at the elevator pressed the button for me when he saw me coming and by the time I was standing at the doors, they opened. I stepped in with a small smile of gratitude and hit the button for the lobby. The Mayfield had a casino and several restaurants and bars on the ground floor and that was where I was headed first. A cold, alcohol laced drink was exactly what I needed.

I wasn't someone who usually turned to drink to solve my problems, but tonight I just wanted a little relief from the internal dialogue that was on repeat in my head. I wanted the kind of relief that only alcohol could give me.

I stepped out of the elevator and the buzz and energy of the crowd bumped up against me, beckoning me forward. It was then that I realised I was on Le Beau. Which sounded weird, but the truth was, until now it had only been a theoretical knowing. Now I could feel the party atmosphere that infused the island. I had never been to Le Beau, but I had heard the stories. It was the Las Vegas of the Mediterranean and I would have missed it all if I had stayed in my room and sulked. We were only here for two days before we set sail again and I had been so caught up in my own problems that I could have missed it completely.

I changed my mind about getting a drink in one of the hotel bars and walked out the front doors instead. The sun was shining and I slipped my sunglasses on, letting a smile cross my face as I took a deep breath. I set off on foot, heading down the strip that was lined with more decadent hotels and casinos than I had ever seen in one place. Long, sleek limousines glided gracefully along the road beside small, compact rust buckets that weaved in and out of the slow moving traffic, horns blaring in contempt. I felt like a kid at Disneyland. There was so much to look at and so many things I wanted to do but I didn't know where to start.

My stomach growled and I realised I hadn't eaten in hours. So, food. I wanted to start there. I looked around to see what took my fancy. I saw a sign for a dessert bar. Dessert. Bar. Two birds, one stone. I strode inside and was greeted by a smiling hostess.

"Table for one?" she asked.

"Just a seat at the bar," I replied.

She nodded and then led me deeper inside. The bar was all dark leather and wood. It took a moment for my eyes to adjust to the low lighting, but by the time I slid onto the stool at the bar I was already feeling much more relaxed. The hostess handed me a menu and then left me to peruse. There was a page of just desserts and a page of cocktails. But my favourite page was the one that combined the two.

Dark chocolate brownie drenched in crème de cacao, topped with Irish cream ice cream.

Tiramisu laced with Tia Maria and Frangelico cream.

Fruit salad soaked in red wine and served with Champagne jelly.

Melon balls marinated in Midori and served with coconut rum sauce.

My mouth watered and I didn't know where to start.

"What can I get you?" the bartender asked, coming to stand in front of me.

"I can't decide," I replied. "It all looks good."

"Can I suggest the Drunken Mess?"

I looked up at him and grinned. "Drunken Mess?"

"Like an Eton Mess," he said with a grin matching mine, "But with alcohol."

I closed the menu and nodded enthusiastically. "Yes," I said. "That."

He winked at me and walked away to place my order. I took a moment to look around the near empty bar. I suppose I was a bit early. A dessert bar seemed like a late night thing and the sun hadn't even set yet.

"Can I get you a drink while you wait?" the bartender asked, coming back to stand in front of me.

"Yes," I replied.

Jamie

MY MOOD WAS NO BETTER WHEN I LEFT THE MEETING WITH Benjamin. We had a clearer understanding about what was happening on Kalopsia, but still no idea how we were going to change anything. By all reports, the country had descended into a pit of corruption and destitution. The people were suffering. The innocents and those most in need were being discarded and forgotten about. General Anastas, as he was calling himself, was a despot. His rule was worse than anything he accused my father of. The whole thing left me wanting to punch holes in walls. What I really wanted to do was storm the castle and take it by force, but my hands were tied. This was about more than just me and my need to see justice served. A diplomatic solution needed to be floated first and then I could look at a show of force. Except...me and what army? I was a displaced prince living in a country that was not mine and without a security force of my own. I couldn't ask Merveille to go to war on my behalf. And truly, would a war even be the answer? Hadn't there been enough bloodshed?

All I wanted right then was to hold Meredith in my arms. There was something about having her close that soothed the raging tempest inside me. I stalked into the suite, alone. I refused Danika's attempts to accompany me. I needed to speak with Meredith and I needed to do it without interruptions.

The suite was empty.

I stalked from room to room looking for anything that might give me an indication of where Meredith might have gone, but there I couldn't find anything. No note. Nothing. I pulled out my phone to check for a message but there wasn't one. I strode back across the suite and flung the door open.

"Where is she?" I asked the guy on the door.

"She left a couple of hours ago," he replied. "She didn't tell me where she was going."

I stepped back inside the suite and slammed the door, not caring what the guard thought of my tantrum. I ran a hand through my hair, tugging at the ends hoping to release some of the pent up anger and worry that I felt. I pulled out my phone again and called Cody.

"Do you know where Meredith is?" I asked without any preliminaries when he answered.

"I haven't seen her," he replied.

I stabbed at the screen to disconnect the call and then pulled up another number.

"Meredith is gone. Did you send her somewhere?"

"No," Benjamin answered.

I disconnected from him and paced around the suite. Finally, not able to stay inside the room any longer, I crossed to the door and flung it open again. I crossed the hall and pounded on the queen's door, ignoring the guard who stood there. Scott opened the door and gave me a disgruntled look.

"Is Meredith in there?" I asked.

"No," he said. "I haven't seen her."

"Dammit," I growled. "Where the hell is she?"

"She left the building," the door guard said.

I turned to him. "Left the building? Where did she go?"

He shrugged. "No idea. All I know is that she left and headed out onto the strip."

I growled low in my throat and took off down the hall. The elevator doors opened as I approached and I got in and stabbed the down button. Where would she have gone? Why the hell had she left without letting anyone know where she was going? It wasn't like Meredith to be so irresponsible. The last thing I needed right now was to be traipsing around Le Beau looking for her. Didn't she understand that?

I charged out of the elevator when it finally opened on the ground floor and headed straight for the front doors. The strip was a hive of activity, but I didn't take any of it in. My focus was wholly and solely on finding my partner. I looked up and down the street, hoping that she would just appear. Of course she didn't. Nothing in my life ever happened easily. I took a punt and headed down the street, glancing at the buildings that I passed. The island may have been relatively small, but with the amount and size of the buildings along the strip, it could take days to search each and every one of them for her. I didn't even know what frame of mind she was in when she left. Did she come out here to find something fun to do or was she running and hiding from me?

We had never even been out on a date, so I didn't even know what she might want to do for fun. Our relationship had been after hours in the training room and the occasional stolen moments while we were on shift together. I didn't even really know what she liked to eat or drink. Our food was provided at the palace and it was usually something ridiculously healthy to ensure that we were always on top of our fitness. Even while we had been on tour, the food had been served with little input from us. We just ate whatever was placed in front of us. So I had absolutely no idea where she would go when left to her own devices.

With no clear idea of where to even start, I walked into the first bar I came to. It took four such forays before I finally found her. I heard her first. Her laugh to be exact. It gripped my gut and clenched hard. Relief and anger coursed through me, tinged with jealousy as I spotted her sitting at the bar and smiling at the bartender who was regaling her with some story.

I stalked across the bar, ignoring the hostess.

"Meredith," I said, my voice a low, growly warning.

She swung around to face me and her eyes narrowed. She tossed her hair over her shoulder and then turned back to the bar.

"What do you want?" she asked without looking at me.

"You left."

"I did."

"Nobody knew where you were."

"By design. I wanted to be alone."

I gripped her arm and she swung back around to face me, her blue eyes flashing dangerously. "Get your hands off me."

I dropped my hand and dropped my head. I squeezed my eyes shut and huffed out a breath. When I looked back up at her, I was calmer.

"Meredith," I said softly. "Please. We need to talk."

"I know what you're going to say and I don't want to hear it."

I quirked an eyebrow at her. "I don't understand."

"I get it, okay? You needed a way to break things off with me. I just thought you would be a bit more of a man and speak to me rather than just hooking up with *her*."

"No. Meredith, no—"

"I saw you! I saw the two—"

I pulled her to me and slammed my mouth down on hers. It was an effective way to shut her up and it went a long way to calming the storm inside me. She tasted of something sweet and heady and I lost myself in her kiss as she melted against me. This is what I needed. Just her. Just this. It made everything else seem insignificant and all my insurmountable problems suddenly felt not so impossible any more.

Meredith

I COULDN'T BREATHE. EVERYTHING INSIDE ME FELT LIKE IT WAS going to explode. I should be pushing him away and demanding he never touch me again but...Oh god. His kiss. He stole all the air from my body when he pressed his lips to mine and now I was more confused than ever. Why was he there kissing me instead of wherever *she* was?

I found the strength I needed to push him away. He looked down at me with those stormy eyes and it was like looking into the very essence of him. There were no walls. No shuttering. He left himself open to me, not shying away from whatever it was we were both feeling. It was everything I wanted and too much at the same time. I turned my head away and slid back onto the bar stool. He climbed up onto the one beside me.

I'd had enough to drink that the edges of my hurt and anger had become fuzzy but I lifted my hand and called the bartender over anyway. There was no way I could get through this conversation without more alcohol.

"Gin and tonic," I said.

"Boilermaker," Jamie said, and I turned to him, surprised.

He shrugged his shoulders. When the bartender placed the beer and the shot in front of him, he slammed back the shot before lifting the beer to his lips. I sipped my gin, watching as he swallowed large mouthfuls of his beer.

"What?" he asked when he lowered his glass. He lifted his hand to the bartender for another one.

"What is going on?' I asked. "You wanted to talk. You tracked me down, so talk."

He waited until another shot was placed in front of him and then he swallowed it without looking at me.

"What you saw," he began, still not looking at me, "in the suite with Danika? It wasn't what you thought."

"You had her in your arms," I said, trying to keep the hurt and anger out of my voice. "What was I supposed to think?"

"I didn't have her in my arms," he said, taking a long swallow of his fresh beer. "I had her in a *hold*."

"You expect me to believe that you were showing her some grappling move?"

He turned to look at me then and the abject sadness on his face said more than his words ever could. "Yes," he said, "because it's the truth."

We stared at each other, the rest of the bar fading away. He lifted his hand to tuck a stray curl behind my ear. I closed my eyes at the feel of his fingers as they caressed my cheek. I couldn't help leaning into his palm and rubbing my cheek against him like a cat.

"Meredith," he said, his voice a rough whisper. "Don't you understand how I feel about you?"

My eyes popped open and I knew we had to have 'the talk.' I

moved my face away from his hand and he let it drop to his lap. I took a fortifying sip of my drink and without looking at him, I said, "My mother sent me a list of potential suitors."

Out of the corner of my eye I saw his hand tighten around his glass until his knuckles turned white and I worried for the integrity of the glass.

"And a whole itinerary of events that I will need to attend when I return to Merveille. All of them require an escort. I'm to be paraded around like a piece of prime beef."

Jamie drained his glass and then turned to me, twisting my seat so that I faced him too.

"No," he said, the word choked out with emotion. "I don't want that. I don't want you seeing anyone else."

I searched his eyes. I was completely on board with that plan, but I just didn't know how to make it a reality.

"I don't have a choice," I said softly.

He leaned forward and kissed me slowly, deeply.

"You do have a choice," he said when he lifted his head. "You have me."

"Is that what you want?" I asked. "Am I what you want?"

I held my breath as I waited for him to answer. His eyes softened and the corner of his mouth tipped up.

"You are everything I want," he said, and then kissed me again.

When he lifted his head from mine again, I sighed and rested my forehead against his.

"How?" I whispered.

He threaded his fingers through my hair and ran his nose alongside mine. "Marry me," he whispered and then kissed me again.

"What?" I managed to mumble, pulling away from the intoxication of his lips.

"Marry me," he repeated.

"Jamie," I said, "we can't."

"Why not?" he asked. "We are on Le Beau. We can get a marriage license within the hour and can be married as soon as we find someone to officiate. It would solve both our problems."

"I'm not going to marry you to solve a problem," I said. The idea was crazy, ridiculous, insane, but... But what if...

"Then marry me because you love me," he whispered in my ear. "Marry me because I love you."

I sucked in a breath at his words as he continued to nuzzle my neck. He loved me? I closed my eyes and rolled the words around in my head. Jamie was in love with me? Could it be true?

"Come on *agapoúla mou*. Say yes."

I opened my eyes and stared into his. They were dark swirls of charcoal and silver. I didn't think I had ever seen him so intense or so serious. Jamie always managed to have a spark of mischief about him, even during a mission. But not now. Not in this moment as he stared back at me.

"Yes," I said.

CHAPTER 10

Meredith

The sun was setting and the sky had turned fiery red. I stood in the outdoor chapel on top of the tallest hill on Le Beau, the cool breeze dancing around me. It was surreal and beautiful and I felt like I was in a dream.

There had been other chapels down amongst the hotels and casinos of the strip, but Jamie had brought me here. We were met by a little man in a black cassock. He smiled and greeted Jamie as if he had known him forever and then they disappeared into the man's small cottage, leaving me to stand and marvel at the view. The alcohol still hummed in my veins, but my head was clear. I was going to marry Jamie. We already had the license and the rings - simple gold bands with no embellishment - and now all we needed was an officiant.

I turned as the door to the cottage opened and Jamie came out, smiling shyly at me, his cheeks an adorable pink from whatever he and the priest had discussed. They had spoken a language I didn't know, Greek maybe. I knew French, Italian and German, along with English, but I hadn't ever learned Greek. I hadn't ever needed to.

"Father Felipe says he can marry us," he said, taking my hand and keeping his gaze on mine. "He would just like a few words with you first."

I felt my eyes widen as I looked from Jamie to Father Felipe. I leaned forward and whispered to Jamie. "I don't speak Greek."

Jamie laughed and pulled me into a hug. "It's okay," he said into my hair, "he speaks English."

I followed Father Felipe into his cottage, feeling like I was going to see the principal. His cottage was small and only consisted of one room. A small bed was pushed into one corner and a wood stove took up another corner. He had a single armchair beside a side table with a lamp and a wooden dining table with four wooden chairs. The room was clean and sparse but looked comfortable and well-lived in.

"Sit," Father Felipe said, indicating one of the chairs around the table.

I took a seat while he bustled over to the stove in the corner and filled a kettle with some water from the tap that I hadn't noticed.

"Tea?" he asked and I shook my head no.

He shrugged and placed the kettle on the stove anyway before coming over to sit opposite me.

"You wish to marry the... ah, Jamie?"

I nodded. "I do," I replied, feeling nervous.

"You love him?"

Did I? I looked over the priest's shoulder to the small window that looked out over the chapel. Jamie stood there, his body in silhouette against the setting sun. My chest filled with an unidentifiable emotion as I watched him. He stood so strong and sure. He had always been that way. There was something just so dependable about him. To other people that might seem like a rather boring trait, but it was that quiet inner strength that drew me to him. I hadn't lived a life of chaos; my life and formative years had been steady and sure. If anything I was the wild one. Freddie may play the part of the carefree jet-setter - well, before he married Alex - but it was, and had always been, an act he perpetuated for the press. He once told me that people underestimated him because of his reputation and that made negotiations more fun. I was the one who didn't really fit the mould of the Bingham family. I was the one who kicked against the goad. Even now, instead of doing what my mother wanted me to do and marry a man with a title and who could be deemed a suitable match for my newly elevated status, I was choosing to marry a man who was a body guard. And where it should have felt wrong or rebellious, it just felt right.

"I do," I said, breathing out the words in a rush of revelation. I was in love with Jamie and it didn't matter where either of us had come from, only that we had managed find one another.

Father Felipe smiled at me and in his eyes I could see understanding. No doubt my whole thought process had been displayed across my face as I puzzled out the answer to his question.

"He loves you too," he said, "very much."

I dragged in a deep breath and then let it out slowly. Had I doubted Jamie's declaration of love? Perhaps. I wasn't used to being the object of a man's affections. I was the tomboy. I was the girl who could beat up most of the boys who ever even tried to get close to me. But now here was a man who was willing to get past all my prickles so he could know me better. I knew I wasn't the easiest person to get along with and according to my mother, I was impossible to love. But here was a man who loved me, warts and all.

"The road ahead won't be easy," Father Felipe said.

I nodded, my eyes finding Jamie again as he waited for me. The road ahead would be anything but easy. My mother was likely to have an apoplexy when she found out.

"You will need to cling to one another through the storms to come."

I nodded again. I had no doubt that Jamie would stick by me. He would be my rock as we faced the tempest that would be my mother. All her plans were going to be ruined tonight and it was the first time since she had informed me that I would be leaving the guard that I felt a weight lift from my shoulders. It didn't matter what she threw at me, I knew Jamie would not leave my side and in fact, he would be my champion.

"You will need to be prepared to forgive when necessary and fight for one another and for what you have found together."

I hoped that Jamie could forgive me for what I was about to put him through. I knew my mother and I knew that she would do whatever she could to try and break us up. My marrying a body guard was not in her plan and there would be a lot of fighting in our future. I just hoped that Jamie was prepared. He knew both my parents, had had dealings with them, especially when Freddie had asked Jamie to be in his wedding party. I had seen the distaste in my mother's face when Freddie had announced that little tidbit. That would be the tip of the iceberg once she found out that we had married.

"You still want to marry him?"

I turned my gaze back to Father Felipe and smiled. "Yes," I said. I had never been more sure of anything in my life.

Jamie

NOTHING FELT AS SURREAL AND YET SO COMPLETELY RIGHT THAN standing in the open chapel waiting for Meredith and Father Felipe. For the last ten years I'd had to keep my true self locked down for fear of being discovered. As I stood on the precipice that served as the chapel and looked down over the island of Le Beau, for the first time in so long I felt truly like myself. My life had been the epitome of the struggle portrayed by Plato's chariot allegory. Training the dark horse and the white horse to work together had been a daily fight within me. Trying to keep my chariot from falling as I battled with the two sides of who I was and who I was meant to be. Until that moment. For the first time it felt like my chariot was soaring, my horses in accord, their wings fully formed and beating in unison.

I heard the door to the cottage open and I turned from the view to see Meredith walking toward me. Nothing in my life had ever felt so fortuitous. It was as if everything that had come before was to bring me to this particular place and time. Destiny and serendipity converged to create the perfect moment. Nothing would ever be the same from this point on.

She smiled shyly at me and I felt my heart fill to bursting. It may have taken alcohol to lower our inhibitions enough to even consider such a spontaneous action, but there was no denying the truth of what

I felt for this woman and that I wanted her to be my wife, whatever the future held for us.

I took her hands in mine and we stood facing one another. Le Beau was at our feet and the sunset turned the sky into a blazing light show as if the gods themselves were celebrating our wedding. Father Felipe spoke words in English and Greek, praying a blessing over us as he joined us in holy matrimony.

Father Felipe knew me, knew who I really was. He had known me from a child and had helped me escape the castle after General Anastas had taken it by force. He had travelled with me to Merveille and then come here to Le Beau - his own form of exile. He knew the struggles that we would face and he had questioned my desire to do this thing here and now. But I had convinced him of the depth and strength of my feelings toward Meredith and she must have similarly convinced him of hers for me. He was a good man and I knew that if he agreed to marry us, then he believed that the two of us were meant to be together.

Most of the wedding traditions of Kalopsia were absent from our ceremony but Father Felipe did include the crowning. He pulled two beautifully worked silver crowns from his robes - more circlets than what most people would consider a crown. They were joined by a thick white ribbon and he placed one on each of our heads. He swapped the crowns three times before instructing us to walk around the altar three times. Then he blessed us and our union.

I turned to Meredith and cupped her face with my hands. I knew there were things about me she didn't know. I knew that our life so far had been built on a lie. But when I looked into her eyes, I knew that none of that mattered. What I felt for her was not a lie. What I felt for her was bigger than whatever we were each facing at home. I lowered my head to hers and kissed her, sealing our marriage, binding our future. There would be recriminations ahead for this stolen moment, but I had no doubt that we would not only face them together as a united force but that we would also emerge victorious. How could we not?

I lifted my head and her eyes were wide and open. She stared at me as if she could see into my very soul. I let her look. I revealed myself to her. My wife. My partner. She smiled tentatively and the rest of the world dropped away. There was no one but the two of us on that mountain top. There was no General Anastas or Duchess Caroline. There were no queens or princes or prime ministers. No earls or dukes or security chiefs who were going to try and tear us apart. It was just Meredith and Jamie. Two people who were in love. It was the eye of the storm and it didn't matter that our worlds swirled around us in a tempest. The place where we were was calm. If only I could keep it that way for the rest of our lives.

I felt the pull of the horses. My metaphorical chariot stumbled as the world rushed back in. There were obstacles in our path that Meredith didn't even know about. I had a moment of panic as I thought about what she would say when she found out, but I pushed it aside. Those things were for the future Jamie and Meredith to deal with. The present Meredith and Jamie needed to celebrate. I kissed her again. Because I could. My wife.

"*Agapiméni gynaíka mou*," I whispered against her lips. "*S'agapo. Se latrevo*." My darling wife. I love you. I adore you.

"CHRISTOPHE JAMES ALESANDRO KOSTOPOLOUS." MEREDITH SPOKE my name haltingly as she read it from the marriage license. No one had spoken my full name in ten years and I had to force down the shiver that attempted to take over my body. Hearing my name fall from her lips did unimagined things to me. "That's certainly a mouthful."

I grinned over at her. We were in the back of a limousine that I had ordered to pick us up from Father Felipe's chapel. We were both drinking from the chilled bottle of champagne that had been waiting for us. We were, in fact, on our second bottle.

Neither one of us felt like going back to the suite, but neither did we want to go to a club or bar. We opted for having the limousine drive us around the island. We drank our champagne and talked about inconsequential things as we each came to terms with what we had just done. I had sent a text to Benjamin, letting him know that I had found Meredith and then I had shut my phone off. I didn't want the world to intrude on this time with her. We so very rarely got time just to ourselves, and I wanted to keep real life at bay for as long as possible.

"And now you are *Missus* Christophe James Alesandro Kostopolous."

She screwed up her nose adorably. "Meredith Kostopolous," she said.

Something bloomed inside me when she added my name to hers. I leaned over and kissed her. I could do that now. She was my wife.

"So now you understand why I go by Jamie Kosta," I said.

"It certainly rolls off the tongue a lot easier," she said. "Does that make me Meredith Kosta?"

"It makes you Princess Meredith Kostopolous of Kalopsia," I whisper in her ear.

"Mmm," she hummed, nuzzling my cheek. "Princess huh? Are you my prince come to rescue me from the evil dragon?"

"No," I whispered, breathing in the scent of her as I held her close. "You are the fair maiden who has rescued the exiled prince and given him the will to claim his birthright."

I wanted to tell her everything. I wanted to tell her about my father and about my country and the island that I called home. I wanted to share every part of myself with her.

"I like that," she mumbled against my throat. "I like that I am the one rescuing you."

If I was honest with myself, I did too. I closed my eyes and gently manoeuvred us so that it was more comfortable. Meredith leaned against me, her head nestled on my shoulder and her face turned into my neck. My arm was around her and I liked the way she fit beside me. I closed my eyes and leaned my head back against the seat, my body relaxed and content.

"I grew up on a small island nation called Kalopsia," I said quietly. "I know you've probably never heard of it. Most people think we are part of the Greek Isles. Our island is not big, but it is beautiful." Meredith snuggled closer to me and sighed. I reached up and wound a strand of her hair around my finger. "My father was the king. I lived in the castle with my parents and my two younger sisters. My childhood was idyllic. I knew that one day I would rule my small country and I was eager to learn all I could from my father in order to be the kind of ruler he was. The people loved my father and my mother. Or that's what I thought."

"Is this the part where I rescue you?" she asked, her voice soft and thick with weariness.

I smiled. "No," I said. "That comes much later."

"Okay," she breathed.

"I thought the people loved us, but I was wrong," I went on. "There was an uprising. I remember the day the General came to lay charges of corruption against my father and his advisors. It got ugly. My mother and sisters were killed. I somehow escaped and watched from a hiding place while they led my father away in chains. I didn't know who to trust or where to turn. Father Felipe helped me. He got me off the island on a small fishing boat. It took days to reach the coast and then more hiding and travelling by night across the land. We crossed borders in the dead of night and stole food when we needed to eat. It was a long and arduous journey and I don't remember the half of it because I was so out of my mind with worry and fear. I had seen my sisters cut down. Their bodies bloody and lifeless. I don't know how I managed to survive and I would have willingly given my life if only I could bring them back."

Meredith's hand gripped on the fabric of my shirt, but she didn't speak. I turned my face, my eyes still closed, and pressed a kiss to the top of her head. I breathed in her scent. The turmoil that had risen inside me as I talked about my past eased as I inhaled the very essence of the woman in my arms.

"Father Felipe brought me to your father. He organised to keep me safe and hidden in Merveille. I owe him my life."

As I spoke the words, I realised just how true it was. And then I was hit with remorse. What would he say when he found out that I had married his daughter?

Meredith murmured something and I opened my eyes, looking down at her. She was asleep. She hadn't heard anything I had just told her. Secretly, it was a relief.

CHAPTER 11

Meredith

I was hot. Someone must have turned up the heat while I slept because I was seriously sweating. My mouth was dry and I knew, even before opening my eyes that I was going to regret whatever happened last night. The details were sketchy but I knew there was alcohol involved. A lot of alcohol.

I groaned and rolled over. I froze. There was another body in the bed with me. A big, solid, strong body.

I took a couple of deep, calming breaths. I didn't need to open my eyes to know who it was. His scent was familiar to me. The feel of his body next to me was familiar. The rhythm of his breathing was as familiar to me as my own. The temptation to roll closer to him was strong and I almost gave into it, but my rational brain caught up with what was happening and I was out of the bed and standing, looking down at him horrified, before I could even realise what I was doing.

I looked down at myself. I was still wearing the clothes that I'd worn last night. Jamie was also dressed. My heart rate slowed somewhat at this discovery. We hadn't crossed the line. Okay. That was okay. We had a few drinks and...

I couldn't remember what happened after that. I knew that I should. I knew something had happened last night, it was niggling in the back of my mind, but I couldn't remember what. I paced silently around the bed. I didn't know what to do. Should I wake him and demand an explanation? Would his memory be any better than mine?

I closed my eyes and tried to remember. I was in the dessert bar. Jamie came in and we fought. He kissed me. He kissed me! Right there in front of everybody. I sighed at the memory. He'd done it to shut me up because I wouldn't listen to him. I thought he was going to tell me it was over between us. But that wasn't what he wanted to tell me at all. He'd come to explain about Danika.

I let out a long slow breath and opened my eyes. Okay. I had jumped to conclusions when I'd walked out and saw him with his arms around her. I'm sure she had orchestrated that. I had the insistent and perhaps premonitory feeling that she was trying to come between us. I did not like her.

I reached up to run my hands through my hair and they tangled in the knots. I was sure it must look like a rat's nest. I couldn't wake up Jamie looking like this. I padded into the ensuite and grimaced at the mess of my reflection. My makeup had smeared - not that I had worn much in the first place. Mascara ringed my eyes and I had pillow creases in my cheek. My hair was a tangled mess and my clothes were rumpled and askew.

I ran some water and washed my face before tackling my hair. I should just have a shower but I couldn't do that while Jamie was asleep in my bed. I blushed at the thought. I grabbed the brush and lifted it to my head. Using my other hand I separated pieces of hair out so I could untangle it bit by bit. Something glinted in the light and my hands froze. What was that on my finger?

Slowly. So, so slowly I brought my left hand down in front of me. I watched my own eyes in the mirror, not yet willingly to look at what I knew would be there on my finger. I took a deep breath. My reflection looked back at me and she was not afraid. She looked at me like she wanted to say something, like she wanted to reassure me. I blinked my eyes a couple of times and then looked. There was a plain gold band on my left ring finger. I knew what it was. In a rush, the memories flooded back in. The hilltop chapel. The sunset. The priest with his kind smile. The words Jamie and I said to one another.

My stomach turned over at the enormity of what I'd done - what we'd done. I rushed to the toilet and threw up whatever alcohol was left in my stomach. Tears streamed down my face, but I refused to sob. I breathed through the panic attack that threatened and swallowed around the lump in my throat. Confident that my stomach wasn't going to revolt again, I walked back over to the sink and quickly brushed my teeth. I washed my face again and took a few deep breaths.

Jamie and I were married.

Married.

I married Jamie Kosta. Except...his name wasn't really Jamie Kosta. It was something else. Christophe James...something...Kostop...something. My brain tried valiantly to remember the mouthful moniker that was now mine. I didn't even know my own married name. Sobs threatened again, but I forced them back. It was okay because it wouldn't stay my name for much longer. As soon as Jamie woke up we would undo this. We could get an annulment. Simple. Le Beau was notorious for its quickie, drunken marriages. Surely they had some quickie, buyer's-remorse annulments too. There should be a thirty day cooling off period. Something to ensure that what we had done last night wasn't permanent.

Except...what if? I sucked in a breath and closed my eyes remembering how it had felt to say the vows that had tied me to Jamie. The ceremony had been perfect. I wouldn't have changed anything except maybe have my friends and family there. When I had stood up beside him and looked into his eyes, I had meant every single word. If it weren't for the fact that I knew how disappointed my father would be in me, then would I take this chance to be with Jamie?

I wished it could be that easy. I wished I was in a position to tell everyone else to butt out of my life. I wished we could just hide away from the world forever. I turned to look out the ensuite door to where Jamie still lay sleeping in my bed. What would it be like to wake up beside him every morning?

I forced myself to look away. I couldn't do that to my dad. He was counting on me to take up that title and support the initiatives that he and Alyssa were trying to get through Parliament. I would do anything for my father, even if it meant walking away from Jamie. So. An annulment it was.

Now that the panic wasn't pressing down on me I could take a moment to remember how it felt to stand in that outdoor chapel and marry the only man who had ever meant more to me than my job. I closed my eyes. Mrs. Jamie Kosta. If only we weren't who we were. If only it could be possible for us to actually make this work.

My eyes popped open and I looked at my reflection. There was a sadness in her eyes as she looked back at me. It didn't matter how much I might want to fantasise about Jamie and me, there was just no way it could possibly work.

Jamie

"JAMIE."

"Jamie."

"Jamie."

The persistent whisper finally pierced through the fog of sleep I was in and my brain registered that someone was trying to get my attention. Years of being a member of the royal guard had me arcing up off the bed and crouching in a battle ready position before my eyes even opened.

"Jamie." Not a whisper this time.

I opened my eyes to see Meredith standing in front of me, her arms crossed and her foot tapping. What was she doing in my room? I straightened and took a slow look around. Correction. What was I doing in her room?

"Meredith?"

"What do you remember?"

I closed my eyes briefly as I tried to think back over last night. I grinned. I remembered. I remembered everything. I stalked toward Meredith and she uncrossed her arms as she took a step back. I rushed her then and picked her up, swinging her around before I kissed her. A big smacking kiss on the lips.

"Good morning wife," I said, a big grin splitting my face.

"Put me down," she said, slapping my shoulders.

I let her slide down until her feet touched the ground, but I didn't let her out of my arms. Meredith didn't exactly look excited to be married to me. Had I gotten last night all wrong? Didn't she feel about me the same way I felt about her?

"Meredith?"

She twisted in my arms, trying to get away, but I wouldn't let her go.

"Talk to me, Meredith," I said. My voice brooked no argument and she stopped wriggling and looked up at me.

"Jamie," she said, "we got *married!*" This last bit was hissed in a furious whisper.

"I know," I said. "I still don't see the problem."

"You don't see the problem? Seriously?"

I dropped my head so that our foreheads touched and I ran my nose along the side of hers. "Meredith," I said softly. "*Agapiméni gynaíka mou.*" I tried to kiss her but she turned her face to the side.

"Don't say that," she whispered, her voice thick.

I leaned my head down into the crook of her neck and took a deep breath. The night before had felt so right. How could it feel so wrong now?

"*S'agapo. Se latrevo.*" I whispered into her neck.

"Jamie," she whispered, "don't."

I lifted my head and looked down into her eyes. "Why?"

"We can't do this."

"Again, I ask, why? Why not?"

"Jamie," she pleaded with me. "You know why. This - us - you know it's not going to work. My mother—"

"This has nothing to do with your mother," I said, losing my patience. "Meredith, I love you."

"Jamie—"

"No. You need to listen to me. You need to understand. I love you. I want to be with you. I want this. I want us."

Her eyes filled with tears and she rolled her lips together. She didn't tell me she loved me. She didn't tell me that she wanted what I was offering her.

I dropped my arms.

I turned away from her.

I ignored the pain in my chest.

I walked over to the window and stared out at the view, unseeing.

"Jamie," she whispered as she approached me softly.

She laid a hand on my back and I closed my eyes against the need to turn around and gather her into my arms. I clenched my fists so that I wouldn't reach for her. I clenched my jaw so that I wouldn't kiss her until she forgot all her objections.

"We were drunk," she said. There was a wobble in her voice despite her attempt to sound reasonable. "We were both upset. I was looking for a way to escape. I wanted to get lost in the fairytale. Us getting married doesn't solve any of the problems that I am facing. I am going to be a countess. I have responsibilities to the title and to my family, to my father and Alyssa. Maybe down the road, when things settle down, something could happen between us..." she trailed off.

"Princess," I said, turning around to her. "You are a princess, not a countess."

She furrowed her brow. "I'm not a princess," she said and then shook her head. "It was a pretty fantasy. You filled my head with the fairytale, Jamie, but it's not real. It's not the truth. I am not a princess that can rescue you. You are not a prince in need of rescuing."

She didn't remember anything I told her last night. She had fallen asleep in my arms, but she hadn't heard anything I'd said. She still didn't know who I was or what I was.

"You don't want to be my wife because I am a royal guard and you are a countess?" I asked.

She lifted her hand and cupped my jaw. "I don't care that you are a guard and I am a countess," she said and I could see the truth in her eyes. "But my mother will. My father will. The queen will."

She had no idea what she was saying. But at the mention of her father and the queen, I had a moment of pause. They would care. They would not want me to bring Meredith into the storm that I was facing.

As much as I wanted her by my side, I also wanted her far away from what I knew was coming for me. I would die before putting Meredith in danger. There was no doubt in my mind that General Anastas would use her against me if he ever got the chance. If he found out that she was my wife, it would put her in danger. I refused to have her dragged into the war that was coming.

"Fine," I said, resigned. "I will see what I can do to get it annulled." The words hurt as they crossed my tongue. The last thing I wanted was to sever this tie between us. But I would. I would do it to save her. I would do it so that she would be safe. "It doesn't change anything, though," I said, pulling her toward me. "I still love you. If things were different..."

She pressed up on her toes and slid her lips across mine. She may not have said the words to me, but her kiss told me all I needed to know. She loved me too, even if she couldn't admit it.

I stood at the registry office, Meredith beside me, and looked at the woman in shock.

"Excuse me?"

"There is a thirty day waiting period," she said again.

"Hang on a minute," Meredith said. "We can get a marriage license in an hour, but to get our marriage dissolved, we need to wait thirty days?"

"That's correct."

"Even if there are extenuating circumstances?" I asked, still not quite sure I was comprehending what I was hearing.

The woman nodded. "Even then."

"I don't understand," Meredith said. "Isn't this backwards? Shouldn't there be a waiting period *before* someone gets married you know, in case it is a spontaneous drunken decision?"

"The onus is on the officiant to decide whether two people are ready to get married," she said. "We only issue the license, but it's the officiant that decides whether to actually make it official."

I blew out a breath and ran a hand through my hair. Father Felipe could have denied us. He could have said no, but he didn't.

Meredith turned to me and poked me in the chest with her finger. "You did this," she yelled. "This is all your fault."

I grabbed her finger and pulled her against me, wrapping my arms around her. "Calm down," I whispered in her ear. "We will figure this out. We'll go and see Father Felipe and see if he can do something."

Meredith huffed out a breath and pressed her forehead against me chest. "What are we going to do?" she whispered.

"Shh," I whispered into her ear. "I'll get it sorted. I promise."

She thumped her fist against my chest and then pushed out of my arms. "Okay," she said, straightening her shoulders and taking a deep breath. "Let's go."

We walked back to the car and I directed the driver to the chapel where Father Felipe lived. I wanted to reach over and take Meredith's hand in mine but I doubted that she would appreciate the gesture. I knew this was what she wanted, but even though I knew it was probably the best thing for both of us, I didn't want to dissolve our marriage. I hadn't been as drunk as she'd thought when we came here last night and she wasn't either. I knew what I was doing and I did it of my own free will. I thought she had too. I was sure that she must have because she had convinced Father Felipe to marry us.

There were so many things I wanted to say. I wanted to tell her that everything I told her last night was true. I want to tell her about my country and what I was facing. I wanted to ask her to stay by my side so that we could fight the coming battles together. But that wasn't fair. I couldn't guilt her into staying married to me. I didn't even know how long I was going to be stuck in this weird limbo that I had found myself in. We could get back to Merveille and I could still be required to stay in exile for another ten years. It wasn't fair of me to dump everything on her when there may be no end in sight. And she was right. If nothing changed in my situation, then she would be the countess who married a body guard. It would reflect badly on her and her family. The fact was, I may never hold the title of prince again. There was a very real possibility that I would stay a displaced person, exiled from my country for the rest of my life. I couldn't expect Meredith to hitch her wagon to that.

The car came to a stop and I got out, offering my hand to Meredith. She brushed my hand aside and got out of the car, striding up the path to the little cottage where Father Felipe lived. I followed her, the dread a hard rock in my stomach. How would I possibly explain to Father Felipe that we needed to annul the marriage barely twenty-four hours after he joined us?

Meredith pounded on the door. I looked out over the island below us. It was a different view during the day. The night before, as the sun was setting, the vista had seemed magical. As I looked at it now, it was still beautiful, but it was also more real. It was like seeing behind the wizard's curtain. I could see the flaws - the smog, the lower income areas, the garishness of the strip of hotels and casinos. The twilight had covered everything with a soft light, but the harsh light of day exposed the cracks. Much like my very short-lived marriage.

Meredith pounded on the door again but there was still no answer.

"Maybe he's in the garden," I suggested.

Meredith spun around and glared at me, but she didn't say anything. When I didn't move she held her arm out as if to tell me to lead the way. I shook my head and sighed. Meredith had a famously short fuse but it usually burnt itself out pretty quickly. I just had to weather the silent treatment and death-stares until she calmed down. Surely she couldn't blame me for this entire mess? We were both present here last night. We both made promises. Promises that she was all too willing to break.

I walked down the path that led around to the back of the cottage and saw a hat bobbing on the other side of a hedge. I headed in that direction hoping to find the priest but instead found a woman.

"Excuse me," I said, "do you know where we can find Father Felipe?"

"He's gone," the woman replied, turning back to her weeding.

"We know that," Meredith said, her voice tight. "But we were wondering if you could tell us where he had gone and maybe when he would be returning?"

"He's gone," the woman said, straightening again and giving us a look like we were wasting her time. "He won't be back for two weeks."

"What!?"

I reached out to lay a calming hand on Meredith's arm but she shook me off.

"Two weeks?"

The woman nodded. "He has gone to the mainland. It's his annual trip to the Vatican."

Meredith slammed her hands down on her hips and glared at me.

"Did you know?"

"What? No. Of course not," I said.

She glared at me as if she didn't believe me and then stormed off toward the car. I thanked the woman and then followed after Meredith. I had no idea what we were going to do now.

CHAPTER 12

Meredith

The next twelve hours were tense. When we arrived back at the hotel, we had very little time before we had to board the yacht that would take us to Barcelona. I headed straight to my room to pack - not that I had any packing to do. My maids had already packed my bag and were waiting for me so they could dress me. I submitted to their ministrations without complaint. I was still in shock. I couldn't believe I'd married Jamie and there was nothing I could do about it for thirty days.

That could be a good thing.

I ignored the little voice in the back of my head that was trying to convince me that marrying Jamie was actually a blessing in disguise. I had been ignoring that voice all day. I ignored it when it prompted me to move closer to Jamie in the car. I ignored it when it told me to reach out and take his hand. And I continued to ignore it because it didn't matter that there was a part of me that was thrilled with being married to him, the fact was that it just couldn't happen. Despite what romance novels and fairytales would have you believe, love was not enough.

When the maids finally left me, I let out a long sigh and sat on the end of my bed. Jamie told me he loved me - more than once - and I couldn't bring myself to say it back. Not because I didn't love him, because I did love him and I knew I did. I couldn't tell him because if I did, I knew he wouldn't let anything come between us. The problem was that there were other people to think about. My life was not my own. I had known that all my life, as much as I tried to ignore it. My father had run interference with my mother so that I could at least have the illusion of freedom, but I knew that that was coming to an end. It was time for me to grow up and stop running from the responsibilities of my birth. I may not have chosen to be born to a duke and duchess, but I couldn't escape the reality of it. I was only ever kidding myself by pretending I could have a normal life.

I slept fitfully on the yacht. I told the team I had a headache and didn't want to be disturbed. I couldn't bear to sit around watching Jamie from across a table and pretending that everything was fine. Everything was decidedly not fine and I just didn't have it in me to keep up the pretence. What I wanted was to have my girls around me and tell them everything. I wanted to hear them tell me that this whole mess would get sorted out. I hadn't realised how much I had come to enjoy having a group of friends until they were no longer there. I didn't even care that they would tease me about falling for Jamie. I just wanted someone to talk to. I hadn't even seen Alyssa, my closest friend. Being her body double meant that we couldn't be seen together, which meant I couldn't even talk to her about what was happening.

It was early morning when we docked. I let myself be hustled off the yacht and into the waiting car. My maids rode with me, thankfully, with Jamie in another car. I just wanted to get to the hotel and escape into my room. I had no interest in taking in the sights of Barcelona - I would have ample time to do that tomorrow when Jamie and I did our little impersonating thing again. This time we were to walk the streets of the city, body guards in tow, and show everyone just how in love Alyssa and Will were. Meanwhile Alyssa and Will would be elsewhere, doing god knows what.

"Meredith," Benjamin said as I got out of the car at the hotel.

I stopped and waited for him.

"Team meeting in fifteen minutes."

I nodded and then continued on into the hotel. So much for me escaping again. I took the elevator to the top floor and let my maids fuss over me as we got settled into the new suite. I didn't make eye contact with Jamie when he came to sit at the table opposite me. Cody was already there, as were Danika and Daniel. Cody and Daniel would be our visible guards tomorrow, with Danika taking up the rear guard. I still didn't trust her. Something about her just felt fake. And I definitely didn't like the way she sat next to Jamie, close enough so their shoulders touched. I watched her hand disappear under the table and wished for laser vision so I could burn a hole through her face. I looked away and took a deep breath. I needed to chill.

Benjamin began the meeting but I couldn't concentrate on a word he was saying. I could feel Jamie's eyes on me and I looked everywhere else but at him. I knew what I would see if I gave in and let my eyes wander to him. I knew that if I looked at him, I would buckle and give him everything he wanted. But I had to stay strong. I had to resist him, even if it broke my heart to do so.

"What is going on?"

I snapped out of my misery at the sharpness of Benjamin's voice.

"What?" I asked, feigning innocence.

"Tomorrow is going to be a public relations nightmare if the two of you don't work out whatever is going on between you."

I looked at Benjamin, still not strong enough to glance Jamie's way.

"I don't understand."

Benjamin actually rolled his eyes at me.

"Lover's spat," Cody said with a grin, and Jamie shot him a glare. Cody held up his hands in surrender. "Whoa. Calm down, I was just joking."

"I'm not feeling great," I said.

Benjamin eyed me but didn't comment.

"It will be fine," Jamie said. "Now if we're done? I'm going to the gym."

"I'll go with you," Danika said jumping up.

I ground my teeth together. Of course she was going to go with him. He could have her for all I cared.

Jamie

I STEPPED OFF THE TREADMILL AND RAN THE TOWEL OVER MY HEAD to mop up the sweat. Danika had followed me down here but I had declined her offer to spar. The last thing I needed right now was to have Meredith walk in and see something she could misconstrue. The woman had me tied up in knots - and not in a good way. I knew she was angry, but I was angry too. I was angry that I had finally found someone who I wanted to spend the rest of my life with and she didn't want me.

I moved from the treadmill over to the bench press. Danika had given up on me and left. I was thankful for the solitude. I needed to get my head sorted out before the op tomorrow - not that we expected any trouble. By and large Alyssa and Will were well liked and apart from the usual crazies, there hadn't been any threats against them. Tomorrow was just a precaution and a way to give them some alone time, which was something they didn't get a lot of. The problem was me...well, and Meredith. If we couldn't get our heads in the game then we could very well give the paps a story that wasn't there. I could see the headlines now - "Trouble in Paradise - the queen and her consort fighting in Barcelona." That was the last thing we needed.

I set up my weights and lay down on the bench. I'd added a few extra weights - nothing I couldn't handle - just enough to make my body work. I needed the strain to take away from all the crap going on in my head. I gripped the bar and pushed up, holding it for a moment before lowering it and pressing up again. It was heavy and my chest and arms protested, but I kept focussed, counting out the reps. I did ten and the pressed up to put the bar back on the stand. A pair of hands came into my line of vision and Benjamin helped me seat the bar safely. I sat up and swung my legs over to the side, wiping my face with the towel he handed me.

"Benjamin? You need something?"

Benjamin walked around the weight bench so that he stood in front of me. He crossed his arms and looked down at me, his face stoic. The guy had a killer poker face. I could never tell what he was thinking.

"What's going on with you and Meredith?"

My heart stopped. I'm pretty sure I died for a moment and all the air was sucked out of my lungs. He knew. Somehow Benjamin knew. I didn't know what to say or do or...

"Whatever it is, you need to apologise to her and do whatever it is you need to do to get her out of her snit."

My heart resumed beating. Life-giving oxygen returned to my lungs and my near-death-experience faded as I realised that Benjamin didn't know what was going on.

"I have apologised," I said. "But she won't listen to me."

Benjamin sighed and took a seat on the bench next to me.

"Should we call off the op?" he asked.

"No, I—"

"I can't have the two of you out there behaving like you did in the meeting. The last thing we want is to start rumours in the press."

"I know—"

"I know Meredith can be a pain in the—"

"It's okay," I said, feeling irrationally angry that he would say something like that about Meredith to me. I knew exactly how much of a pain she could be but I didn't like hearing it from someone else. "I'll go and talk to her and see if I can smooth things over. We both know how important this mission is and we're both professionals."

He turned his head to look at me and I had to stop myself from squirming under his examination.

"Are you sure? Is it something I need to know about?"

I kept my face passive and shook my head. "It's fine. Meredith is just being...Meredith." I sighed.

Benjamin kept his eyes on me for a moment longer before huffing out a breath and getting to his feet. "Okay," he said. He gave me another long look before he walked out of the gym. I exhaled roughly and spun around to lay back down on the bench. Maybe I should have told Benjamin to call off the op. I had no idea if Meredith could compartmentalise this whole situation, not if the way she couldn't even look at me throughout the team meeting was any indication.

As much as I wanted to be with Meredith, the last thing I wanted was for it to impact on our job. This whole situation had made us both distracted. Not a good mindset to be in when we were heading out to an op. The timing probably hadn't been the best - not that there would have been a perfect time for any of this. The other night had been a perfect storm of situations to make us do what we did. Our inhibitions had been lowered and we were both feeling the pressures of circumstances that were out of our control. Not to mention the chemistry loaded emotions between us. But no matter how mad Meredith was at me and how much she might regret what we did, I didn't. For the first time since my world fell apart ten years ago, I felt like I was doing exactly what I should be doing. Marrying Meredith felt right and I wouldn't apologise for that or for the way I felt about her. I would do what she wanted and I would get the marriage annulled, but I would do it under protest. I had thirty days to convince her that we could make this work. How I was going to do that? I had no idea, but I had thirty days to work on it.

Meredith

I MANAGED TO HIDE FROM EVERYONE THAT NIGHT BUT I COULDN'T avoid the team meeting at breakfast. I walked along the sideboard that had been set with all the breakfast foods that a team of muscle-bound men could possibly want. I wasn't hungry, but I put stuff on my plate anyway. My stomach was too tied up in knots to eat. I hadn't slept very well, with thoughts of Jamie and our elopement going around and around in my head. There was part of me that wanted to just tell everyone in my life to get lost and let me have what I had inadvertently started with Jamie. Alyssa had gotten to marry the man of her dreams, and Freddie had married the woman he fell in love with even if she wasn't exactly who my mother would have picked for him. The other girls in the entourage were falling in love too. It was so unfair that I couldn't have what I wanted - *who* I wanted - too.

Jamie came to stand beside me. I couldn't deny the reaction of my body whenever he was close. There was something very real and powerful between us and whatever *it* was didn't care that we couldn't be together. I supposed in a perfect world we could just let this thing between us happen organically. But we didn't live in a perfect world and I couldn't just give in to the whims of my heart. I had to use my head. I had to be smart.

"Are you ready for today?" he asked as he piled scrambled eggs onto his plate.

"Of course," I snapped. I hadn't meant to, but what could I do? I was trying to keep everything else together, but it all felt like it was falling apart around my ears. I took a breath and pushed all the emotions back down. "I'm sorry. I didn't mean to snap. Yes. I am ready for today."

He looked at me then and I could feel the pain and confusion he was experiencing as if it was happening to me. I supposed it was happening to me too and I wondered if he could see it mirrored in my eyes.

"Meredith—" he began but was interrupted by *her*.

"Hey Jamie," Danika said, pushing between the two of us as she reached for some toast. "Thanks for last night. I really appreciate you spending the time with me."

My fist clenched around the knife I was holding and I was inches away from plunging it into her kidney. The red haze of violence that descended on me surprised me. I didn't like her, that was no secret, but the way she flirted with my husband was beyond the pale.

Whoa.

My husband.

I was jealous because she was flirting with my husband.

I spun away from the two of them, trying to get my bearings. This possessiveness was so uncharacteristic for me. Wasn't it? I had never been in this situation before, so there was no way to tell. I couldn't deny that I wanted to do her harm. I wanted to push her out of the way and scratch her eyes out and claim Jamie publicly as my own. I looked down at my hand and noticed the ring I was still wearing. Despite my protests, I hadn't taken off the band he had slid on my finger during our wedding ceremony. A quick look over my shoulder confirmed that he was still wearing his as well. That quick look over my shoulder also revealed that Danika had pressed herself up against him and was looking up at him with big, adoring eyes.

I didn't mean to do it.

Okay, maybe I did.

My feet moved of their own volition and I was headed in their direction. My elbow came out and I landed a nice, tight jab to her ribs. I pretended to stumble and followed through with my shoulder. She was shoved out of the way and I felt myself being pressed up against the hard chest of *my husband*. His arms came around me to steady me and I looked up into his eyes. I saw the flare of dark, stormy fire and I knew I had overplayed my hand. It may have looked like an accident to everyone else, but Jamie knew the truth.

"We need to talk," he whispered to me before helping me to right myself.

I smiled - grimaced - before turning to Danika. "Oh, I'm so sorry," I said, fake concern dripping from my words. "I tripped."

Danika pursed her lips and crossed her arms across her chest. She cocked her hip and tossed her short dark hair. "You can't help being clumsy," she said.

It took all of my training and self-control not to jump her. I must have tensed or given myself away because I felt Jamie's hand close around my elbow and steer me away.

"Why don't we go and discuss some of the logistics of today," he said loudly enough that everyone could hear.

I clamped my mouth shut and let him lead me away. He closed the door to my room, shutting us in, and then turned to me, his eyes snapping.

"What the hell was that?'

"I didn't like the way she was flirting with you," I said before I could filter myself. "She throws herself at you constantly and today, the way she was pressed up against you...it was disgusting."

"You didn't like the way she was flirting with me?" Jamie said, his voice low and dangerous. "And why is that?'

He had stepped closer, crowding against me. My heart was racing as I looked up into his eyes that had turned the colour of storm clouds. "It's unprofessional," I said. It came out as little more than a whisper. I wet my suddenly dry lips.

Jamie took another step closer to me and I took one back, but there was nowhere for me to go. The wall pressed up against my back as Jamie pushed up against me, holding me captive. I had to fight against the desire to close my eyes and melt into him. He hadn't been this close to me since we had sealed our marriage with a kiss. It had been more than twenty-four hours since he had held me in his arms and my body missed him. Keeping this wall around myself to protect against how I felt about him was hard. I didn't want to, not when he was right here in front of me. It would be so easy to just let go and give in to all these feelings.

"Meredith," he said. His voice was gentle but it was also dark and husky.

I suppressed a shiver and turned my face up to his. I couldn't help it. I wanted him to kiss me.

He growled low in his throat before lowering his lips to mine. His kiss was hard and punishing and exactly what I needed. I gripped his shirt and pulled him closer. We might not be able to have a future together, but for right now he was my husband. For better or worse. I kissed him back, revelling in this small sliver of time and showing him exactly how I felt.

CHAPTER 13

Meredith

I stepped inside the *Mercado de La Boqueria* and let the sights, sounds and smells of the famous food market wash over me. Jamie stood beside me. Cody and Daniel, dressed as civilians, were a few steps behind us trying to not look like body guards. Jamie laid a hand on the small of my back and I fought the urge to grimace. Not because I didn't like his hand on me but because I did and I was trying really hard to hold on to my mad. I didn't want him soothing the anger that I kept trying to stoke. I needed it to keep burning inside me to remind me that we couldn't happen; that I couldn't give in to the temptation that he represented.

I knew he was annoyed at me too, and that was fine. Good. Great. Exactly what I wanted. After a moment of insanity when I had allowed myself to give in to the kiss, I had pushed him away. It had taken all of my will power to do so, but my self-preservation response had kicked in. It would be too easy to lose myself in him and what he offered. I kept saying that my being a countess and him being a body guard was the reason that we couldn't be together, but we both knew it wasn't the truth. I hadn't even accepted the title yet. I didn't have to accept the title. My mother would be mad but I knew that if I really wanted to be with Jamie then my father would make a way. I could turn my back on my responsibilities and hide in the anonymity that Jamie offered.

But that would be the coward's way out.

Taking up my grandmother's title wasn't exactly going to be a walk in the park. There was a lot riding on it and me. My father and Alyssa were hoping that I would be a case study for Parliament. The first unattached female to take up a title and make it work. Knowing that I was doing something to help both Alyssa and my father made the whole thing more palatable. What I was not looking forward to was the all the expectations that went along with the title. Despite what Daddy and Alyssa wanted, my mother would make sure to inundate me with events and commitments with the express purpose of finding a suitable match for me. Being already married to Jamie would negate everything that my father and the queen were planning. It would only prove Parliament's point that a single woman couldn't hold the title.

And besides, if I walked away from it, what would I do with myself all day? I would no longer have a job in the royal guard. That was non-negotiable. Whether or not I accepted the title of countess, I would still have to resign my post. I could no longer be part of Alyssa's ladies in waiting. Those positions in Alyssa's inner circle were only for peers. If I turned my back on my title and decided to marry - *stay married to* - Jamie then I would no longer be a peer of the realm and that would mean I could no longer be one of Alyssa's confidantes. We would still be friends; I knew Alyssa well enough to know that she wouldn't care, but our relationship would be different.

I stopped to look at an amazing display of colourful chilies. I wasn't really seeing them, though. My mind was too caught up in the mess I was in. I was barely even aware of my surroundings. The arguments I was using to justify my desire to dissolve this ill-conceived marriage to Jamie were weak. They were excuses and not really valid. It didn't matter whether I was a countess or a daughter of a duke with a courtesy title, Alyssa would still be my closest friend. It didn't matter if I was a part of the ladies in waiting, all of them would still love me and treat me no differently. They would still be my friends. My father wouldn't care that I married Jamie, well apart from him not being able to walk me down the aisle. Even my mother, with all her bluster and carrying on would eventually calm down and accept Jamie as part of the family.

So why? Why was I trying to get out of this? What was really going on?

I let Jamie steer me through the crowds. The market was teeming with people and if this had really been an outing for Alyssa and Will, there would be no way we would have let it go ahead. There were too many people to truly keep them safe. For my part though, I was thankful for the crowds. I was thankful for the disguise that had taken my maids an hour or more to complete. I needed the anonymity that came with being just another patron amongst the many who had crowded into this building.

It hit me with all the subtlety of a tank rolling down a hill. I was scared. The way I felt about Jamie petrified me. I had always prided myself on my independence and my strength. I was not a girl who swooned or looked to a man for comfort or security. And yet being around Jamie brought out all those feelings.

My life was in flux. I was being forced out of the guard - the only place that I had ever felt that I truly belonged - and forced into a life as a peer in my own right. A life that I had never wanted. Now Jamie wanted to put another label on me. Wife. I had never had the fairytale dreams of finding my soul mate, getting married and living happily ever after. If I was honest with myself, I never really expected to even fall in love. I wasn't beautiful or elegant. I didn't have grace and poise - much to my mother's eternal disappointment. I was a tomboy who knew how to fight. I was brash and outspoken and about as cultured as tap water.

How could Jamie even love someone like me?

I looked over my shoulder and caught a brief flash of Danika. Her eyes were trained on Jamie and there was a hunger in her gaze that made my gut clench. As much as I disliked her, I couldn't deny that she was beautiful. There was something about her that was inherently feminine - unlike me. Her hair was cropped into a short, curly bob, but it was anything but harsh. It curled softly around her delicate features and gave her an air of elegance and fragility. Unlike me. My hair may be long, but I wore it pulled back in a tight bun or ponytail. My skin was freckled, my hands had callouses and I carried about fifty-two knives on my person. I could kill a man with my bare hands and it showed. Unlike Danika, who looked like she wouldn't hurt a fly.

Why would Jamie choose me when he could have her? Why would he want me with all my hang ups and neuroses when he could have a simple life with a woman like Danika?

I stepped away from the comforting pressure of Jamie's hand on my back. I moved into the crowd, out of his reach. I needed to get out of his orbit so I could think clearly. I needed to get lost in the crowd so I could find space where I could breathe freely. Being so close to Jamie made the walls seem like they were closing in on me. I finally understood why I was so scared of giving in to my heart and getting lost in Jamie. I would never be enough for him and I knew it.

Jamie

I COULD FEEL MEREDITH PULLING AWAY FROM ME - AND NOT JUST physically.

There had been a moment earlier, when we were in her room together and she was in my arms that I felt like she was finally giving in to what I knew she felt toward me. I thought that finally I had gotten through to her and that she understood that I meant what I said when I told her I loved her. But as the morning went on, I could feel the distance she was putting between us. It was even more obvious now as she moved away from me and into the crowds. I tried to keep her in view, but the crowds closed around her and swallowed her up.

My gut clenched and my eyes darted around. I could see Danika over my shoulder but Daniel and Cody had been absorbed by the crowd too - not an easy feat when they were both large men with scowling faces. I only hoped that they had eyes on Meredith.

Benjamin had suggested we wear earwigs and microphones but both Meredith and I had objected. There were things we didn't want the rest of the team knowing. I rued that decision now as I tried to find Meredith in the crush. At least if we'd had ear pieces then I would know that she was safe.

I had no reason to think that she couldn't look after herself. She was a skilled fighter in both armed and unarmed combat. We had sparred enough times for me to be confident in her abilities. But still... There was a protectiveness that squeezed my chest because I didn't have eyes on her.

The crush of the crowd seemed to pull me away from the direction that she went. I fought against the flow. I didn't want to get separated from her. I stopped and people cursed as they had to go around me, but I didn't care. I took a moment to survey the crowd and then I spotted her head as she headed for one of the exits. She was running from me.

I swore under my breath and headed in her direction. I didn't bother trying to signal Danika or Cody and Daniel. They would just have to keep up. I needed to get to Meredith. Apart from the fact that we were supposed to be impersonating the queen and prince, her putting distance between us was a problem. I didn't like to think about what it meant for us or for our future.

The crowds parted for me slowly. I felt like I was swimming against the tide and she got further away from me. Her smaller figure meant she could slip through the crowds easier. I became increasingly annoyed as the distance between us grew. She was freaking out and if she wasn't careful she would blow this mission. We were supposed to be a loving couple and we looked the least like a loving couple right now. If the press got a hold of this, it could be bad for the royal couple.

Whatever was going on in her head, she was letting it cloud her judgement. She was letting it make her a coward who ran instead of facing whatever the issue was. I refused to draw parallels to my own life. I had been forced to run. I had been a boy. I'd had no choice.

But I was a man now.

I forced the little voice in my head back. Yes, I was a man now but that didn't make me any more powerful than I was when I was forced from my home. My hands were still tied when it came to my birthright. I was still in exile and there were still people who wanted me dead.

I was still running. I was still hiding. I was still that little boy who did what he was told instead of doing what he knew was right. Was marrying Meredith just another way for me to hide? I had tied myself to her and to Merveille. Had I done that because I was too afraid to face up to my responsibilities? Was I using Meredith as an excuse to avoid the truth of what I needed to do?

It was long past time for me to make my move. All reports from Kalopsia were that the current regime was floundering. The people weren't happy. It was the perfect time to reveal myself and take back the country of my birth. It was way past time for me to stand up and become the man my father had wanted me to be. Whether he was alive or dead, I was shaming him by continuing to hide in the safe little world I had created. I couldn't do that while yoked to Meredith. It was tantamount to hiding behind my mother's skirts.

Here I was accusing Meredith of being a coward when I was the cowardly one. I had been running from my responsibilities for ten years. Now, instead of stepping up, I was using Meredith as an excuse to avoid those same responsibilities. I couldn't deny that I loved her, but why hadn't I told her the truth about who I was? I could lie to myself and say that I had tried to tell her, but that was just another excuse. I should have made sure she knew who I was before we had gotten married. I should have sat her down in Father Felipe's cottage and explained everything to her. I should have given her the choice of hitching her wagon to mine instead of marrying her under false pretences.

I finally broke through the crowd and followed Meredith down a tunnel that ostensibly led to the outside.

"Meredith!" I called out to her, but she didn't turn around.

I hurried after her, reaching out to grab her elbow. She turned to me and I dropped my hand. The woman wasn't Meredith and she was holding a gun on me.

Meredith

"MEREDITH!"

I heard Jamie call my name and turned, but he wasn't looking at me. He was headed down an alley in pursuit of someone dressed just like me. My gut clenched and my spidey-senses started tingling. Someone was luring Jamie away and that didn't feel right. I scanned the crowd looking for Cody or Daniel, I'd even settle for Danika, but I couldn't see anyone. I changed direction, heading after Jamie, not caring as I pushed people out of the way in my haste and determination. I broke through the crowd and headed down the tunnel. I could see Jamie ahead of me and he stood with his arms raised in a non-threatening posture. Was that woman holding a gun on him?

"Whoa, hey, sorry," Jamie said. "I thought you were someone else."

"You need to come with me, Your Highness," the woman said.

Oh god. She thought he was Will. She was trying to kidnap Will.

I slowed my steps and tried to keep myself hidden behind Jamie's large frame. The woman hadn't seen me yet and if I could get close enough, I would have the advantage of surprise.

"I think you may have me confused with someone else," Jamie said, trying for the affable tourist, his voice holding no threat.

I imagined he was smiling at the woman too in an attempt to disarm her with his charm. Stupid man.

"I know exactly who you are," she said.

Jamie stiffened. The easy-going act was gone and he seemed to stand straighter.

"Who are you?" he asked, his voice a command.

"All will be revealed soon enough," she said, "but you need to come with me. Now."

"Does that line ever actually work?" I asked, coming up to stand beside Jamie. "I mean, really. It's like a line from a bad movie. 'All will be revealed.'" I rolled my eyes. "Seriously."

The woman sneered at me, but I had achieved my objective, she was now distracted. Jamie and I had run this drill thousands of times. It was two against one. We now had the upper hand. I stepped toward her and she waved the gun in my direction.

"I wouldn't do that if I were you," she said, and then two goons stepped out of the shadows behind her. "We just want the prince and we don't want any trouble."

The odds had changed. It was now three against two plus a gun and not in our favour. Not that they were insurmountable odds. We had also run this drill. I didn't even need to look at Jamie to know what the plan was. I moved when he did and we each engaged the goon closest to us leaving the woman with the gun with no immediately identifiable target.

The guy in front of me was big and thick with muscle. I had fought men his size before and it wasn't about strength, but physics. I just had to get in the right position and hit him in the right place. I was quick and agile and what I lacked in strength I made up for in bloody-mindedness. I had expected my opponent to be all brawn and no brain, but the guy had skills. He was a trained fighter but more pugilist than MMA. Thankfully I had been training in all sorts of hand to hand combat since I was old enough to take a punch without running home to my daddy.

We grappled wordlessly. I got in close to him so that he couldn't use his powerful swing to knock me to the ground. I needed to stay upright. The minute I hit the ground, he would have the advantage. I think I surprised him by the ferocity of my attack. I don't think he was prepared to fight a woman. Guys usually weren't. Even the guys in my team tended to go easy on me - not Jamie, but the others. It had been ingrained in them that they should never hit a woman and they struggled to overcome that internal value even when it was their job to do so. This guy was no different.

I pressed my advantage, not even looking to see how Jamie was fairing and then just as I gained the upper hand, the guy turned and ran. I dropped my arms and watched as he, the woman and the other guy who had been wrestling with Jamie took off down the tunnel. I looked over at Jamie then and noticed a cut above his eye, the blood running down the side of his face. He was breathing hard and it suddenly hit me that we had both been in very real danger. In all the years of training, I had never actually been in a serious, life and death fight. We had run drills and sparred and run as many scenarios as we could in order to be battle ready, but we had never had to face a real life threat. My body started to shake as the shock set in.

In two steps, Jamie was picking me up and wrapping his arms

around me. We were both breathing hard and I think tears were running down my face. I searched for his lips, needing to feel them on mine. I needed reassurance that everything was okay, that he was okay. It wasn't professional or regulation and it went against everything that I had been trained to do but I didn't care. Jamie had been threatened. The man I loved had been in danger and he was hurt and bleeding and I needed the reassurance that he was okay. I wrapped my arms around him and breathed him in. I could feel his heart beating against mine and I relished the way he held me tightly as if he was just as shaken up as I was. Neither of us was behaving as elitely trained royal guards right now. We were two people who had feared for the other's life.

"Jamie? Meredith?" Cody's voice broke through the bubble that had wrapped around us and Jamie let me down slowly, but he didn't let me go entirely.

"There was an incident," Jamie said. "We need to get back to the hotel ASAP."

CHAPTER 14

Jamie

"Where's Daniel?" I asked as Cody hustled Meredith and me back to where the car was waiting.

"I don't know," Cody replied. "I can't find Danika either."

"I just don't get it," Meredith said, her arm through mine. "Why were they after Will?"

She had a point. All the scenarios we'd run centered around Alyssa being taken. No one had ever expected Will to be the target.

"What did that woman say to you?" Meredith asked, looking up at me. "How did she get you to follow her?"

"I thought she was you," I replied looking down at her. "She was wearing the same clothes as you, the same hair."

"I was following someone who was dressed as you as well," Cody said. "That's how I managed to lose you. When the two of you split up and went in different directions, I followed who I thought was Meredith and Daniel followed the Jamie look-a-like."

"There was someone who looked like me?" I asked as we stopped at the car.

"Yes," Daniel replied, stepping up beside me. "Led me on a merry chase too. I was too far away from you when I realised I was following the wrong person."

"This wasn't random," Meredith said.

"No." I couldn't get the woman's voice out of my head. It had sounded familiar. Not exactly familiar like I knew the woman, but the accent was familiar and one I hadn't heard in a long time.

Daniel opened the door of the car and I indicated that Meredith slide in first. "Where's Danika?" I asked Daniel quietly.

"I don't know," he said, "but we're not waiting for her. This was the rendezvous point if things went south. She will need to find her own way back to the hotel."

I nodded and then slid into the car beside Meredith.

I know exactly who you are. The woman's words ran in a loop around my head. When she had spoken those words I had the uncomfortable realisation that she wasn't talking about me being Will. She wasn't even talking about me being a body guard impersonating Will. There was the distinct threat that she knew who I really was. She knew I was Prince Christophe. That had to be what she meant.

"Here," Meredith said, holding a cloth up to show me. "You're still bleeding."

I turned to her and lowered my head so she could press the cloth to the cut. She rolled her lips together and wouldn't look me in the eye. Her face was pale and she had a little smudge of dirt on her cheek. I reached up to wipe it off and let my finger linger on her skin for a little longer than necessary.

"Are you okay?" I asked quietly.

She nodded, but kept her lips pressed tightly together. Her eyes were glassy but she didn't let the tears fall.

"Are you sure?"

"You're the one who's bleeding," she snapped. She closed her eyes and took a deep breath. "Sorry."

"It's okay." I hated that we had to be so careful with one another. I hated that I couldn't pull her into my arms and just hold her. I think we both needed it. We both needed the reassurance that the other one was fine. I knew I needed to feel her warm body against mine as reassurance that she was okay.

The car cruised to a stop and the door opened. I reluctantly slid away from Meredith and then reached in to help her out of the car. We still had to keep in character. We were dressed as the queen and prince of Merveille and until we got behind the closed doors of our hotel, then we would need to continue the ruse. I tucked Meredith under my arm, holding her close to my body, and we walked, head down, into the hotel, Cody and Daniel flanking us tightly. There were no press, thankfully. The attempted kidnapping - or whatever it was - hadn't been leaked to the media yet.

Cody was on his phone, leading us through the lobby, and Daniel crowded in behind us. Of all of us in the guard, only Daniel and Carlos had been involved in anything like this before. That had ended in the tragic deaths of Alyssa's father and brother. I could tell by the set of Daniel's shoulders and the grim look on his face that he was remembering that day and was probably kicking himself for the near miss of today. Today's attempt had been well coordinated. Professional. Planned.

"We have a leak," I said as the elevator doors closed.

Daniel nodded once. He had come to the same conclusion. It was the only explanation for why there were multiple people dressed in the same clothing as Meredith and me. Clothing and wigs that were so close to what we wore that it was enough to fool the body guards tasked with protecting us. There was no way a random person could know the details of what we would wear. It had to be someone within our entourage, someone with intimate knowledge of our mission. Someone who would also have had to have known that I wasn't really Will. If they knew what we were going to wear, then they would definitely know that we weren't who we were dressed up as.

They weren't after Will.

They were after me.

Meredith

I FELT LIKE I WOULD NEVER BE WARM AGAIN. COLD HAD SEEPED into my very bones and only Jamie's body heat kept me from shivering uncontrollably. I pressed into his side and his arm tightened around me. While I had been in the fight, I hadn't thought about what was happening. My body had just responded with muscle memory. It was why we trained. It was why we ran scenarios. I had kept my head and I had done what I was trained to do. What I hadn't been prepared for was the after effects. I wasn't prepared for the excess adrenalin in my system. I wasn't prepared for the crash that came after the spike. And I wasn't prepared for the emotional response of seeing Jamie in danger, of seeing Jamie hurt and bleeding.

He tightened his arm around me and I had to suppress the need to melt against him. The last thing I wanted to do right now was to go into a meeting where I had to relive what had just happened. I wanted to go to my room and be alone with Jamie where I could just have him hold me so that I knew he was alright. Maybe then I would be alright too. But I couldn't do that. I couldn't fall apart. This was my job. This was what I had been trained for all my life. This was what I was fighting with my mother over. If I fell apart I would just prove all the naysayers right. I needed to be strong.

The elevator doors opened and I stepped away from Jamie, although it killed me to do so. I followed Cody, walking in front of Jamie, putting distance between us. I had to do it for my own preserva- tion. I needed the distance so that I could find the calm, cool Meredith that could deal with a crisis. I did not need Benjamin, my boss, or Alyssa, my real boss, to see me falling apart. I had to show them that I was worthy of the confidence they put in me, even if inside I was falling apart.

We didn't need to discuss where we were going; we all knew that nothing would happen until after we had briefed Benjamin. Cody had been on the phone to him already and he was waiting for us. We all trouped into his room and took our seats around the table. There was a laptop open and Von Bartham was on the screen, looking back at us.

"Tell me what happened," Benjamin said, all business, no pleas- antries.

"We got separated," Jamie said, taking the lead.

"How is that even possible?"

"It was crowded," I said, glad that my voice wasn't shaking. "I moved away from Jamie to look at something and the crowd seemed to surge around me, carrying me further away from him."

"I followed her," Jamie said, shooting me a look, "but when I got close enough, the woman revealed herself not to be Meredith. She had lured me away specifically."

Jamie and Benjamin shared a long look that I couldn't interpret.

"And what about you two?" Benjamin asked, shooting quick glances at Cody and Daniel.

"I was following Meredith," Daniel said, "but again, it wasn't Meredith."

"And I was following Jamie, except..."

"It wasn't Jamie," Benjamin said with a sigh.

"They knew we were coming," Jamie said, his voice hard and cold. "They knew exactly where we would be and what we would be wearing. They knew where Cody and Daniel would be in relation to us. This was a well-coordinated attempt."

Benjamin nodded, his eyes on Jamie. I got the feeling that something was going on between them that I didn't know about.

"Where's Danika?" Von Bartham asked from the laptop.

"We don't know," Cody answered. "After the attack we rendezvoused back at the agreed place but she didn't arrive."

"It had to be her," I said. I never liked her and certainly never trusted her. It seemed that my gut was right about her and it wasn't because of the way she threw herself at Jamie...well not *just* because of the way she threw herself at Jamie.

Benjamin made us run through it several more times, asking specific questions and interrogating us until he was satisfied. Then he dismissed us. I was exhausted and just wanted to go and collapse on my bed.

"Jamie, a moment?"

I turned to see Benjamin looking at Jamie with that weird expression and I slowed. Why did Benjamin need to speak to Jamie alone?

"You can go, Meredith," Benjamin said, and I nodded.

I walked out of the room and headed for the elevator and my suite.

I walked into the room just wanting to fill the tub with hot water and bubbles and sink into it before crawling into bed and letting the exhaustion take me. But before I could even get two steps into the room I was enveloped in a hug.

"Oh my God! Meredith! Are you okay?"

I squeezed my best friend hard and finally allowed the mask to drop. A sob escaped my throat and the tears that I had been holding back began to flow freely. I wasn't having a break down, this was just the excess adrenalin leaving my body. I was a professional. Professionals didn't cry.

"I'm okay," I said when I finally pulled back from Alyssa. "I'm fine. I wasn't the target."

Alyssa held me by the shoulders and inspected me, taking in my appearance and the mess the tears had made of my face.

"They didn't go after you?"

I shook my head. "They were trying to take Jamie - or Will, I suppose."

Alyssa took a step back and sat with a thump on the sofa. "They were after Jamie?"

I sat beside her. "Yeah. A woman had a gun on him and wanted him to go with her."

Alyssa turned to me and furrowed her brows. "But why? Why would they want Will?"

"A cheese coup?" I asked, trying for levity and failing miserably.

Alyssa turned back to me, her eyes concerned. "Are you sure you're okay?"

I nodded. "A bit sore. That guy was big, probably had a hundred pounds on me."

"You had to fight someone? I thought they were after Jamie."

"They were, but I came to his rescue. There were these two big guys, I stepped in and took on one of them while Jamie took on the other one. We would have beaten them too, but they turned tail and ran."

Alyssa shook her head slowly before dragging me back into a hug. I was feeling better, much more like myself. See, I was a professional. I wasn't an emotional wreck because the man I was in love with had been in danger. I wasn't freaking out because he had been bleeding and had had a gun pulled on him. I was perfectly fine.

"Are you okay Mer?" Alyssa asked. "You've gone really pale."

I nodded jerkily and tried to smile. "I'm fine," I said, "just exhausted."

"Oh of course. You probably want to shower and crawl into bed. I'll let you be. We'll talk later."

I nodded and was able to hold it together until Alyssa left the suite and I was all alone. Then I began to shake and the cold enveloped me. It was shock. Just shock, that's all. I made myself stand and head to the bathroom. I needed a hot bath and rest.

Jamie

"WHAT'S REALLY GOING ON?" BENJAMIN ASKED AS SOON AS WE were alone.

"The woman said she knew exactly who I was," I said slowly, imbuing my words with meaning. "She knows who I really am."

Benjamin nodded. "I figured as much. There is no logical reason to try and kidnap Will. Why not just go for Alyssa?"

"Exactly," I said.

"So if she knew that you are Christophe, what was her end game?"

"Could she have been one of General Anastas' spies?" I asked. "I mean, she had to have inside information. Has the general been able to infiltrate us?"

Benjamin wasn't surprised and I knew he must have already considered this scenario.

"And where is Danika? She was the only person apart from the three of us and Alyssa and Will who knows the truth. Is she the mole?"

Benjamin sighed. "I suspected she might be," he said.

"Hang on. What? You suspected?"

He nodded. "I didn't expect her to make her move so early, but I did expect her to try something. It's why I brought her in."

I shook my head, my brain running at a hundred miles a minute.

"You knew she was a potential mole and yet you brought her along anyway?"

"Keep your friends close and your enemies closer."

"So, she works for Anastas?"

Benjamin shook his head. "We could never tie her to him. She was definitely working for the Greek government, though. We know the government has been financing Anastas. We just assumed that she was with him even though we couldn't find any associations."

"So what happens now?"

"Maybe I can answer that."

I spun around to find Danika walking in the door. I jumped to my feet.

"What the hell are you doing here?" I was so angry I could spit. She had not only endangered me but she had endangered my whole team. More than that, she had put Meredith in danger and for that I couldn't forgive her.

"It's not what you think," she said with a sigh, walking over to the table and sitting down.

I looked over at Benjamin who was sitting calmly but I wasn't fooled. Benjamin was like a coiled cobra, ready to strike.

"I don't work for Anastas," she said, practically spitting his name. "I am working against him."

"You are with the resistance," Benjamin said - not a question but a statement of fact.

She nodded once.

"And today's stunt?" I asked indignantly. "What was that all about?"

"We think it's time to make our move. Anastas is weak. Greece has pulled its funding and is wiping its hands of the whole matter. He has nothing left. The people hate him and resent what he has done to the country. They want their king back. They want you, Prince Christophe." She looked right at me when she spoke. "And we can help you."

"And you thought the best way to do that was to kidnap me?"

She shrugged. "We needed to push you. You are comfortable here with your job and your girlfriend and your cushy life. We needed to force your hand."

"You didn't think that maybe you could just, I don't know, *ask me?*" I was so angry. I was angry that she hadn't even come to me and at least stated her case.

"Would you have listened? Would you have been willing to leave all this? To leave Meredith? No. You needed a push and now we have provided it."

"What do you mean?"

Benjamin's phone started beeping and he frowned when he looked down at it.

"What did you do?" I asked staring at her with barely contained fury.

"I outed you," she said with a shrug. "It is about time the crown prince of Kalopsia stood up. Your people need you. Your country needs you and yet here you are hiding and pretending to be someone you are not. It is time for you to be the man that your father trained you to be."

"While I admire your commitment to your country," Benjamin said, "I can't say I am all that enamoured with your process. We would have helped if you had only come to us." He shook his head. "Now you have tied our hands. You have outed the prince and we will have to distance ourselves from the fallout."

I looked to Benjamin, a cold dread filling me. "What does that mean?"

He looked at me with something like sympathy. "We can't protect you anymore, Your Highness."

"You're kicking me out?"

"It's the only way," Von Bartham piped up from the laptop. Not helping, Von Bartham.

"Surely there is something—"

"I really like you, Jamie," Benjamin said. "You have been an asset to our team, but we all knew that this day would come. You can't serve as a guard when everyone now knows that you are the crown prince of Kalopsia and Merveille can no longer hide you. Like it or not, you need to face this, head on."

Two emotions warred within me. Excitement that I would finally be able to stand and hold my head high and let the world know who I really was, and fear. Absolute fear that as soon as I stuck my head out of my hiding place it was going to get shot off. I wanted to be the man who saved his country from the evil overlords, but I also wanted to live to see my next birthday and I wanted...Meredith. I wanted Meredith. I wanted her beside me. I wanted her fighting alongside me. There was no way that was ever going to happen now. I would be lucky if she even ever spoke to me again.

CHAPTER 15

Meredith

I had barely gotten in the tub before there was a persistent knocking
on the bathroom door. I wanted to ignore it but with everything
that had happened today I knew I couldn't.

Huh. I just discovered one of the perks of being a countess. I could
tell everybody to just leave me the heck alone and not bother me.

But I wasn't a countess yet.

"What is it?" I called as the knocking started up again.

"A security meeting has been called," Collette called through the
door. "Andrea and I are here to dress you."

"They want me to dress as Alyssa?" I asked, puzzled.

"Ah...no. We just—"

"Then I can dress myself," I said, standing up and letting the water
sluice off me. It was a shame too, because I was enjoying my bath. The
water was that perfect temperature of hot enough to give that satisfying burn without being so hot that it scalded.

I dried off and stepped out of the ensuite and into the bedroom.
Collette and Andrea were waiting for me.

"I told you I could dress myself," I said.

They looked at each other before Collette spoke up.

"Lady Bingham told us—"

I sighed. I should have known my mother would be trying to control me from afar. I would even wager to guess that these two reported back to her on everything I did. My mother should have had a career in espionage. She could have ruled the world.

"Fine," I said, exasperated.

I really didn't have it in me to argue with them. I also didn't want to get them in trouble. My mother wouldn't accept any excuse for her orders not being carried out. It was just easier for all concerned if I just gritted my teeth and put up with their ministrations. One thing was for certain though, I would be hiring new maids once I left the guard and took up my title. The last thing I wanted was for my household staff to be loyal to my mother and not me.

Instead of my regular plain black pants and black shirt, Andrea and Collette dressed me in a pair of skinny jeans and a silky green top. It was not what I was expecting at all. I thought that if they were working for my mother then they would be putting me in demure floral dresses and twisting my hair up into complicated chignons. The wedge sandals and chunky jewellery were a surprise and not very practical, but I liked them. They left my hair down and only applied the barest hint of makeup. Maybe I would keep them after all...if they could promise to be loyal to me and not my mother.

I walked out into the suite, but it was empty. Cody and Jamie must have already left for the meeting. I nodded to the guard that was posted outside the door of the suite and then headed back down to where Benjamin had set up his headquarters. I knocked once and the door opened. Cody, Daniel, Scott, Aiden and Carlos were all inside and turned to look at me when I walked in. I couldn't see Jamie, but I could hear raised voices coming from the other room.

"That is unacceptable!"

That was Jamie's voice. I could hear a lower murmur which sounded like Benjamin but I couldn't make out the words. And then there was a female voice who I could only assume was Danika. I clenched my jaw. Where had she been when all this went down? We had definitely been compromised and the only one who had the intel to pull it off was one of us. I trusted the other guys with my life, but not her. She had the opportunity to be the mole, my only question was why? And what was she doing here? Why hadn't they arrested her?

The door to the other room flew open and Jamie stood there looking like he was ready to commit murder. His eyes tracked around the room until they landed on me and some of the tension eased out of his body. I wanted to go to him. I wanted to slide my arms around him and hold him until the rigidity that had him so wound up was gone. I wanted to comfort him. I wanted to make sure he was okay. He still had a small bandage covering the cut above his eye, and I wanted to know that he didn't have any other injuries.

We stared at each other across the room and I could almost feel the way his breathing slowed. The slightly crazy air about him eased the longer we looked at one another and if I couldn't go to him and hold him, I could at least know that just my presence was enough to calm him. I tipped the corner of my lips up in a small, encouraging smile and he seemed to relax further.

There was movement behind him and I saw her. Danika. I felt my face change. The soft, relieved expression on my face hardened as I made eye contact with the woman I didn't trust and who I thought was completely responsibly for the events of that afternoon. I made a move to stand. I wanted to confront her. I wanted an explanation for what had happened and what part she played in it. I had no doubt she was involved somehow and I needed everybody to know that they couldn't trust her. But before I could make a move, Benjamin came through the door.

"Take a seat," he said.

I thought Jamie would come and sit beside me, instead he stayed next to Benjamin. Danika would have too if Benjamin hadn't given her a look. She took a seat, but Jamie remained standing beside Benjamin and my stomach clenched. I didn't like this. I didn't like this at all.

"We have some information about this afternoon's...attack," Benjamin said. "The target was not the prince." Benjamin and Jamie shared a look before Benjamin turned back to the assembled group. "Not Prince Will at any rate."

"I don't understand," I said, looking between Jamie and Benjamin. "They were after a prince, but not Will? Then who were they after?"

Jamie and Benjamin shared another look and Jamie sighed.

"Me," he said. "They were after me."

Cody scoffed. "What would they want with you?"

"There is a small island nation off the coast of Greece called Kalopsia," Benjamin said. "Ten years ago there was an uprising and the young prince was smuggled out of the country in order to protect him."

"And the attackers thought you were this prince?" Daniel asked, his eyes on Jamie.

Jamie gave a short, sharp nod. "Prince Christophe James Alesandro Kostopolous."

My stomach turned over as I heard Jamie say the name. The name I knew. The name that was now also mine. His eyes didn't leave mine as he spoke, but it didn't help me comprehend them. Jamie had told me I was a princess who was rescuing the prince. He was the prince. I had married a prince. My mind was about to shut down and I had the sudden and intense need to run from the room or go up and punch him or something. I needed to move. I stood and Jamie made a move to come to me, but I quelled him with a look.

"I don't understand," Cody said, stopping me from leaving. "Why would they think you were this prince?"

"Because I am," Jamie said without taking his eyes off me. "I am the exiled prince. I was brought into Merveille for protection and hidden from the world."

No. No, no, no, no. This couldn't be happening. I remember the first time Jamie came to my house when I was younger. I remember the shy boy with the haunted eyes.

"My mother and sisters were killed. I watched them being murdered and could do nothing to help them. My father was falsely accused and then tried in a corrupt court before being imprisoned. A priest helped me escape."

"Father Felipe," I said softly and Jamie nodded. His eyes still hadn't left mine as he told his story.

"He brought me to Merveille and Lord Bingham and King Edward agreed to hide me."

"Alyssa knows," I said. "Freddie knows. My father knows."

Jamie nodded.

"All this time?" He nodded again and I looked to Benjamin. "And you knew too. You knew and didn't tell us."

Benjamin nodded. "It was safer that way. We had to protect the prince from exposure. Nobody would think to look at one of the royal guard and think him an exiled prince. When we formed the team to accompany Alyssa to the States for school, it was the perfect way to keep him hidden."

"But you didn't tell us," I said, my voice rising. I may have screeched but I would deny it if anyone accused me of it. "All this time we had no idea? Don't you think that was something that we, as a team, should have been aware of?"

"We felt it more prudent to keep the knowledge contained," Benjamin said.

"More prudent?" I said and shook my head. "You didn't think that having him among us would endanger the queen?"

"That was the reason we felt it better not to tell the team. If they knew Jamie's real identity then their loyalties would be divided. By keeping his identity a secret, everyone was able to focus solely on Alyssa, as it should be."

"And you," I said, turning back to Jamie, "you didn't think it was something to share with your wi...team mates?"

"I was under orders."

"But you are a freaking prince! I don't think Benjamin has any authority over you."

"Meredith, please," he said, taking another step toward me. I backed away, holding my hands up in defence. He stopped and his face fell. "I am a prince in exile. I have no authority. Merveille took me in and hid me when I had no one and nowhere to go. Of course I was willing to submit to the authority of Benjamin and Von Bartham and the queen. I owe them my life."

"And what about me?" I asked softly. "Don't you think you owe me?"

"If we could get back to the issue at hand," Benjamin said.

I turned away from Jamie and squeezed my eyes shut. I would not cry in front of everyone. They were tears of anger and frustration but there was no way I was going to appear weak in front of my team.

"The attack this afternoon was an attempted kidnapping by a resistance group who are determined to restore the royal family of Kalopsia."

"Do we know who they are?" Carlos asked.

I turned around and caught the look Benjamin gave Danika.

"We do," Benjamin said.

Danika stood. "I am part of the resistance. It was my job to get intel to the team so they could execute their mission. We never had any intention of harming the prince. We just want to see him on the throne and the usurper General Anastas imprisoned for his crimes. Our country is straining under the weight of a despot and we are desperate. The people want their prince back and now is the time to strike when the general has lost the support of his financiers and the people. I won't apologise for my actions. I believe in my cause."

"The problem now, however," Benjamin said through a hard jaw, "is that Jamie's identity has been leaked to the press. We can't contain this. Jamie has been outed and Merveille needs to distance herself from the fallout."

I didn't think my stomach could drop any further than what it had. Merveille was distancing herself from the troubles in Kalopsia and that meant we were distancing ourselves from Jamie.

"We will be returning to Merveille first thing in the morning. The queen thought it best to end the tour now and to make a statement once we reach sovereign soil."

"And Jamie?" Cody asked.

Benjamin looked at Jamie, whose eyes were still on me.

"The prince is going home."

I fled the room. I couldn't take anymore.

Jamie

I WATCHED MEREDITH LEAVE, HELPLESS TO STOP HER. I HAD TRIED to get to her before the meeting. I wanted to explain it all to her, to tell her in private and tell her that it changed nothing between us. I wanted her to know that I wanted her as my princess. I wanted her beside me while I navigated the mine field that I was walking into. The last thing I wanted was to blindside her like this. But I couldn't get away. There had been so much to discuss and plans that had to be made. I was no longer a royal guard, I was a prince with all the responsibilities that went along with that title.

After the meeting with Benjamin, we had met with Alyssa and Will to discuss what the next steps were. In her official capacity, Alyssa assured me that Merveille would support my bid for the throne but they would need to distance themselves from us until we had attempted to diplomatically resolve the conflict. As a friend she had offered to help me in any way she could behind the scenes. I appreciated her offers and knew that I would make use of whatever she had to give me.

From that meeting we went into another one to address the small detail of me needing my own royal guard. Danika had presented a strong case for using herself and her team. I had been against it. The woman might be loyal to me but she had caused me no end of problems - and not only by outing me to the world. She had come between Meredith and me time and again and the last thing I wanted was to drive another wedge between my wife and me. But I had been overruled. Was that even a thing now? I had given in to the superior knowledge of Benjamin and Von Bartham and Danika was now my head of security. She would assemble her team and we would be leaving for parts unknown before the day was done.

But none of that helped me get to Meredith and now she was walking away and I didn't know if I would even get to see her before I left.

I should come clean. I should tell Benjamin and Von Bartham that Meredith and I were married. I should insist that my wife go with me to wherever Danika was whisking me off to. But I didn't. Despite my desire to have her close to me and for her to never leave my side ever again, there was a part of me that needed her to be safe. As long as our marriage was secret, then she would be safe. The moment our relationship became public was the moment I painted a proverbial target on her back and I couldn't do that to her. I couldn't put her in danger even when it was killing me to let her walk away. Somehow I knew we would be together in the future. I had to believe that. It was the only thing that was stopping me from running after her and begging for her forgiveness. A little pain now would pay off in the future when I could offer her a life away from the demands of her mother. A life where she could be a warrior queen. I knew that things in Kalopsia would take a long time to settle and I would need someone by my side who was fierce. Meredith was that person. I just had to bide my time. It was the only thing that kept me rooted to the spot.

The door slammed and I took a breath before turning back to the rest of the team still assembled.

"I know I owe you an apology," I said.

Cody shrugged. "You really don't," he said. He looked at the other guys and they all nodded in agreement. "We get it. We get the need for secrecy and we understand that it was never personal. This job is not easy and if we had known who you really were it would have made our job harder."

"Thank you," I said. "Really, thank you. For the most part even I forgot who I was. I couldn't have asked for a better place to grow up and I couldn't have asked for a better teacher and mentor than Benjamin. Being a part of this team has meant the world to me. You all gave me a place to belong when I had nothing and could rely on no one. You will never know just how much that has meant to me."

"If there are no other questions?" Benjamin said. When everyone shook their heads, he dismissed them. "Wheels up in twelve hours. Check your tablets for updates to the itinerary."

Each man stood in turn and shook my hand. I was humbled by their support. These men had become friends and I would miss them. I was about to go into a hostile situation and none of the people I trusted would be there to back me up. I would be in the hands of a brand new team who I knew nothing about. What I wouldn't give to have these guys in their stead.

When the room was empty, Benjamin turned to me and stuck out his hand.

"It has been an honour," he said as he shook my hand.

"The honour has been mine," I replied.

"You have my number," he said. "If you ever need something, anything, don't hesitate to call."

I nodded once, my throat thick.

"We need to go," Danika said.

"I need to speak to Meredith," I said, turning to her.

"We don't have time," she replied. "The transport is waiting."

"Go," Benjamin said. "I will talk to Meredith."

They didn't understand and I couldn't make them without outing us. And I couldn't do that without talking to Meredith first.

I let Danika lead me from the room. I would find a way to talk to Meredith and explain. When all this settled down, I would make a way for us to be together. If she would still have me.

CHAPTER 16

Jamie

I was on a boat. In the Mediterranean. The sky was blue and there was just a hint of a breeze. The water lapped gently against the hull as we sat at anchor. It should be the perfect scene for a romantic rendezvous. It wasn't. I was surrounded by people I didn't know, people who looked at me curiously. I felt like an exhibit in a museum. To them I was a unicorn, an enigma, something they never expected to see in their life time.

I was completely out of my depth.

What had ever made me think I could be the king of a country? I knew nothing about these people and I had spent the last ten years hiding from them. Now they expected me to come charging in and save them all. I didn't know where to even start.

"The latest intel we have is that Anastas is preparing to run," Danika said.

"Run?" I asked. "Why would he run?"

"Greece has officially cut ties with him and they are calling in their loans. He is up to his eyeballs in debt and he has no way to repay them - or anyone else he has borrowed from." She stopped and took a slow breath. "There's something else," she said, looking straight at me. "We believe..."

I clenched my fists as she paused and looked at one of her team members before continuing.

"We believe your father is dead."

It shouldn't come as such a blow. Hadn't I thought that he must have been dead all this time? It still knocked me a little off kilter as I came to the reality that my father was not going to somehow stride in and rescue me. In the back of my mind I suppose I had always thought that he would somehow be the victor in all of this. Now it all came down to me. The last of the Kostopolous line. The last of the royal family. The fate of my nation now rested squarely on my shoulders. I shifted, rolling my shoulders and straightening my spine as if I could feel the new weight of the mantle that had just landed on me.

"How sure are you?" I asked, my voice tight.

Danika shared a look with her colleague again. "Almost one hundred percent certain. We have...an associate inside the castle. By all reports, after your father's trial, he was incarcerated in the castle dungeons. From what our associate is telling us, he died from his injuries not long after."

"He has been dead all this time?"

"Yes. It would seem so."

"So why didn't Anastas come out and say so? He told the world I was dead, quite gleefully I might add, so why keep it hidden that my father was dead?"

"To keep the population in line," she said. "Your father's sentence was not a lifetime sentence, it was twenty years. General Anastas used it to quell the people. If they thought that one day the king would be released, then they wouldn't rise against the new regime."

"And yet here you are."

She smiled briefly. "Here we are."

"So what makes you different?"

"We didn't grow up under the rule of a benevolent king. We have only ever really known the tyranny of a despot. But we have heard the stories of the old men as they sit around and talk about the 'good ole days.' Many of them never believed that you were dead. You became a bit of a legend to me and others my age. While the old men believed that the king would be released from prison and would resurrect the monarchy, those of us younger ones believed that you would be our saviour."

I could definitely feel the weight of their expectations now.

"How did you find me?"

"A lot of trial and error," she said with another quick smile. "There were reports of a fishing boat leaving the harbour that night. There was no official record of it, just people who had seen it and drew conclusions from it. I think for a lot of people it was wishful thinking. They wanted you to be alive. They wanted you to have escaped."

"How did you keep all this from Benjamin and Von Bartham?"

"To be honest, I don't think I did."

My eyebrows popped up at that. Had Benjamin and Von Bartham known all along who Danika really was?

"It seemed too easy," she went on, "but I went with it. I didn't think I would get so close to you so quickly. I thought they would play a few mind games with me first and test my backstory. We were prepared for the long game."

"If Benjamin let you close and knew what you were going to do then he must have more intel than you do," I said, convinced I was right. "He must know something you don't."

"It's entirely possible," she replied with a nod.

And if Benjamin thought it was time to make a move, then it must be. I had come to trust the man and his spooky intuition. I remember the day that we got the news about Alyssa's father and brother. He had been twitchy all that morning as if he knew something was going to happen. Now he was pushing me to do this, to step up. He wouldn't have pushed me out of the nest unless he knew I was ready.

"Okay," I said with a long exhale. "What's the plan?"

Meredith

I WAS SULKING. I KNEW IT AND I DIDN'T CARE. JAMIE HAD LEFT without even saying goodbye...not that I would have seen him anyway, but he could have at least *tried* to see me. He owed me an explanation. Not that I wanted one or would listen to one. He had lied to me - to all of us. I knew there were extenuating circumstances, but I was his wife! He should have told me the night we got married.

Something niggled in my brain and I flopped back on the bed. I couldn't sleep. I didn't care that I would look like a swamp monster tomorrow. My days of impersonating the queen were done. I was angry and sad and I wanted to hit something. I sat up in bed and swung my legs over the side. That's what I needed to do. Hit something.

I dressed quickly and quietly before sneaking out of the suite. I couldn't sneak past the guard who stood watch outside the door so I didn't even try.

"I'm going down to the gym," I said and he gave me a short, sharp nod.

The gym was dark when I opened the door but as soon as I stepped inside, the lights came on. I was thankful for the solitude as I made my way across the floor to the heavy bag hanging in the corner. I should probably warm up first, but I was too keyed up to sweat it out on the treadmill first. I needed to hit something hard and I didn't think this uncomfortable feeling inside me would leave until I did.

I wrapped my hands and pulled my gloves on. I started with a few light jabs until I could feel my muscles loosen and then I started hitting harder. The thwack of leather on leather was strangely cathartic. I got lost in the rhythm and let my mind wander. It was almost self-hypnosis - the repetitive action of the punching bag and just letting go of all conscious thought.

"I grew up on a small island nation called Kalopsia. I know you've probably never heard of it. Most people think we are part of the Greek Isles. Our island is not big, but it is beautiful. My father was the king. I lived in the castle with my parents and my two younger sisters. My childhood was idyllic. I knew that one day I would rule my small country and I was eager to learn all I could from my father in order to be the kind of ruler he was. The people loved my father and my mother. Or that's what I thought."

"Is this the part where I rescue you?"

I paused mid swing. I remembered Jamie telling me this story the night we got married. I was tired and snuggled up against him in the back of the limousine. There was something special and dream-like about that moment. I thought he had been just telling me a story. He had called me princess earlier and I thought this was just him being romantic and making up a fairy story where I rescued him. But it wasn't a fairytale.

Jamie was telling me the truth.

I didn't remember what he told me after that. I had dozed off in his arms with my head full of an exiled prince and a small, beautiful island that mourned his loss. I leaned back against the wall and let my legs buckle, sliding down the wall until I sat on the floor. Jamie had tried to tell me the truth that night, but I fell asleep. It didn't explain why he didn't tell me the next day or any of the days since that night. I know I freaked out when I woke up that morning but surely he could have...

Who was I kidding? I pretty much made it clear to him that I didn't want to be married to him. I even used the excuse that my mother wouldn't think he was good enough for me. He was probably laughing at me the whole time. He was a prince and here I was telling him the great Lady Caroline Bingham, Duchess of Monterey, would find it unacceptable that her daughter married him. If my mother only knew.

God. If my mother knew then I would never hear the end of it. She would make such a production out of it all. Her daughter married to a prince.

I dropped my head to my knees. There was no way the two of us could be together now. I had seen the internet and all the news sites that were breaking the story of the lost prince who everyone assumed was dead. It was a fairytale all of its own. Jamie - *Prince Christophe* - hadn't done any news interviews yet, but there was lots of speculation. The spotlight had been shone on Kalopsia and I knew that he would have the support of his people if he chose to go back and take control from the guy who was currently leading the country.

He didn't need me. He didn't even ask me to go with him. He was going to be the king and I had no doubt that he would do whatever he could to dissolve our marriage. I was a fine wife when we were two royal guards living a very non-extraordinary life, but now that he was exposed and famous, he had no further use for me. I wouldn't fit into his world.

I snorted out a harsh laugh. It was ironic really. Or pathetic. I had been the one who was convinced he wouldn't fit into my world. I had been worried what people would think if the prime minister's daughter married a royal guard. But all this time he had been a prince and not just a prince, but the heir apparent. Crown Prince Christophe of Kalopsia married to me, a royal guard who wasn't even going to be that much longer. But even a countess wouldn't be good enough for him, no matter that I wanted to be. A countess marrying a prince was not out of the realm of possibility, but when that prince was the ruler of a country in flux? There were all sorts of political ramifications for tying Merveille to such an unstable country. Alyssa would never sign off on it. That's even assuming Jamie still wanted me.

Which he didn't.

I climbed back to my feet and swung half-heartedly at the bag, but the need to hit something was gone. Now I just wanted to crawl into bed, curl up in a ball, and sob. I'd had my chance at happiness and I'd blown it. Jamie wouldn't want me now that he was reinstated as the prince. Not when he thought I had rejected him because I thought he was below my station.

I was an idiot.

"MEREDITH," BENJAMIN SAID COMING UP BESIDE ME.

I pulled the earbuds from my ears and looked up at him from my seat. We had boarded the private plane that would take us back to Merveille. I hadn't slept more than a few minutes and I was cranky and annoyed.

"Alyssa wants to see you."

The temptation to put my earbuds back in, close my eyes and ignore him was strong. I probably would have done it too if the whole team hadn't been within hearing distance and were looking at me expectantly. Yes, Alyssa was the queen and my boss, but she was also my friend and right now I wasn't feeling very friendly toward her.

With more attitude than was entirely appropriate, I got up and tossed my earbuds on the empty seat. I would like to say that I didn't swagger like a teenager getting called into the principal's office, but I would be lying. I may have even had a scowl on my face and felt the need to chew gum sardonically.

I knocked on the door to the private office that was at the back of the plane and waited for her to give me permission to enter. I couldn't hide my anger. Maybe it was the redhead thing, but as soon as she looked up at me I knew that she knew everything I felt...maybe not *everything*. I hoped that she didn't know how I felt about Jamie, but with all my emotions so close to the surface, anything was possible.

We stared at each other for a moment and then she lifted her hand and indicated the chair in front of her desk. "Take a seat."

I sat, with as much contempt as someone can. I couldn't help it. Alyssa was my best friend and she had kept this from me. I was still reeling from being kept in the dark for ten years about Jamie's real identity, but the fact that even Alyssa hadn't told me really stung. We didn't have secrets. That's what it meant to be best friends.

"Look," she said, "I understand—"

"No," I said, "I don't think you do."

"I didn't have a choice. It wasn't my secret to tell."

I crossed my arms and looked away. Her rational explanation did nothing to cool my ire. I still felt betrayed and not just by her. Von Bartham, Benjamin, and my father all knew and didn't tell. How could I trust anything anyone said when something like this had been kept from me? What else were they hiding?

"You didn't think that the team that lived and worked with him should be told? You didn't think that something like that could endanger a mission because we were unaware?"

"The danger would have been if you had known," she said. "Your loyalties would have been split at worst, and at best you would have been distracted by it."

"I don't agree. If we had known right from the start, we would have..."

"What? Gotten used to it? Even you're not that naïve, Meredith. It would have always been there in the back of your mind. You would have treated him differently and then how long would his secret have been kept? It was for *his safety*. When he came to us, he was running for his life."

"How long have you known?"

"Since we got back from the States," she said, looking down at her desk. "It was part of my security briefing as the new head of state."

"And how did you feel when you found out that it had been kept from you?" I asked. "Did you maybe feel a little betrayed like maybe it was something you should have known about? He was part of your team. We were like family. It was us against the world. Surely when you found out that one of your security detail was holding a secret as big as that, you felt a little of what I feel now."

Alyssa locked eyes with me and I felt like she could see more than I was willing to show her. I looked away first.

"I was shocked," she said carefully, "but I understood." She paused for a few heart beats and then, "What's really going on, Mer? Your reaction is out of proportion—"

"Out of proportion?" I jumped to my feet. "I've just found out that I've been lied to for the last ten years. Fair enough that it was kept from the rest of the team, but *you* kept it from me too. You, who tells me everything. Alyssa, we don't have secrets. That was our pact, remember?"

Alyssa stood as well. "You don't have secrets from me?" she asked and I froze. "Are you telling me that you don't keep anything from me, Meredith?"

"I—"

"Because I have noticed that you and Jamie have been really close lately, and I'm not the only one. Even Savannah mentioned the way the two of you seemed...friendly."

I swallowed and tried to keep my face from betraying the turmoil inside me. She was right. I had been keeping my relationship with Jamie a secret. And now we had an even bigger one. One that may even cause an international incident.

"Are we done here?" I asked. I couldn't do this. I was tired, cranky, and too emotionally unstable to match wits with her right now.

Alyssa walked around the desk and stood close to me. She reached out and laid a hand on my arm. I just barely managed not to flinch but she must have seen me tense.

"Meredith," she said, and it wasn't the queen speaking, but my friend. "You know you can tell me anything. It's obvious that Jamie's revelation has been hard on you. For what it's worth you can come to me and I promise just to listen, be a sounding board or just let you vent. I love you and I know you're hurt, but you're also better than this. You know why I couldn't tell you and you know why he couldn't either. Cut him some slack, okay?"

"If you're finished?" I said, stepping away from her.

She gave me one last, long look and then nodded.

I turned and walked out the door. I didn't make eye contact with anyone as I moved down the aisle to my seat. I sat, put my earbuds back in and closed my eyes, shutting the world out. I just wanted to go home. Maybe I could escape to the country estate of my new title and just forget about the pain of my heart as it shattered in my chest.

CHAPTER 17

Jamie

It wasn't exactly a triumphant return. We slunk into Kalopsia in the dead of night. I was hustled through the dark street, a heavy cloak over me obscuring not only me, but my first view of a country I hadn't seen in ten years. Not exactly how I imagined I would return to the country of my birth.

A door opened and I was ushered inside. It was all very cloak and dagger and I wondered if maybe it was a little over the top. I shucked the cloak that had been covering me and squinted in the dim light. The room was crowded with people and they were all looking at me with a mixture of awe and disbelief. There may have even been a scowl or two.

I know I didn't look like a prince. I was wearing black cargo pants and a black t-shirt - my standard uniform as a royal guard. I had never been one to dress up or worry too much about the clothes I wore. It was a running joke amongst the rest of the guard about my lack of fashion. It wasn't what you wore that determined who you were, that was something I was very aware of. But these people looked at me like they expected something more.

"Prince Christophe," a man said, stepping forward. He extended his hand in greeting and I took it and shook it. I recognised him. He was the current prime minister, or what would have been a prime minister if General Anastas hadn't installed himself as *Próedros*. He still had the title of prime minister even if his authority was impotent. He had been elected by the people and his presence here among the resistance spoke volumes. I just wasn't sure whether to trust him or not. These people obviously did, but he and the rest of Parliament had let General Anastas have free reign over the country since he had wrested control from my father.

"Prime Minister Theodorou," I replied.

"I cannot express how good it is to see you, here, back in Kalopsia. For many years we believed you to be dead."

"And my father alive," I said.

He grimaced and nodded. "Yes. We were all led to believe that your father was alive. It has come as a shock to all of us of his passing. But the grief is tempered by the news that the prince lives."

I ran a hand through my hair and exhaled roughly. I hadn't expected this homecoming to be so emotional. There was so much anger still inside me with the way my family had been ripped away from me - anger I thought I had long since put behind me.

"So what happens now?" I asked. I needed to focus on the tasks ahead and not let myself dwell on the murky pool of feelings. This was not the time to show my sensitive underbelly. These people needed a strong leader, not a bleeding heart.

"A press conference," Theodorou said. "We need to announce your return. The people want to see you. They have been lied to for too many years and will not believe you have indeed returned until they see your face."

I felt every eye on me as the prime minster spoke. He smiled a small, tight smile and shook his head. "You look just like him, you know?"

I knew. Every morning when I looked in the mirror I saw my father looking back at me. It was why I had grown the beard. The last thing I needed was for people to recognise me because of a careless photo while I was guarding the queen. Being Freddie's groomsman had been the stupidest thing I'd ever agreed to.

"And what about Anastas?" I asked. "Won't he have something to say about me just turning up here and giving a press conference?"

Theodorou looked over my shoulder at Danika before looking back at me. "The *Próedros* has disappeared."

I raised my eyebrows and looked behind me to Danika. "You said he was preparing to run, has he already made his escape?"

"It appears that way," she said.

"And do we know where he is? For all we know he could just be in hiding, waiting for me to reveal myself so he can do to me what he did to my family."

"We have reason to believe he has made for Greece," she said.

"He's just walking away? I don't know whether I believe that."

"He really doesn't have much choice," Theodorou said. "The men who bankrolled him are calling in their loans. General Anastas has not exactly been a good steward of the money entrusted to him. He has been defaulting on these loans for years and now that Greece is suffering their own financial crisis, they need the money owed them."

I shrugged. "It's not like they can do anything—"

"That's where you are wrong," Theodorou said. "The Greek government didn't officially support Anastas. Prominent men in high places did and they did it through questionable means. They are now being pressured and are in turn pressuring Anastas."

I tilted my head to the ceiling and clenched my jaw. What was I walking into? My country was broke and the government appeared to be in shambles. I had known it wasn't going to be easy, but it sounded like I had nothing to work with. I wished for the millionth time that Meredith was here with me. I needed someone who I knew was loyal to me. Someone I had known longer than five minutes who I could talk to. I couldn't even pick up the phone and call Freddie because there was too much chance that I would draw Merveille into a fight that wasn't theirs. I needed to do this on my own with people I didn't completely trust. Talk about going from the frying pan and into the fire.

Meredith

I KNOCKED ON THE DOOR OF BENJAMIN'S OFFICE.

"Come in," he called.

I took a deep breath and pushed through the door, keeping my emotions in check.

"Have a seat, Meredith," he said.

I nodded and sat in the chair opposite his desk. He leaned back in his chair and looked at me. I tried not to fidget. I had known this day was coming. It was time for me to leave the guard and as much as I had protested against it, now I just wanted it over with.

"I suppose you know why you're here," he said.

"Because it's time," I replied flatly.

"You know I wish this didn't have to happen."

I shrugged. It didn't matter what Benjamin wanted or what I wanted. It was bigger than both of us and it was past time I understood that.

He sighed and looked down at a document on his desk. "So, the plan is to transition you out. We are already short-staffed. Although the new transfers are slotting in well, it's not the same as having people like you."

And Jamie. His name hung in the air between us, unsaid, but we both knew that his leaving had created a hole.

"If it's alright with you, I'd rather just go. Alyssa's schedule is clear and there really isn't any need for me to stay."

"Go where?"

"I'll move back into Château de Monterey. There is no need for me to stay."

"You're still a lady in waiting, Meredith. You don't need to leave the palace."

"I am taking the title of my grandmother, Countess of Bellemere. I need to spend time learning the role. I think it would be best if I did that at Monterey."

Benjamin was silent as he looked at me. I couldn't tell what he was thinking, but it didn't matter. I had made my decision and I knew my mother would make sure I got what I wanted - especially because it was what she wanted too. I hadn't told her I was moving home. I knew she would be ecstatic when she found out. My leaving the guard and taking up the title was a dream come true for my mother and I was sure that as soon as I announced it, she would be all over it. She would employ a stylist and new lady's maids and have me tricked up in no time. Oh joy.

"Are you sure there's nothing you need to tell me?" Benjamin asked and my gaze snapped to his.

"Pardon?"

He leaned back in his chair again and steepled his fingers under his chin. Benjamin was shrewd and he had the best poker face I'd seen on anyone. He looked at me now like he could see every single secret I'd ever kept hidden and I couldn't stop myself from shifting in my seat.

"The night in Le Beau when you disappeared," he said, "I sent Jamie after you."

I nodded but didn't trust myself to speak.

"What happened?"

I swallowed and looked at a spot over his shoulder. "We got drunk."

"And?"

My eyes snapped back to his. "And nothing. I was upset and so was Jamie, although at the time I didn't know why. We had a few drinks together. Rode around in the limo for a bit and then went back to the hotel."

Benjamin didn't say anything and I held myself as still as I could, trying not to give myself away. He couldn't know, could he? We had used a random car company and we hadn't told anyone. There was no way he would know, not unless he'd followed us. I was pretty sure he hadn't done that, surely I would know if I was being followed.

"I need to get back to my packing," I said, standing. If I stayed much longer, I was likely to give myself away.

"Meredith."

I stopped, but didn't look at him. Benjamin had always been a good leader. He had trained me and we had been together for a long time. There was a bond that grew between people who worked in such close quarters as the royal guard had. Unfortunately, finding out that he had been lying to me for all this time had damaged that bond. My trust in him had been battered. I knew he had his reasons, and that Jamie's life had been at risk, but still, I was hurt. It hadn't seemed to faze the other members of the team, so maybe it was because I was a woman. Or because I had fallen in love with Jamie. Prince Christophe. Whatever. It didn't matter. The fact was, I was still angry and upset and I wanted to just put the whole sordid mess behind me and move on.

He sighed. "You still remain a part of the guard for the next six months, even if you aren't on the rotation. It's part of your contract that I can call you up at any time for any mission until the six months is complete. At the end of that six months we can decide to extend it for another six months."

I laughed. It was humourless and rough. "Good luck explaining that to my mother."

"The duchess really has no say in the matter. The crown spent an awful lot of money training you and your contract was for fifteen years. It is only because the circumstances have changed and you have become a person of interest that we are terminating your contract early."

"Because I became a liability, don't you mean?"

"Yes. But part of your transition out of the guard is that you remain available for recall for the next six months. At that time, we will review."

"Fine," I said with a sigh. I was tired and I was done with all of this. "Can I go now?"

"There's nothing you want to say to me?" he asked and I finally looked over at him.

"It's been real."

I turned and walked away, closing the door behind me and refusing to look back. Onward and upward. Looking back was for chumps.

"WHAT THE HELL, MER?"

I looked up from the book I wasn't reading and squinted at Freddie. He stood in the doorway of my suite, arms and legs akimbo and a scowl on his face.

"And hello to you too, brother. Please, come in. Make yourself at home."

He rolled his eyes and stepped across the threshold. I had been back in Château de Monterey for a week and a half and was just about to kill my mother. I knew how to do it and make it look like an accident too. I could probably get away with it except that too many people knew of my skills. Matricide was frowned upon these days. Pity.

"What are you doing here?" Freddie said, falling into an overstuffed armchair opposite me.

I held up the book that I had been trying to read. "Reading," I said, although I used the term loosely. I had been on the same page for an hour or more.

"I don't mean here in this room, but here in the castle. Seriously? You moved home?"

I closed the book and put it on the seat beside me. Freddie had only just returned from his honeymoon and I hadn't yet had a chance to talk to him about Jamie.

"I was kicked out of the guard," I said primly. "Where else was I supposed to go?"

"You stay at the palace with all the other ladies in waiting," he said, his exasperation clear. "Why come back to the viper's nest?"

"I'm to be the Countess of Bellemere," I said as if it answered all his questions.

"So?"

"Well, I -ah, that is, Mother needs me here."

"Rubbish."

I nodded, warming to my theme. "Of course she does. How else am I to learn all about my new title and estate if not at her knee? She needs to teach me everything she knows. Our mother is one of the most well-respected peers in the country. I am privileged to have her tutelage."

"Balderdash!"

I slumped back in my seat. It was no use trying to convince Freddie that I was here because I wanted to be. The fact was, I was hiding. I was hiding from my friends and especially from the queen.

"Alyssa is worried about you," he said as if he could read my thoughts.

"I don't care," I said.

"Oh come on, Mer. You're going to turn your back on a life-long friendship because she had to keep state secrets from you?"

"Yes."

"So what about me? Are you going to cut me out of your life too because I knew?"

"Yes!" I jumped to my feet and pointed my finger at him. "You should have told me!"

"Sit down and stop being so melodramatic. Of course I knew. Jamie and I were friends from the start. Have you forgotten that he lived with us for a while? He was a scared boy who had just lost his entire family and we were friends. He told me everything."

"And you didn't tell me?"

"Why would I?"

"Because...because..." Because I am his wife! But I couldn't say that. I couldn't tell Freddie that I had fallen in love with Jamie either. As far as he was concerned, we were only colleagues. "Because you're my brother," I finished lamely and then sat back down on my chair.

Freddie snorted. "Yeah, because I tell you everything. Come on, Mer, what's this really about?"

"I feel betrayed," I said. "Everybody was lying to me."

"More an omission than a lie and it was to protect Jamie. Have you even seen the media storm that has come out of the debacle in Barcelona? The poor guy is being eaten alive by the press."

I shook my head. I had purposely stayed ignorant of any and all mentions of Jamie in the press. I didn't read the newspaper and I didn't watch the television. I had made the mistake once and had spent the next two days crying myself hoarse. I had told my mother I was sick and had stayed in bed, sulking. I couldn't risk another meltdown like that, so I stayed away from anything that might inadvertently mention Jamie and his country of Kalopsia.

Freddie sat forward and rested his elbows on his knees. "Talk to me Mer. What's really going on?"

I bit my lip as I looked at my brother. I loved Freddie but more than that I looked up to him and respected him. If I was going to confide in anyone, it would be him. I opened my mouth to say the words and then snapped it shut. I couldn't say it. How could I tell my brother that I had snuck off and gotten married to a guy who was soon to be the king of his own country? How could I tell Freddie that I had fallen in love with his best friend?

I sighed and closed my eyes, leaning back against the chaise. "Nothing," I said. "Nothing is going on. I'm just tired and grumpy. I've been kicked out of the guard and forced to become a countess. I have to endure endless criticism from Mother as she points out all of my flaws and tells me constantly how much work she still needs to do before she will even entertain the idea of presenting me to the rest of the peers. My whole life has been upended and I don't know which way is up." My voice had risen as I spoke. "So I'm sorry if I'm not the fun-loving, joy-filled bundle of sunshine that you expected to find when you returned from your blissfully perfect honeymoon. I'm sorry that I am maybe a little upset that my whole life and everything I've known to be true has fallen down around my ears like a house of cards while you get to marry the woman of your dreams and live happily ever after like some sappy romance hero." I was standing now and I didn't even remember getting out of my chair. I was breathing heavily and my throat was tight. Tears filled my eyes but I refused to let them fall and I glared at Freddie with hurt and anger. He looked back at me with shock, which would have been funny if my world didn't feel like it was crumbling around me.

"Mer," he said, standing and wrapping his arms around me.

It was too much. I clung to him and the sobs I had been holding back burst out of me, wracking my body.

"It's going to be okay, Mer," he murmured as he stroked my back.

I wished that I could believe him, but from where I was standing, nothing would be okay again.

CHAPTER 18

Jamie

I stood in the entrance hall of the palace I once called home. It was empty and I was alone. The tapestries and paintings that had hung on the walls for generations were gone. As I turned slowly, my movements echoed in the cavernous space making me feel more alone than I ever had in my life.

I had been back in Kalopsia for a month now. There had been political wrangling in Parliament to reinstate the monarchy. It wasn't a done deal yet, but the signs were positive. General Anastas had disappeared. Danika had set someone on his trail to hopefully find him and bring him back to face a trial of treason. Those of his cronies who had stayed in Kalopsia had been rounded up and even now were facing similar charges. We weren't through the woods yet, but there were definitely positive signs. Meanwhile, the island of Kalopsia held its collective breath to see what type of man I had become and what kind of king I would be.

It didn't feel how I imagined it to feel. I didn't feel victorious, I just felt sad and empty. My family was gone. Buried in unmarked graves. The people surrounding me were still wary of me and I, them. I had known most of them less than a month, and the ones I had known longer...well, I had only known them two months at the most. Danika was the only person I had known longer and I still had reservations about her. I didn't like the way she forced my hand and I had issues with the way she tried to come between Meredith and me.

Meredith.

It had been six weeks since I'd seen her. Six weeks since we'd argued. Six weeks since I had felt her in my arms. I missed her. I missed seeing her, talking to her, sparring with her. I had been required to sever all contact with Merveille until my government was stable. I pulled out my phone and looked at it. Today was the day. Parliament was letting me move into the palace and I had been encouraged to reach out to any country that might be friendly. I knew I could count on Alyssa, but she wasn't the person I wanted to speak to. I dialled the number and waited. It rang several times before a recorded voice informed me that the person I was calling was unavailable and asked if I would like to leave a message. I pulled the phone away from my ear and disconnected the call.

"Everything alright?' Danika asked as she walked through the front doors.

"Of course," I replied. "I was just wondering what happened to all the artwork."

Danika looked around. "I had never been in here before, when your family was on the throne, but I have seen pictures."

"I assume he sold off what he could to finance his lavish lifestyle but there was no way he would have been able to get their true worth. Some of those vases were priceless."

With one last look around, I headed further in to the palace. It was a surreal feeling to be walking these halls again. My memories were overlaid on the present with unexpected clarity. It was like stepping back in time... almost.

Before I knew it I was standing before the door of my father's office. I stopped and leaned my head against the wood for a moment, wishing for my father to be seated behind his desk like he had been all the times before when I was a child. But I knew he wouldn't be there, just as my mother wouldn't be in the drawing room with my sisters trying to teach them how to needlepoint or instructing them on the finer points of etiquette and deportment. They had been precocious little girls who had much preferred to be outside than sitting inside and learning to be little princesses.

I hadn't thought about my family in years, mostly because it hurt too much. Being surrounded by the familiarity of the palace had caused a barrage of memories to assault me and I was reeling with the force of it. I felt Danika's hand on my shoulder and realised I was still leaning against the door. I took a breath and straightened. I couldn't show any weakness, not now, not when the eyes of the whole country were on me. I needed to show these people that they could trust me and that I could be a strong leader. The country was in ruins and I needed to be able to pick up the pieces and show the way in the rebuilding. There was no place or time for sentimentality.

I pushed open the door and stepped across the threshold. It was almost exactly how I remembered it. My many-times great-grandfather's portrait still hung on the wall behind the desk and looked down on me disapprovingly as he always did. I wondered, not for the first time, if the man ever smiled. The desk was the same, but strangely devoid of the clutter that had characterised my father's rule. Not that it was tidy. It looked to have been rifled through and draws stuck out at odd angles. The photographs of my mother and sisters were gone as was the in-tray and out-tray that would normally be overflowing with paperwork.

The bookshelves that lined the room were intact and the books looked undisturbed for the most part. With a small smile I crossed to one particular bookcase and selected a blue, leather-bound tome. I pulled it out about halfway and listened for the tell-tale click before swinging the hidden door open. It was a panic room that had been designed so the reigning monarch could hide in case of the palace coming under attack. It had never been used as such and my father had often let me play in there, even setting up a child-sized desk and chair so I could work alongside him sometimes. It was exactly the same as I left it. General Anastas must not have discovered the secret room. A fine layer of dust covered everything and I staggered against the memories as I walked inside. I ran my finger over the desk, seeing my childish handwriting as I made a list of things that I felt the nursery needed.

I squatted down and reached under the desk to the little cubby where I used to hide my most precious things. My hand closed around the little statuette of a soldier on a horse and I pulled it out, the weight and shape of it familiar in my hand. As I did so, an envelope fell to the floor and I picked it up before standing. I looked at the small figurine and smiled before turning my eyes to the envelope. It had my name written on it in Father's flowing script. My jaw clenched against the emotions the threatened to overwhelm me. I took a deep breath and shoved the envelope in my pocket before stepping back out into the office and closing the door to the secret room.

Now was not the time. There would be time enough later when I was alone to read the last words of my father.

Meredith

I SLID DOWN FROM THE HORSE AND PATTED HIS NECK A FEW TIMES before handing over the reins to the groom. I drew in a deep breath of the fresh country air and turned my face up to the weak sun that shined down. Winter wasn't far off and already I could feel the chill in the air.

"Lady Meredith," a voice said, interrupting the few moments of peace that a ride through the paddocks had given me.

"Yes Pamela?" I asked, opening my eyes and turning to face my personal assistant. Oh, yes. I had one of those now. Chosen and assigned to me by my mother. My whole staff were selected by her and I knew every one of them were her little spies. Apart from my two lady's maids. They were mine and I knew they were loyal to me.

"I need you to look over the seating chart for dinner tonight."

I sighed. The woman needed my approval for everything. I thought that by having an assistant I wouldn't be bothered by the details, but I was wrong.

"Okay, fine."

I fell into step beside her as we returned to the house. I had moved into Bellemere a few weeks ago and it still didn't feel like home. It was an hour out of Calanais so that my mother couldn't just drop in casually, but it didn't stop her from trying to run my life. Tonight's dinner was one such machination of hers. I had wanted just a quiet meal with my friends. She had turned it into some big to-do. Yes, the queen and her consort were coming for a visit, but that didn't mean it had to be a state dinner.

Jacques scowled at me as I entered the foyer in my dirty boots. The old butler hated me, but I was pretty sure he held a candle for my mother. I smiled sweetly at him as I passed, but I got no pleasure out of it. If I thought taking my grandmother's title was going to be a walk in the park, I had been sadly mistaken. By all accounts, my grandmother had been a formidable woman who ran the household with an iron hand, yet remained graceful and elegant. I was neither graceful nor elegant and the staff didn't respect me. That probably had more to do with them being my mother's little spies than anything else.

I plopped down in my chair behind my desk and waited for Pamela to begin. She spread the seating chart out in front of me and I looked at the names of the people who would be attending tonight. My friends. The ones I had run from in my haste to escape the fallout from Jamie. I hadn't seen them since I moved into Bellemere, but we had spoken on the phone. The women who had become my friends weren't so quick to let me leave the fold and I was grateful for that, even if I grouched about it.

"It looks fine to me," I said.

"But—"

I tuned her out. She would no doubt give me an entire spiel about why it wasn't working. I didn't particularly care who sat where. We were all friends and we would all no doubt end up with our shoes off and sitting on the comfy couches I had installed in the drawing room - much to my mother's disgust.

I picked up my cell phone idly while Pamela prattled on. I had a missed call from a number I didn't recognise. There was no voicemail, but I knew who it was. The thirty days were long past and I had been waiting, holding my breath, for when the call would come that would dissolve our union.

I squeezed the phone in my hand until my knuckles went white. I hadn't heard from him in six weeks. I tried to deny how much I missed him. I tried to tell myself that I was still angry at him and that I would be glad when this call came. We needed to bring this whole thing to its conclusion. I needed closure. It would be a relief, really, to finally have it dealt with and then maybe I could get on with my life instead of waiting for the other shoe to drop.

"Are you listening to me, Lady Meredith?"

I looked up at Pamela and smiled. "Whatever you decide will be fine," I said. "I trust your judgement." I looked at my wrist and my non-existent watch. "I think I might head upstairs and start getting ready. Our guests should be arriving soon."

"Of course," Pamela said.

I escaped her disapproving scowl and headed up to my room. A long, hot soak in the tub sounded like the perfect thing right now. Anything to get the memories of Jamie out of my head. I had even been dreaming about him. In my dreams he was calling out to me, asking me to come, telling me he needed me. The prince in need of rescuing. Except he was going to be king now and he had his own royal guard to protect him. He didn't need me or my particular brand of crazy in his life.

The only good thing to come out of this was seeing my mother when she found out who Jamie really was. The look on her face had been priceless. She had berated Freddie for including Jamie in his wedding party but now she had had to eat her words. It was entirely too satisfying to watch. I wish I could tell her that I was married to him, just to see the look on her face.

Yeah. That's the only reason.

The lie didn't even sound convincing to me. I had been holding on to the secret of our marriage like a security blanket. It was something I clung to, knowing that Jamie had cared enough for me to want to make me his wife, even if I knew it wasn't true and couldn't last. In my fantasies he came for me. I knew it was sentimental and ridiculously childish to imagine him riding up on a white horse to sweep me off my feet. But it didn't stop me from wishing, which was why I needed to end our marriage. Soon. As long as I had the fantasy, I would never move on. It was time to let the dream go.

I SIGHED AS DESSERT WAS PLACED IN FRONT OF ME. THE NIGHT HAD not gone as planned. The conversation was stilted - when there was any conversation at all. I knew it was my fault. I was the one who left the palace in a huff without talking to my friends and now they didn't know how to behave around me. I didn't know how to behave around them either.

We finished our dessert in mostly silence. They were all staying the night; the house at Bellemere was big enough and it was a long drive back to Calanais. I'd invited them all because I wanted to make up for the way I behaved when I returned from the tour and everything that happened with Jamie. I wasn't doing a very good job of it. My mother would be appalled if she were here to witness my complete failure as a hostess.

"Okay," I said as I stood. "Boys, off you go. Go and do boy things in the library. The girls and I need to talk."

Freddie led Will, Dom and Drew out of the dining room and I could almost hear their sighs of relief at not having to be present any longer.

"Come on ladies," I said, walking to the door, "it's to the drawing room for us. Jacques, bring the wine."

I waited until everyone had a seat and a drink in their hands and then excused Jacques. I looked at each of my friends in turn and sighed, shaking my head.

"I'm sorry," I said. "I know when I came back from the tour I was rude and moody and just plain awful to be around. None of you deserved the way I treated you and for that I am sorry. Forgive me?"

Alex was the first to break ranks. She crossed the room and sat beside me, taking my hand in hers. "Of course we forgive you," she said. "That's what friends do."

"But," Priscilla said, "we need an explanation. What on earth happened while you were away?"

The others looked at me and then at Alyssa and then back to me. I sighed and dropped my head. I desperately wanted to tell them about Jamie. I wanted to bare my soul to them and have them tell me it would all work out and that I could have my happily ever after. But the fact was, I knew that wasn't in the cards for me. My mother was already making noises about setting me up on dates with men who not only didn't interest me, but in most cases bored me. I didn't want anyone else, I only wanted Jamie, but that was impossible.

I looked up at my friends, making eye contact with each one. Half of our group had found their true love - more than half. I knew if I told them how I felt about Jamie they would try and find a way for us to be together. I wanted that more than life itself, but that wasn't fair to Jamie. He and I came together before this whole thing blew up in our faces. The last thing he needed was a new wife to deal with when he had an entire country to try and fix. I just couldn't do it to him.

"I think it was just a whole lot of things that combined to make a perfect storm," I said softly. "I knew before I left that I would be leaving the guard and I wasn't happy about it. I was even less happy that my mother had all these plans for me. And then the whole Jamie thing—"

"Oh my goodness," Jeanette said. "How did we not know that Jamie was a prince?"

Everyone looked at Alyssa and she held her hands up in defence. "I couldn't tell you," she said. "We needed to keep it a secret to protect him."

Jeanette sighed and nodded. "Yeah, I get that, but what a shock. I mean, the guy has been around us all this time and none of us had a clue."

I frowned. "He was a really good liar."

Alex patted my hand. "Oh no, honey, no. That wasn't it at all. I think the Jamie we knew is the real man. Have you seen him on the news? He looks so severe and unhappy. Nothing like the fun-loving Jamie that we all knew."

"Maybe that's the real him," I said.

Alex shook her head but it was Alyssa who spoke. "Come on Mer, you know better than that. The media are watching him like a hawk. He has to do more than convince his Parliament that he should reign, he has to face the court of public opinion as well. Remember what it was like for me? I had to wear a mask so that no one could see what I was really feeling."

"He's hurting, sweetheart," Alex said softly. "He has no friends or confidantes. He is surrounded by people he hardly knows and probably doesn't trust. A lot of these same people were there when his family was murdered and they did nothing to stop that General guy. The Jamie we all know and love is still in there, he's just had to hide that part of him for self-preservation."

"She's right," Alyssa said, looking at me strangely. "The Jamie we're seeing all over the news is still Jamie, it's just another side of him."

"I feel sorry for him," Margaret said, almost in a whisper. "I can't imagine what it would be like to have his whole life turned over like that. He had no say in how or when his identity was revealed. His choices were taken away from him and now he's on the back foot and just trying to do the best he can."

We all stopped to stare at Margaret. That was the longest speech she had ever made in a room with this many people. She turned bright red and dropped her head so that her mousy brown hair fell forward to hide her face.

"Margaret's right," Savannah said, speaking for the first time. "Jamie is just doing the best he can."

CHAPTER 19

Jamie

I stood in front of Parliament and listened to the prime minister as he spoke on my behalf. It had taken some political wrangling but Parliament had finally agreed to accept my claim as legitimate heir. A thorough investigation of the constitution had shown that General Anastas hadn't thought to change the law that said Kalopsia was to be ruled by one of royal blood. He had just assumed control of the country and no one had been prepared to stand up to him. Now he was gone and the country was in tatters. In a way, Parliament was happy to have someone else to foist the problems on to.

I touched the breast pocket of my jacket and the envelope crinkled under my hand. I hadn't read the letter from my father yet. I couldn't bring myself to break the seal. I would, one day. I just needed to get through the next few months and build a trusted enclave around me and then, when I felt secure in my new position, I would read the letter. If I did it before then, I was sure to lose the mask of calm that I had cultivated.

The 'ayes' from the parliamentary floor brought me back to the issue at hand. This was my coronation. I was to be officially crowned as

King Christophe today. There was no fancy coronation ceremony or a fancy dinner. The country couldn't afford it and I didn't think the people wanted it. They just wanted stability and that's what I wanted to give them. With the Parliament in agreement, all that was left was to repeat the words and vows of the office.

I knelt before the prime minister and spoke the words, my voice strong and true. There could be no weakness, not now. I was the last surviving relative of the royal blood line and I needed to assure the people of Kalopsia that they could trust me to rule them. They needed to feel secure with me at the helm and not worry that I might be some despot king that would take the little that they had and turn it to dust.

As it was placed on my head, the weight of the crown was more than just a physical weight. I felt the metaphoric weight settle on my shoulders as I was charged with my duty.

I had been fortunate to have been with Alyssa when she had walked a similar journey. I had learned a lot from her and the way she had handled being thrust into the limelight. I wasn't as fortunate to have a tight group of supporters around me, but I was slowly finding them. My initial distrust in Theodorou had been unfounded and now I held a deep respect for him. Danika had built a security team around me and I was slowly getting to know those who supported me and those who had a more 'wait and see' attitude. That was fine with me. I knew I would have to prove myself to these men and women who had suffered at the hands of the General.

I just wished I had someone to go home to at night. Someone I could talk to who would just listen. Someone I could share my fears with and not worry that they would be turned into ammunition against me. Someone like a wife. My wife. Meredith.

The prime minister bid me to stand and I rose and turned to face the Parliament. There was applause and handshakes and a general air of celebration, but still there was something missing for me. As time went on and we got farther from that moment when Meredith and I had pledged our lives to one another, my affection didn't lessen. It grew. And a longing grew along with it. A longing that things could be different. A longing that I had been honest with her from the start. But most of all, a longing for her to be here with me now. I wanted to raise my eyes and see her standing there with a smile on her face as she supported me as the new king of Kalopsia.

I let the prime minister usher me forward and out of the government building. The people had crowded the sidewalk in front of the building and a podium and microphones had been set up so that I could address the people. Theodorou had offered me his speech writer for this but I had respectfully declined. If I was going to rule this country then these people needed to hear words from me, from my heart, not a crafted statement designed to hit all the pertinent political beats.

I took a breath and touched my breast pocket again, the crinkling of the envelope a calming influence on me.

"Thank you, people of Kalopsia," I said and the crowd got quiet. "I stand here before you a king, but my heart is humble. I am reminded of the kings who came before me and the generations of peace and prosperity that our country enjoyed under their rule. These past ten years have been hard. I will not even try to imagine what it was like for you to be subjected to such harsh treatment by a man who only had his own interests at heart. I could stand here and promise that it would only be clear skies and sunshine for the rest of our days but I wouldn't insult you like that. We all know the road ahead will be tough, but I ask you to trust me and join me in my efforts to make Kalopsia great again. It is not going to happen overnight, but I have a long view and I know that we can make the changes we need to bring back the Kalopsia that our fathers and grandfathers knew. Will you stand with me? Will you support me in my efforts to make right the wrongs that have been done?"

The crowd cheered and my heart lightened just a bit under their encouragement. I knew I would have detractors and that even though the people cheered for me now, they may curse me tomorrow. I let myself be led away, touching the envelope in my pocket once more. My other hand was in my pocket and I fingered my phone, wanting to call her. I wanted to hear her voice. With a sigh, I withdrew my hand and waved to the crowd before slipping into the dark interior of the waiting car. I leaned back against the seat and closed my eyes. One hurdle completed. Just about another five thousand and forty-two to go.

Meredith

I WOKE UP FEELING ALMOST NORMAL FOR THE FIRST TIME SINCE I had been told the news that I was to leave the guard. It probably helped that my sleep had been undisturbed - something I couldn't remember happening for a long time. It may have been the alcohol, but I was more inclined to believe that it was reconnecting with my friends. When I finally crawled into bed last night, it felt like a weight had been lifted off my shoulders. The six of us had talked long into the night, staying up even after the men had retired for the evening.

I headed downstairs in search of breakfast and stopped when I heard the television on in the media room. I poked my head in to see Freddie sitting there watching a press conference. I joined him on the couch and he put his arm around me companionably.

"Look at him," Freddie said with a proud smile.

I turned my attention to the screen and saw Jamie standing there, speaking to the assembled press.

"Parliament just had his coronation and crowned him king. It looks good on him, don't you think?"

My throat was too tight to talk so I just nodded. My eyes were glued to the screen and the man who had been haunting my dreams and every waking thought. My husband, who was now the king. I swallowed thickly.

He did look good, if a little tired around the eyes. He didn't smile, but he didn't scowl either. He was in a suit that fit him to perfection. The only other time I had seen him in a suit was at Freddie's wedding. Except that wasn't true now. He had worn a suit when he was impersonating Will, although that was different. He hadn't been Jamie then. The royal guard didn't wear suits like some other countries' secret service did. The royal guard dressed like soldiers, albeit all in black. Black cargo pants, black shirts and black boots. Jamie looked good in a suit.

"I knew that one day he would be king. He doubted it, you know. We had a lot of conversations about it and about his doubts that he would ever make it back to Kalopsia."

I listened as Freddie talked. He had never spoken to me about Jamie and the friendship they shared. I suppose the giant secret they had been keeping meant that it was more prudent for Freddie not to mention him at all. I had even forgotten how close they had been until Freddie had asked Jamie to be in his wedding party.

The press conference on the television finished and Jamie stepped down from the podium. He was now the king. My husband was the king. What did that make me?

I laid my head on Freddie's shoulder. I felt like weeping. Jamie looked so lonely. He had no one in his inner circle that he could really trust. He couldn't even call Freddie or Alyssa without causing an international incident. I didn't know how long it would be before he could be seen to have connections with Merveille, but until then, did he have anyone he could truly rely on?

He had called me yesterday and I had ignored his call. Was he reaching out to me because he needed a friend? Or was it simply because he needed to have our marriage annulled? I couldn't imagine the scandal that would arise if it was found out that we were married. The press would use it as ammunition against him.

"So what's going on between the two of you?" Freddie asked, turning to me and shifting so he could see my face.

I looked away and wiped the unshed tears from my eyes before looking back at him. "Nothing." Now.

Freddie searched my eyes and I knew he didn't believe me, but what could I say? I didn't know how Freddie would take the news of the elopement. It would come as a shock, that was for sure. Jamie and I hadn't been dating publicly so no one had any reason to suspect that there was anything going on between us.

"You two used to spend a lot of time together."

"Yeah, because we worked together."

"No, but, you also trained together, outside normal training hours, I mean."

I shrugged. "I had to work harder than everyone else," I said, looking down at my lap and playing with a loose thread in my jeans. "He was helping me."

"So you were friends, too?" Freddie looked at me curiously and I was afraid he was seeing far more than I wanted him to see.

"Of course we were friends," I said, and then stood. "I'm starving. Have you had breakfast yet?"

Freddie held my gaze for a moment longer and I wasn't sure he was going to let the conversation go, but then he sighed and stood. "Not yet," he said. "I was waiting for Alex but someone kept her up way too late last night and she was still comatose when I came down earlier."

"Well, come on then," I said, "let's see what the kitchen has prepared for us."

I led Freddie from the room and I knew that I couldn't leave this thing with Jamie hanging in limbo. The thirty days was up and we both needed to get on with our lives. The sooner we could get the marriage dissolved, the better for both of us. The only problem was that I would need to see Alyssa and tell her the truth. She was the only one that had the wherewithal to get the marriage annulled quickly and quietly.

I KNOCKED ON ALYSSA'S DOOR AFTER BREAKFAST AND WAITED FOR her permission to enter. Freddie, Will, Dom and Drew had headed out on horseback to look over the grounds. The other ladies in waiting were either still at breakfast or not out of bed yet. Alyssa had come down to breakfast with Will but had come back to her room after he'd left. I wiped my sweaty hands on my jeans as I waited.

The door opened and Bridgette blinked at me before stepping aside and letting me in.

"Would you like me to ring for tea?" she asked.

"No, I'm good," I replied.

Alyssa looked up from a document in her hand and smiled at me. "Come and sit," she said. "Thanks Bridgette, we'll be fine now."

I waited for Bridgette to leave and then took a seat opposite Alyssa. I don't think I had ever been this nervous about talking to her. Even when I went to her to intervene on my behalf so that I wouldn't be kicked out of the guard, I hadn't felt so sick to my stomach with apprehension.

Alyssa's eyebrows puckered as she frowned at me. "Are you alright?"

I swallowed and shook my head. "I - ah - have something of a delicate nature to talk to you about."

She put the papers she had been reading down on the coffee table and gave me her full attention. "Is this a friend thing or a queen thing?" she asked.

I huffed out a small, humourless laugh. "A little of both."

She nodded and folded her hands in her lap. "Okay. Lay it on me."

I took a breath. "Something happened when we were on Le Beau," I said. "Something I need help with undoing."

"O-kay," she said slowly. "You didn't get arrested or anything did you?"

"No, worse," I said. "I got married."

It was a credit to all the training Alyssa had had in maintaining her composure that she sat there and barely reacted at all. Her eyes widened and her nostrils flared as she breathed in deeply. I held my own breath as I waited for her to say something, anything.

"Who?"

It wasn't the question I expected, but it was a valid one.

I dropped my head and felt the tears fill my eyes. When I looked back at her, all my walls were stripped away and my pain was on full display. "Jamie," I whispered. Fat tears rolled down my cheeks.

I didn't think Alyssa's eyes could get any wider. "Wow," she breathed. "Just...wow."

"We were both a little under the influence and a lot annoyed with what was happening in our lives. I was upset with my mother and her machinations and Jamie was upset about...well, I didn't know at the time but I suppose in hindsight, he was upset about the whole Kalopsia thing."

"No wonder you were mad when you found out."

I sighed and looked down at my hands. "The thing is, he did try and tell me. That night, the night we got married. He told me he was a prince in exile and that I was rescuing him. I didn't believe him. I thought he was just being romantic."

Alyssa stood and began to pace. "Okay," she muttered to herself. "Okay. This is okay. This is something we can work with. This is good. We just—"

"No, no, no," I said, standing too. "You don't understand. I want to get this annulled. Quietly."

Alyssa stopped pacing and looked at me. "What? You don't want to be with him?"

"No. Well, yes, but no. I'm not queen material. He needs someone beside him who has been raised to be a queen."

"You were raised by a duchess and you're my best friend. That makes you perfect queen material."

I shook my head and moved away from her, walking over to the window and looking out over the estate that was now mine. "The last thing Jamie - King Christophe - needs right now is to deal with me and our elopement. We need to get this annulled before the press get wind of it and cause a media storm. He is in a precarious position right now and I don't want to do anything to jeopardise that."

"Standing beside him as his wife is the best thing you can do right now," Alyssa said, her voice taking on the tone of authority that only a queen could have, proving once again that I was just not cut out for the role. "He needs you. He needs someone who has no stake in the politics of Kalopsia."

I turned to her, upset that she wouldn't do this for me. Upset that I couldn't do what she wanted me to do. "Look at me, Lys. I am the last person he needs standing beside him. I am a body guard, not a queen."

"You are a countess, but more than that, you are a wonderful, loyal, beautiful woman." She took a breath and her gaze drilled into me. "Do you love him?"

I collapsed onto the couch. "Yes. God so help me, I do."

Alyssa sat beside me and took my hands in hers. "Then go to him. Tell him."

I searched her eyes, a little ray of hope birthing inside me and then I thought of what would happen if I were to announce to the world that Jamie and I were married. I dropped my head and shook it.

"I can't," I breathed. "I can't do that to him." I looked up at her again. "Please," I said, "can you do this for me?"

She stared back at me for so long I didn't think she was going to answer and then she sighed. "Are you sure this is what you want?"

I nodded. It wasn't what I wanted but it was what I thought was best.

"Okay," she said.

CHAPTER 20

Jamie

"Lord Frédéric Bingham is here to see you, Your Royal Highness," Fenton said.

I looked up at the man who had once served my father as his butler and smiled for what felt like the first time in days.

"Thank you, Fenton," I replied. "Show him in."

I stood from my desk and stretched. Freddie being here must mean that the embargo between Kalopsia and Merveille was at an end. I walked around the other side of the desk and eagerly waited for Fenton to bring Freddie in. The door opened and I strode eagerly forward, hand out-stretched. Freddie shook my hand but he did not return my smile. I frowned.

"Welcome to Kalopsia," I said. I turned to Fenton. "Thank you Fenton. I will call if we need anything."

The butler nodded and left, closing the door behind him.

"Thank you for seeing me, Your Royal Highness."

"Freddie," I said with a shake of my head. "Come on. Let's not stand on formalities."

Freddie frowned further. "Fine," he said. "Then tell me what the hell is going on between you and my sister?"

I took a step back from him, shocked.

"And don't try to lie to me. Tell me the truth - all of it."

I took a deep breath and indicated that we should sit in the over-stuffed leather couches. He took a seat and I poured us some drinks. This discussion needed alcohol. I handed him a tumbler of whiskey and then sat opposite him, taking a sip before I started.

"I fell in love with her," I said, not hiding anything from the one man who had known everything about me since the moment we met. "It started out as just an innocent flirtation and then along the way I fell for her. I wanted to explain everything to her, and I finally did, only she didn't believe me. She thought I was spinning some romantic fairytale." I looked down at the glass in my hands remembering the night we had ridden around in the limo. It had felt so natural to have her in my arms. My wife.

"There's more," Freddie said, his voice gentler than it was when he first entered the room.

I nodded. "One night on Le Beau, Meredith was upset and she took off. I found her in a bar drowning her sorrows. We were both feeling pretty low about what was going on individually in our personal lives. Meredith was having a hard time coming to grips with leaving the guard and taking up the countess title and I had just had some bad news about Kalopsia. We ended up having a few drinks together and I proposed to her. She said yes." Freddie hadn't said a word and didn't look particularly shocked at what I was saying. "We got a license and got married in a little open-air chapel on a hill overlooking the island. But you already know this."

He nodded.

"Meredith told you?"

He shook his head. "No," he said and sighed. "Alyssa told me. Meredith went to her and asked her to organise an annulment."

I gripped the glass in my hand until my knuckles turned white. "She wants it annulled?" Of course she did. She had from the moment we had woken up and she had realised what we had done. I was kidding myself to think that she had changed her mind, especially after her ignoring all my calls. Somehow I had still held on to hope that she would eventually want me and what we could have together. Obviously I was wrong.

Freddie took a sip of his drink and then placed it on the side table. He pulled out an official looking envelope and laid it on the low coffee table between us. "Alyssa tells me that Meredith is in love with you and after seeing the way she has been moping around the place since she got back from Barcelona, I tend to agree. Alyssa thinks that Meredith is doing this because she thinks it's what you want. She doesn't think she is cut out to be your wife or the queen of your country. This is her way of giving you an escape clause."

I looked down at the envelope but didn't reach for it. Inside held the dissolution of my marriage. The end of a relationship that we had only just begun to explore. I wasn't ready for it to be over, but I didn't want to force Meredith into something she didn't want.

"The ball is in your court now, Jamie," Freddie said, picking up his drink and sitting back. "What are you going to do?"

"How do you feel about Meredith and me as a couple?" he asked. "I know there is some sort of rule about friends dating their friend's sister."

Freddie smirked. "I'll admit I was a little peeved when I found out. Not that you two were an item, but that I wasn't in the loop. Neither of you came to me and told me. I was prepared to come in here and box your ears over it, but then you had to go and tell me you were in love with her. That's all I want for my baby sister. Someone who will love her for who she is, not who my mother is trying to turn her into. Meredith is prickly and ornery and tough. If you can see past all that and love her anyway, then who am I to stand in your way?"

"How long are you here for?" I asked.

"As long as you need me."

"Is Alex here too?"

Freddie smiled. "Of course. We're still newlyweds. I wasn't going to spend any more time away from her than I absolutely had to."

"Please stay here in the palace with me."

Freddie cocked an eyebrow. "Are you sure?"

"As long as it won't impact Merveille negatively. I have missed having people around that I can trust."

Freddie nodded and stood. "Okay," he said. "I'll go and get Alex from the hotel."

I stood too and pulled the bell for Fenton to show Freddie out.

"Lord Bingham and his wife will be staying with us for a few days," I said to the butler when he arrived. "Please see that a suite is prepared for them."

"Very good, Your Highness."

I paced the office after Freddie left, avoiding the coffee table that held my execution - annulment - papers. The ball was in my court but I had no idea what was the best way to proceed.

ALEX HAD HUGGED ME TIGHTLY WHEN SHE SAW ME. I HADN'T expected it. I thought she would be mad at me first for the deception, and then again for what had transpired between Meredith and me. Instead she whispered in my ear, "She needs you." If only that were true. Meredith was an amazing woman who didn't need anyone. I wished she needed me; it would make this decision a whole lot easier. I was in love with her and I just couldn't imagine feeling this way about anyone else. But that wasn't enough. She had to be in love with me too. She had to want to be with me too. Her sending the annulment papers was a big red flag.

I paced the terrace outside my bedroom and breathed in the salty air. Living in Merveille, away from the ocean, had made me forget what it was like to hear the constant susurration of the waves on the shore and the tang of salt in the air. I hadn't realised how much I missed it until I was back here. The night was cool with a hint of autumn in the air. And it was late. Dinner with Alex and Freddie had been long but enjoyable. I felt I could relax for the first time in what seemed like years but was in fact only a couple of months. I seemed to be always on edge lately, waiting for the next blow to come. Having friends, close friends, who I could just be myself with, was a relief.

I pulled out my phone and brought up Meredith's number. Freddie had mentioned that she didn't know he was here. She wouldn't know I already had the annulment papers...or maybe she would. Maybe she assumed that Alyssa had sent someone else to serve me with them. Without overthinking it, I hit the call button and lifted the phone to my ear. It rang several times and then I cursed under my breath. It was the middle of the night. Kalopsia was one hour ahead of Merveille, but it was still too late to be calling. Just as I was about to hang up, the call connected. I waited to hear her voice, but it didn't come.

"Meredith," I whispered into the phone.

I heard a gasp and then the call disconnected. I took the phone away from my ear and just stared at it. I missed her so much. It clawed at me, the need to have her nearby. I wanted to feel the warmth of her skin and taste the sweetness of her lips. I wanted to hear her laugh. I wanted to see her smile. I knew that if she was by my side then I could traverse the next obstacles facing me and Kalopsia confidently. But was that reason enough to not sign the papers? Was what I wanted enough to turn her life upside down?

Some people said that love was a game. I felt like I was the furthest from a game that a person could be. I loved her with every cell inside me but it was because I loved her that I hesitated. I didn't want to force this life on her if it wasn't what she wanted. I wasn't going to force myself on her if she didn't love me too. I wanted Meredith to be happy and I already knew how she chafed at taking the title of her grandmother. How much worse would it be for her to be my wife for real? How much more of a burden would being a queen in a fledgling country be for a woman who cherished her freedom?

And yet...

Despite everything and all the compromises that we would both have to make, I wanted her. I wanted her so much that I was very nearly prepared to walk away from Kalopsia. But I couldn't do that. I couldn't do that to the people who were just beginning to hope that there was something to look forward to. I felt an obligation to these people who had put their trust in me and although it would kill me to be without Meredith for the rest of my life, I had committed to them and I wouldn't renege. I wouldn't renege on Meredith either if only I had some indication that she wanted me in spite of the baggage that came with me.

I stripped from the suit that I wore and pulled on some cotton boxers before crawling into bed. I had sent my valet to bed hours ago and I had been undressing myself long enough that I didn't really need him to help me change for bed. Having someone at my beck and call every minute of the day took a lot of getting used to, especially when I was so used to fending for myself. I lay in bed and stared at the ceiling. I had become intimately acquainted with the fresco that was painted above me. I had been surprised that General Anastas hadn't had it painted over, but from all reports he hadn't made use of this bedroom. It had been my parents' room and there was a bittersweet feeling for me to lie here in the room that had seen generations of happily married kings and queens. And by all accounts they had been happily married. It had been a tradition of Kaolpsia that the king and queen married for love. The country was too small to try and keep it only to the peers and we weren't well known or wealthy enough to have interested royalty from outside out borders.

These were the sort of things that I wanted to share with Meredith. The little tit bits from my heritage, the things that I'd been forced to keep hidden for so long. They burned in me to share with her. With a sigh, I realised that I couldn't just walk away. I couldn't just sign the papers and forget about the woman I had come to love more than my own breath. I needed her in my life and I was willing to beg if that's what it would take. The only problem now was getting her to speak to me. I couldn't very well convince her to make our relationship public if she wouldn't even take my calls.

But that was a problem for tomorrow. Right now I felt the weight of sleep pulling me. Having made the decision had lifted a weight from my shoulders and now that I knew what I was going to do, my brain was ready to sleep. Tomorrow - or later today in fact - I would set a plan in motion. I had no idea what that plan was yet, but I was determined to make one. After some sleep, when I could think clearly and maybe get some help from two people who knew Meredith probably better than I did.

I WALKED INTO THE BREAKFAST ROOM WITH PURPOSE. FREDDIE AND

Alex were already there, which saved me from having to find them. Now that I had made a decision, I was eager to get on with making a plan. I walked to the side board and poured myself a cup of coffee before sitting down at the table with them.

"So," I said and they both looked up at me. "I'm not going to sign the annulment papers."

"What?" Alex said as she dropped her fork with a clatter. "You're married?"

I shot a look at Freddie. "She didn't know?"

Freddie shook his head once. "I didn't want to say anything until you had made a decision."

"Hang on a moment," Alex said. "Who are you married too?" She shot Freddie a narrowed glance before turning back to me. "And if you are married, why were you pursuing Meredith?" Now she narrowed her eyes at me.

"Meredith," I said.

"Yes, Meredith. Why were you pursuing her if you were a married man and how can we have known you all this time and not known that you were married?"

Freddie reached over and covered Alex's hand with his. "He is married to Meredith."

Alex swung her gaze from me to Freddie and then back to me. "You and Meredith are married?" I nodded. She looked at Freddie and he nodded. "How? How did this happen? And why didn't she tell me?"

I took a fortifying sip of my coffee before answering. "We got married on Le Beau," I said, not looking at her. Suddenly my coffee cup was very interesting. "It was a spur of the moment thing and the next morning she regretted it and wanted it annulled."

Alex reached across the table and laid her hand on mine. I looked up at her sincere blue eyes. "But she loves you."

"I thought she did—"

"And you love her."

I exhaled roughly. "I do."

"Then there is no way you are signing those papers."

"He already said that, love," Freddie said with a sweet smile for his wife.

"But how do we convince Meredith?" I asked. "I've tried calling her and she won't take my calls. You both know how stubborn she can be. How do I get her to listen to me?"

"She needs to come here," Alex said. "You need her to be backed into a corner where she has no choice but to listen to you."

"No," I said, "I don't want to force her to be with me. I just want to talk to her."

"Nobody's saying that we kidnap her and tie her to a chair until she listens to you," Alex said. "We simply orchestrate a way that causes her to come face to face with you and the decision she has to make."

"You don't think the annulment papers are her decision?"

Alex shook her head. "That's Meredith's way of protecting herself. She probably feels like you don't want her, now that you're king and have this whole country to put back together. I love Meredith like a sister but she doesn't exactly make it easy to love her."

Freddie snorted and the side of my mouth quirked up in a small smile.

"She needs to know how you feel about her. She needs to know that you want her by your side."

"Okay, so how? How do I do that when she won't speak to me?"

Alex looked at Freddie and they seemed to share a silent communication before she turned back to me. "I think it's time for the queen of Merveille to show its support for the new king of Kalopsia. And what better way to do that by continuing her tour and visiting the new king?"

"O-kay," I said slowly, "but how will that get Meredith here?"

"She is still contracted to the guard for another couple of months," Freddie said. "Benjamin can make sure she comes."

I liked that idea. A lot. I liked that I would finally have a public show of support from my adopted home and I couldn't wait to speak to Alyssa again. But more than that and probably the most important thing, I was desperate to see Meredith again. It was maybe underhanded and sneaky, but I was at a point that I was willing to do just about anything to see her again. I needed her to know how much I wanted her in my life. I needed her to know how much I loved her.

"Okay," I said, standing. "So, how do we get this ball rolling? Should I send an official invitation for Alyssa and Will to visit Kalopsia?"

"You get on that," Freddie said, standing also, "and I will send my own missive to the queen and let her in on the plan."

"Excellent," I said. We had a plan, now we just needed Meredith to follow it.

CHAPTER 21

Meredith

I strode into the palace with a scowl. I wasn't ready to be back here yet. My wounds hadn't fully healed and being back here just reopened them again. Everywhere I looked there were reminders of Jamie and the time we spent together. It was the reason I had been so eager to disappear to Bellemere. There were no memories of him there, only the ones I brought with me.

But here I was, back in Calanais, back at Château de Conte de Fées because I had been commanded by Benjamin. I had tried to get out of it, but he wouldn't take no for an answer and even threatened to bring me in under guard if I refused. I couldn't very well tell him why I didn't want to come back to the palace. Benjamin was not a romantic and he would shudder to think that any of his precious guard were. And there was no way I could tell him that Jamie and I were a thing or that we had eloped while on tour. If my time wasn't already up with the guard, then it sure would be after that and despite running away to Bellemere, I wasn't quite ready to sever all my ties to the guard. Not that I would tell him that.

I knocked on the security office door and was let in by a guardsman that I didn't know. One of the new recruits, I assumed. He led me through to the briefing room where I was surprised to see the rest of the royal guard waiting for me and seated around the large conference table. I smiled at them, a pang of longing making my chest tight as I smiled and greeted them all. I had missed them, not that I would let that get out. But the big, burly guys had been like an extended family to me and I missed our daily banter.

"So should we bow to you now Countess?" Cody asked with a smirk.

"Only if you wish to spar with me," I replied with a sweet smile.

"Alright, let's get started," Benjamin said before we could take it any further. I may be dressed as a lady these days, but I wouldn't turn down an offer to go a few rounds with one of the guys. Working out with a heavy bag wasn't the same as sparring one on one. The bag didn't hit back.

I took my seat and looked down at the packet in front of me. It was a security briefing for a royal tour. It had been a few weeks, but it was only natural that Benjamin would want to debrief the recent tour.

"The queen has been invited to visit the new king of Kalopsia," Benjamin said without preamble.

My stomach cramped as everyone around the table opened to the first page of the security packet. This wasn't a debrief, this was a planning meeting.

"Are you sure you need me here for this?" I asked.

Benjamin looked directly at me and nodded once. "You're coming with us."

"I'm what?"

"You're still part of the guard, Meredith, even if you are hiding away in that dusty old mansion in the country. We are short-staffed and the new recruits are still too wet behind the ears to be of any use to me. We are going into what could be a hostile environment and I need the best team I can get. That includes you."

"When you said I was still contracted to the guard, I thought you meant having to come to meetings and maybe the occasional desk duty. You said nothing about going on active missions."

"Being contracted to the guard means making yourself available to whatever I need doing, whenever I need it done. The queen has accepted the invitation from Kalopsia and that means I need you on the security detail. Kalopsia may seem stable now with the installation of their new king, but we don't really know what we will find until we are on the ground there. I can't take any chances."

"There has to be someone else," I said, standing. "There has to be another way."

"There isn't and there's not. Sit down so we can continue."

I sat. Benjamin used his commander's voice and my response to obey had been so ingrained in me that I didn't even think about it.

"Right, now..."

I tuned out his words as I silently panicked. I may have been sitting at the table pretending to read through the briefing packet, but inside I was running around screaming. How could I go there and see him? I wasn't ready. My wounds were already weeping again and that was just from being back in the palace where the memories of him were strong. I didn't think I would survive a face to face meeting with him. What would I even say to him? Would he even talk to me, acknowledge me?

The other night when he called and I picked up was both a torture and a blessing. The sound of his voice saying my name was like a soothing balm until I remembered that I could never have him in my life again. He was a king now and the little interlude we had enjoyed was over. I was not the type of woman a king married. I was not the type of woman he needed by his side. Even thinking of another woman by his side made me grit my teeth and practically snap the pencil in my hand. But I had no right to be jealous. He owed me nothing. Except our annulment.

I had to swallow down the sob. I refused to cry. I refused to show weakness in front of these guys. I would sit through this meeting and then I would do everything in my power to get out of going to Kalopsia. There was no way I could face Jamie. Not if I hoped to survive.

"THE COUNTESS OF BELLEMERE TO SEE THE PRIME MINISTER," I SAID to the aide who greeted me at my father's office.

"Do you have an appointment?"

"No," I said, "but he will see me."

"Ma'am, the prime minister is very busy."

"Too busy to see his own daughter?" I asked using my best haughty voice. This aide was obviously new and didn't know who I was, which was fine except that I really needed to see my father.

He paled slightly under my gaze and then swallowed. "I'll just see if he is available."

"You do that," I said with a fake smile.

I had sat through the security briefing as Benjamin discussed the upcoming tour to Kalopsia and I nearly held myself together. No one said Jamie's name, but every time they mentioned the new king, I felt it like a stab to the heart. If only they knew the truth. Technically, I was a queen. A queen of a country I had never been to and knew very little about. I wasn't the type to obsess over someone to the point of needing to know everything about them. I was more into self-preservation by way of denial. The less I knew about the new king and his country, the more I could distance myself from the man who had stolen my heart.

The door opened and the aide came out, a blush staining his cheeks.

"You may go in," he said, without looking at me.

"Thank you," I said sweetly and walked past him and into my father's office.

I barely got across the threshold and I was crossing the office and burying myself in his arms. "Daddy," I breathed.

He hugged me tight. My father was a big, bear of a man with a ginger beard and faintly reminiscent of Richard the Lionheart. There were rumours that our family was related to the famous king of England, but no one had substantiated them to my knowledge. It didn't matter. Charles Bingham was my father and I had missed him terribly. When I worked at the palace I would see him regularly, and now that I was sequestered away in Bellemere I hardly ever saw him.

His arms wrapped around me and held me tight. I'm ashamed to admit that a few tears may have leaked out of my eyes before I could get a hold of my emotions.

"Sweetheart," he murmured, "whatever is the matter?"

I took a deep breath and stepped back, surreptitiously wiping the tears from my cheeks. "Hey daddy."

"What are you doing here, my love? Not that I'm not happy to see you."

I blew out an emotional breath. "Can't a girl just pop in and see her daddy?"

"Of course she can, but I might worry a bit when said daughter bursts into tears when she hugs me."

I looked down and tried to control myself. I couldn't tell him the whole truth. He would skin Jamie alive if he knew we had eloped.

"Benjamin has recalled me for an upcoming tour," I said.

"Oh right. I heard something about that. Kalopsia, right?"

I nodded.

"I've been invited too," he said, walking around to sit in the couches by the window.

I joined him and sat demurely, practising the lessons my mother had been drilling into me.

"I'd rather not go," I said, looking him in the eye.

"Oh?" He raised an eyebrow at me. "Why's that? I thought you'd be chomping at the bit to get back into uniform."

My father knew me all too well and under normal circumstances I would be jumping at the chance to leave all this countess nonsense behind.

"Well, of course, but it's just a delicate time for me right now. I'm trying to establish myself in society as Countess of Bellemere, and going away right now could be detrimental to that."

Charles Bingham, Duke of Monterey, Prime Minister of Merveille looked at me shrewdly, his lips flat. "Now try that again without lying."

I huffed out a frustrated breath. My father could be the most infuriating man when he wanted to be. I had never been able to get anything past him. What had I been thinking that I thought I could do it this time?

"Fine," I said. "I don't want to see Jamie."

Both his eyebrows popped up in surprise. "That was not what I thought you were going to say," he said.

"I'm still angry at him for lying to me. In fact," I said, warming to my subject, "I'm still mad at you too. All this time! All this time and not even a heads up?"

Father sighed and shook his head. "Try again, Meredith. I know you're upset about what happened but that is no reason to breach your contract with the guard."

"So you're not going to help me get out of it?"

"Is that what this is? You want me to step in and try and get my daughter excused from her national obligations?"

"Yes," I said and then shook my head. "No. When you put it like that it sounds kind of underhanded. I just really don't want to go."

"Ah, Mer. I know something is going on with you. You haven't been the same since you got back from Barcelona. You know you can tell me anything, right?"

"I know, daddy," I said quietly.

He waited for me to go on and when I didn't he sighed. "I can't intervene," he said. "Benjamin is the commander and he reports directly to the queen. There is nothing I can do. I'm sorry."

"I know," I said, dropping my head. "But it was worth a shot." I stood and Father did too. He hugged me again.

"Whatever it is," he whispered in my ear, "I'm here if you need to talk."

I nodded against his chest before stepping back.

"So are you and mother going to Kalopsia?"

He smiled. "We are."

Of course they were. It wouldn't take much for my father to know something was up between Jamie and me once he saw us together, so I had to make sure he never saw us together.

ONE WEEK LATER, AFTER FIVE HOURS ON A PLANE, WE WERE FINALLY arriving at the palace of the new king of Kalopsia. It was a beautiful Parthenon-inspired building with a tall, white marble colonnade. The entire palace was set on a cliff and had an incredible view of the Aegean Sea that surrounded the small island. I stood for several moments and just stared. It looked like something that would house the Greek gods and not somewhere us mere-mortals could reside. And Jamie had grown up here.

"Stop gawking Meredith," Cody called as he headed up the stairs.

We were the advance party before the queen and prince arrived. We were supposed to be meeting with the head of the royal security to go over the schedule and other pertinent details. The queen would be arriving in a few hours and we needed to make sure everything was secure and safe for her arrival. But my feet were rooted to the spot. I knew that once I stepped inside that building I would be in Jamie's world and I wasn't entirely sure I would find my way out of it again...or if I'd want to.

"Meredith!" This time it was Scott who called to me.

I shook myself out of my stupor and gave myself a pep talk as I walked toward the stairs that would take me into the lion's den.

"You can do this Meredith," I whispered to myself. "You are a professional. Just remember not to make eye contact with him. Look over his shoulder or at his chest...no. No! Don't look at his chest. Look over his shoulder but not at his eyes. Don't you dare look in his eyes."

"What on earth are you muttering to yourself?" Scott asked as I met him on the stairs, and we continued up together.

"Nothing," I said.

"Whatever," he replied, but he didn't look away from me. "You've been acting really weird lately. Has all this countess thing gone to your head?"

I pushed him with my shoulder. "No, it's just being back working with you morons. I'm used to a better class of people these days." I tried for light-hearted but it fell flat.

"Whatever," Scott said again and moved ahead of me.

He was right. I had been different since I'd been back training with them. It wasn't that I didn't want to be there, it was more the reason I was there. It had all been for this. Coming here to Kalopsia, seeing Jamie again. I just wasn't emotionally prepared. I didn't think I would ever be.

I stepped over the threshold and into the dim, cool interior of the foyer. I stopped again to look around. I expected...more. I expected paintings on the walls and precious marble statues and porcelain vases.

The foyer was rather empty - minimalist - with just a heavy wooden sideboard that held an enormous vase of fresh flowers.

"The palace was practically stripped of all its art and artefacts," a voice said and I looked up. My gaze met Danika's and I had to clench my fist at my side so that I didn't take a swing at her.

"Oh?" I replied, taking another look around.

"General Anastas was desperate for money toward the end and he tried to get it where he could."

"That's a shame," I said quietly, and meant it. To some people, the items in the palace might be thought of as frivolous and extravagant but they held the history and culture of the nation. To have them sold off to the highest bidder was a tragedy.

"Come. We are meeting in the conference room."

I followed Danika as she led me along a long hall that was overlooked by a mezzanine. I could feel his eyes on me as I walked and I tried really hard not to look up, but I couldn't help it. Our gazes clashed together and I stumbled. I couldn't read the look on his face. He was standing in shadow above me, but his eyes held me captive.

I wanted to stop, turn around and run to him. My body yearned to be close to his. My hands itched to touch him again. My eyes ate him up greedily. I had seen him on television numerous times now, but it wasn't the same as seeing him in the flesh. There was something different about him and yet so familiar that I was bombarded with melancholy. I knew what he would smell like if I got close enough. I knew what his lips would taste like if he kissed me again. And yet there was something else that I hadn't seen in him before. There was an authority, a dignity. It was in the way he carried himself and the set of his shoulders. I had seen the same transformation in only one other person. Alyssa. She had also grown and changed when she accepted the crown. And just like her, he wore it well.

I tore my gaze away. He was born to be king. I could see it now. He had hidden it well for all the years we'd known each other, but seeing him standing there, I could recognise the royalty that ran in his blood. The man was a king, through and through. He was a man with a calling and a mission. He wasn't free to love me. I had held out hope that maybe, somehow, some way, we could be together. I had sent him the annulment papers to give him an out and when he hadn't returned them, I began to hope. Seeing him now, though, that changed things. I was not the woman he would need by his side. I was not the woman to be his queen. I wanted to be, but even I knew that I was not right for him. He needed someone beautiful and elegant and graceful. He needed a proper lady born with an impressive pedigree and trained in all the gentle arts of a woman of nobility. Not a woman like me. I was a fighter, a soldier, a warrior. As much as it pained my mother, I was not a lady. I was not cut out to be a queen, however much I wished to be.

CHAPTER 22

Jamie

I knew she was coming. I had orchestrated her being here and yet it didn't prepare me for seeing her again.

Her hair was tied back in a long tail and she wore the uniform of the royal guard. She was just like I had seen her a hundred times before, but she was different. Her skin was pale and she had dark circles under her eyes, but even that wasn't what made her seem different to me. There was something in the way she walked, like she carried the weight of the world on her shoulders. She seemed...defeated.

Then she looked up at me.

It was in her eyes. There was a sadness there, a sadness that seemed to burrow deep inside her. Had I put that there? Was I the cause of her sorrow? Was I the cause of her slumped shoulders and dark circles? It killed me to know that I was. I was desperate to make it right. I wanted to take away her pain and hurt and put a smile on her face. I wanted to make her laugh and see the life and sparkle back in her eyes.

She disappeared from view and I took a steadying breath. I felt a hand clamp down on my shoulder and looked behind me to Freddie.

"You okay?" he asked.

I nodded and swallowed, clearing the lump from my throat before I spoke. "Tell me I'm doing the right thing," I said. "Tell me bringing her here is not just going to make it worse."

Freddie turned me so that we were face to face. He stared me down. "Do you love her?"

"You know I do," I said, "but is love enough? What I am asking of her is big. I'm asking her to give up her life and her country and her friends for me."

"It's not as if she will never see her friends or family again," Freddie said. "Or her country. Yes, you are asking her to give up her title, but she never really wanted it anyway. And you are offering her something more."

I snorted disbelievingly. "I hardly think offering her to be my queen is really going to impress her all that much."

"No," Freddie said, deadly serious. "That's not what I mean. You are offering your heart to her."

I searched Freddie's eyes, afraid to ask the question...was my heart enough?

"What if she doesn't feel the same way about me?" I asked instead.

"What if she does?"

I took a deep breath. What if she did? I was so focussed on what I would do if she turned me down flat that I hadn't even considered what I would do if she didn't.

Freddie grinned and then slapped me on the back as he walked away. I turned back to the balcony railing and looked down at where Meredith had been standing. The room seemed darker without her in it.

What would our life together look like? Could I even dare to dream? It was easy to think in abstracts and to get caught up in the daydream of fantasy, but what would the realities be if it turned out that Meredith wanted to be with me as much as I wanted to be with her? We were already married, but the people of Kalopsia would want to witness the wedding of their king and queen. It would go a long way to boosting public opinion and putting a smile on the faces of the people who seemed to have lost their hope. Meredith wouldn't want to make a spectacle and I respected her for that. The country couldn't afford to spend a lot of money on something that would only be a performance.

And there wouldn't be much of a honeymoon either. I had only just come home, I couldn't leave again so soon. Sequestering myself and Meredith away in the palace was not exactly a hardship. We had access to a private beach and there was really no need to leave the compound if we didn't want to. I allowed a small smile as I imagined spending every day and every night with her. Waking up beside her every morning, kissing her goodnight at the end of every day. Those were the thoughts I could get behind. But real life would eventually knock on the door and then what? What would Meredith do while I fulfilled the duties of king? I hadn't really paid much attention to what my mother had done as queen. I had been more preoccupied with trying to be like my father. My faded and vague memories of my mother were of her lunching with other women and organising charity events. Not exactly something that I could imagine Meredith doing. Not that she couldn't do it, just that it seemed more like something her mother would do. Would she be happy with that kind of life?

I raked a hand through my hair. I was back to wondering if I was doing the right thing. What if she ended up hating me? Fairytales may make marrying a prince out to be the perfect life goal, but the reality was a lot different. Meredith had never wanted that for herself. The very fact that she had pursued a career in the guard and not lived the high-life of a privileged peer of the realm was proof of that. What if she said yes to me and then when real life set in after the honeymoon ended, she regretted it? A quick annulment now before our marriage was made public would be a whole lot less messy than a king and queen divorcing in twelve months' time. And then there was the fact that it would break my heart into a million irreparable pieces.

I took another deep breath. I wanted her in my life. I couldn't deny that I wanted to rebuild my country and my family with her by my side. I wanted to make a family with her. What I didn't want was to stifle her and kill the spark that had attracted me to her in the first place.

"MEREDITH!"

She didn't look back at me as she turned the corner and disappeared into the garden. Infernal woman! I quickened my pace and turned the corner, stepping down the three steps into the sunken garden that was overgrown and forgotten. So many things had been left to go to rack and ruin under General Anastas' rule and I was still trying to catalogue everything that needed to be done and then find the finances to do it.

I stopped at the bottom of the stairs and listened. I could hear her moving through the overgrown foliage, even though I knew she was trying to be quiet. Moving as stealthily as I could, I headed in the opposite direction. There was only one way in and one way out of the garden, something I didn't think Meredith knew. The path she was on wound around the perimeter and finished up back at the stairs. I had every intention of intercepting her.

I could hear her stomping footsteps and her muttering before I saw her. She obviously thought I had given up on chasing her down, something that I was looking forward to disabusing her of. I leaned against the wall with one shoulder and crossed one leg over the other while I waited for her like I had all the time in the world. In this moment I did. There was nothing more important than speaking with her and I was willing to take as much time as I could to do just that.

She came around the corner, her head down and a scowl on her face. I couldn't help the lift of the corner of my lips or the sense of absolute peace and rightness that descended on me when I saw her. It cemented my decision when nothing else could. I needed her in my life and I intended to convince her that she needed me too. Finally she looked up and stopped in her tracks as she saw me standing there. Her eyes raked over me as she stood frozen and I could see the need and sadness in her eyes. She turned on her heel, but before she could make her escape, I reached out and took her by the elbow.

Her reflexes hadn't dimmed in the time we were apart and before I knew it we were locked in a sparring match, neither one of us dressed appropriately but neither one of us caring either. With a growl, I pinned her to my body, locking her arms beside her so she couldn't get any jabs in and dancing around so she couldn't stomp on my foot.

"Stop," I hissed in her ear. Her body went taught and then she relaxed against me, but I wasn't fooled. I knew all her tricks and she was just playing possum.

"Am I supposed to curtsy to you now?" she hissed back at me.

The growl rose in my throat uninhibited as I turned her around in my arms and slammed my lips down on hers. Electricity arced between us, stunning us both. She whimpered and I gentled my assault on her lips, but didn't release them. I couldn't. I felt like a dying man being offered a chance at life. Her hands clenched my suit coat as she tried to get closer to me. My hands tangled in her hair, unbinding it from its tie and letting it tumble freely down her back and over my arms. I breathed her in and the knots of tension that had been my constant companion over these last weeks began to loosen.

"Meredith," I whispered against her lips.

She tore herself out of my arms and swiped her hand across her mouth, stepping away from me, her eyes narrowed and furious.

"Meredith," I said again, louder this time and more determined. "We need—"

"King Christophe," she said, executing an appalling curtsey.

"Stop it," I barked harshly.

She straightened and slammed her hands on her hips as she looked at me. "You can't do that," she said.

"You are my wife!" I yelled, frustrated and cranky.

"That doesn't give you the right to do...that!" She flicked her hand around to indicate the embrace and kiss.

I raked a hand through my hair and took a deep breath, letting it out slowly. "Meredith," I said calmly but through gritted teeth, "we need to talk."

"There's nothing more to discuss," she said, her eyes not meeting mine. "You have the annulment papers. This nightmare will all be over as soon as you sign them."

"Nightmare?" I snapped.

She lifted her chin and stared me down. "What would you call it?"

I took a step toward her, not willing to let her reduce what was between us to some flippant comment. She stepped back and her foot got caught on a trailing vine. I caught her as she fell and when her eyes met mine I could see all her fear and worry reflected in her eyes.

"Meredith," I said softly. "*Agapoúla mou.*"

I brushed a soft kiss across her lips and I felt her melt against me. Why couldn't she just trust what this was between us?

"Jamie, I—" Her voice was tremulous as she looked up at me with wide blue eyes.

The scrape of a footstep on the flagstone path had Meredith jumping out of my arms once again, dragging a long suffering sigh from me.

"Your highness," Danika said, coming around the corner, her head down and looking at the tablet that she carried with her constantly. "The queen has arrived." She looked up then and took in Meredith and me. It was a credit to her professionalism that she didn't react to what undoubtedly looked suspicious.

Meredith shot a quick look at me and then back at Danika. "I - I need to go." She turned and fled. I took a step to follow her, but Danika cleared her throat and stopped me.

"Dammit!" I said with a frustrated growl. I took a deep breath and turned back to Danika. "Let's go," I said.

Meredith

OF COURSE SHE HAD TO INTERRUPT US! I THOUGHT AS I STORMED back the way I had come. The foliage slapped at my legs and I took out my frustrations on the overgrown vegetation that had the misfortune of getting in my way. Danika had once again come into my life and ruined everything. From the first moment I had laid eyes on that woman she had been causing me nothing but pain. I knew my ranting wasn't fair, but jealousy and frustration were not rational emotions and I was just out of control enough to let them rage unchecked inside me.

I reached the steps at the entrance of the garden and jogged up them, stopping to take a deep breath at the top. I couldn't go in and greet the queen with all this *mess* inside me. My mother and father were with Alyssa and I needed them to stay blissfully unaware of what was going on between Jamie and me. I needed to get all this stuff inside me under control and locked away tight.

But that kiss...kisses.

Oh my god! All this time I had convinced myself that it wasn't as good as I remembered. I had tried to tell myself that it was just the silly, girlish feelings of a crush and that I had built it all up in my head to be better than it really was. Jamie had just run over all those protests and then backed up and run over them again. One touch of his lips on mine and I was lost. Completely and utterly lost to him.

I heard footsteps and voices as Jamie and Danika approached the stairs from the garden. I took off toward the palace. It was cowardly, I knew, but I didn't care. I couldn't see the two of them together and not feel like tearing the other woman's throat out. I couldn't bear to see their heads lowered together as they discussed the day to day running of the palace and whatever other business that they had to discuss. They shared confidences that I would never be part of and it hurt. Like, physically hurt. I rubbed at a spot on my chest as I took the stairs up to the back entrance to the palace.

I wanted it to be me who he shared those confidences with.

I stepped through the doors into chaos. Maids looked shell-shocked and footman were racing around but not achieving a damn thing. I knew all of Jamie's staff were new. Anastas had dismissed all the original staff when he had stormed the palace and then as funds grew tight, the staff he had managed to employ and keep were slowly let go when he couldn't afford to pay them. From what I could see, no one was in charge and the rest of them had no idea what do to.

With a deep sigh, I clapped my hands sharply, which caused everyone to stop and stare at me.

"What is going on?" I asked. They looked guiltily at one another before one of the older maids answered.

"The queen has arrived," she said.

"And?"

The maid gave a quick look at the others before replying. "They want tea."

I couldn't stop myself from rolling my eyes. Seriously?

"Haven't you served tea before?"

"Well, yes," the maid answered, "but not to a queen and a prince and a duke and a duchess."

"Right," I said. "This is what you are going to do."

I handed out instructions like I was taking point on a mission into enemy territory. I had grown up with being served tea, but I had never been the one to give directions before. I was surprised at just how much I knew. My mother's lessons had obviously rubbed off on me despite my attempts to block them. I spent the next half an hour giving directions and spot checking everything before it went out to the sitting room. When sanity was restored and everyone was safely entrenched in their chores I looked up to see Freddie watching me.

"What?"

He shrugged and smiled as he straightened. "The queen would like to see you."

I looked around and spotted Tonia, the maid who had been brave enough to speak up earlier. I waved her over. She sketched a quick curtsey when she reached us. "Yes, Ma'am?"

"Have you got everything under control?" I asked.

She nodded. I had promoted her to head maid so that she could oversee the others, that way I only had to show her how to do something and she could show the others so I could turn my attention to the footmen.

"I need to go into see the queen. Will you be okay now?"

She nodded and curtsied again before turning around and clapping her hands to get everyone's attention. I hid a smile behind my hand as I turned back to Freddie. "Okay, let's go."

He gave me a shallow bow and swept his hand out for me to go before him. I slapped his shoulder on the way past but couldn't hide my own grin. I had surprised myself and I felt strangely proud of myself. I hadn't done much, really, but still it gave me a warm feeling inside. I might no longer be part of the royal guard and I may be floundering in trying to find where I now belonged, but I could still lead the troops when I needed to, even if they were maids and footmen and not actual troops.

CHAPTER 23

Jamie

"So, how did it go with Meredith?" Freddie asked as he handed me a glass of whiskey, the ice cubes clinking against the tumbler.

I glowered up at him. "Your sister has to be the most stubborn, irritating woman I've ever known."

Freddie just laughed as he took a seat opposite me and then sipped from his own glass. "That she is."

I pushed back from my desk and rocked back on my chair, looking at the ceiling. "We were interrupted before I could actually say what I wanted to say. The blasted woman ran from me when she first saw me and I had to chase her through the garden. Even when I cornered her, she kept shoving the annulment at me." I stopped and shook my head. "It's like she already made up her mind."

Freddie studied me over the rim of his glass. "You didn't think this was going to be easy, did you? We *are* talking about Meredith."

I sighed gustily and leaned forward to pick up my glass. "I know. It's actually one of the things I like about her, her tenacity and her willingness to put others before herself. I just wish she would stop being a damned martyr for one minute and let me talk."

We sipped our drinks in silence for a moment and then Freddie said, "What else is going on?"

I looked at him for a long time before I spoke. I didn't know how to say what was on my mind without offending him.

"Just spit it out," he said, interpreting my silence.

"Okay." I sighed. "What if I get her to listen to me and we move forward and she agrees to stay as my wife and she becomes my queen... what then? Meredith hates everything to do with this life. She turned her back on it for the guard, what would make her want any of this with me? And even if she does, what would she do all day? Meredith needs focus, she needs a goal and to be busy. I can't exactly see her sitting around entertaining other ladies of the peerage."

Freddie tried to hide his smile, but I could see the laughter in his eyes. "You need someone like Meredith by your side," he said. "Your country is in a mess, the last thing you need is a queen who will sit around all day and entertain. You need someone who isn't afraid of hard work and is willing to roll up her sleeves and get stuck in beside you."

He was right. It wasn't that I had forgotten how much work there was still to do, it was more that I hadn't ever pictured someone willing to work beside me to get it done. My mother hadn't concerned herself with the affairs of the king. Maybe if she had, none of this would have happened.

"Meredith would do that." It wasn't a question but a statement of fact.

"She would," he said. "She already has."

I looked at him curiously. "What do you mean?"

"When I went to find her this afternoon, do you know where I found her?"

I shook my head. I had been too preoccupied with greeting the queen and Will.

"She was in the scullery directing the maids and footmen to serve tea. Apparently they were in a right old mess when she'd walked through the door and didn't know which way was up. Meredith got them sorted."

"What?" I barely contained my choked laughter.

"I know," Freddie smirked. "I was a little stunned myself, but from what I gather, she promoted one of your maids to head maid and then proceeded to show them all how to go about serving tea to the queen. Mother would have been so proud."

"I admit I was surprised at how smoothly the tea service went," I said thoughtfully. "They are all new and I don't think any of them have done anything like that before. Come to think of it, dinner service went smoothly as well."

Freddie chuckled. "I think she might have slipped in there and given them a few instructions."

The panic that I had felt earlier, calmed. Meredith wouldn't be anything like my mother as queen, but that was a good thing. I needed a woman like Meredith by my side so that together we could rebuild Kalopsia. More importantly, Meredith wouldn't have time to get bored. There were plenty of things she could get stuck into and none of them involved sitting around and entertaining - although there would be a bit of that and she had proven to be an able hostess even if she hadn't even realised she was doing it.

"Do you need any more convincing?" Freddie asked.

"It's not that I need convincing," I replied honestly. "I love your sister and want to spend the rest of my life with her. My concerns were more that she would say yes and then regret her decision. I want to make sure it is what she wants."

"You are never going to know that unless you ask her," Freddie said.

Meredith

I FELT RESTLESS. ALYSSA AND WILL HAD RETIRED FOR THE NIGHT. Alex and I had chatted for a while but when she started yawning, I left her to get ready for bed. I didn't know where Freddie was, but I didn't think he would be too far away from his wife. I paced my room. It wasn't as grand as the suite I'd had at the palace in Merveille, but it was practical and comfortable. It actually made me a little sad to think about all that Kalopsia had lost under a regime of a despot like Anastas. It was a beautiful country, but I could tell that the people were beaten down. I knew Jamie would be good for them. He would make a good king.

He would be good for me too.

Ugh! Why couldn't I stop thinking about that kiss in the garden this afternoon? Why did it have to feel like coming home?

No! I had to stop thinking like that.

But then why did he kiss me?

Why indeed? And his declaration that I was his wife? What was that all about? I had to admit to myself that it had given me a thrill to hear him say the words. Claiming me. Why hadn't he signed the annulment papers? Is that why he wanted to talk to me?

God! I was sending myself insane with all this thinking. I changed into workout gear and headed into the bowels of the castle. I had been given a tour of the facilities earlier and one of the first things I had been shown was the gym. I needed something physical to work out all this anxiety and frustration. I pushed through the doors and came to a sudden stop. Danika turned from the heavy bag to stare at me.

I hesitated before going any further. She was part of my problem. Coming here and working out while she was in the same room was not exactly going to do anything for my frustration levels.

"Do you want to spar?" she asked, turning to face me.

Okay then. That might do it. I nodded to her and then walked over to a bench that ran along the wall, dropping my gear bag and pulling out some tape to strap my hands.

We circled each other around the mat a few times before I went for her. It was a typical move for me. I always struck first, especially when grappling with a bigger or stronger opponent. I needed to have the advantage and that meant striking first before they could get a hold on me. It helped that I had been wanting to pummel Danika since the moment I laid eyes on her.

We had fought only once before and I remembered she was good. I usually fought men - Jamie in particular - but the other guys on my team too when they would let me. The only other woman I had fought was Alyssa but that hadn't been for a couple of years now. It was different fighting a woman. Her body mass was smaller and she was quicker than I was used to. It didn't take long for me to be sweating and breathing hard. My only consolation was that she was breathing hard too.

I got her to the ground, but she managed to get behind me and before I knew it, she had me in a body triangle. I let myself go limp. It was my only defence. If she thought I'd given up, she might loosen her hold and I could get free. No such luck.

"Giving up?" she asked without releasing her hold.

"No," I replied stubbornly.

"Good," she said, "I'd hate to think our queen would give in so quickly."

I froze. "What did you say?"

She chuckled in my ear, her hold still tight. Her legs locked around my body and squeezed, making it hard to breathe.

"You heard me," Danika said.

"How did you know?"

"I was having you followed the whole time you were on Le Beau," she said.

"Why didn't you say anything?"

"It wasn't my place to tell."

Anger flared in me. "And yet you continued to flirt with Jamie."

She snorted. "It was part of my cover. Besides, I wanted to see what you would do. But you didn't do anything except huff and puff. You could have put me in my place, told me to back off, challenged me to a duel. But you did none of those things. Why? Don't you love him?"

"I couldn't break cover," I said lamely.

Danika snorted again. "Not even for the man you married?"

"We were drunk—"

Danika rolled us over and let the hold go, standing and walking away from me. I got up off the floor, stunned.

"What?" I asked.

She turned on me, eyes blazing. "You are not the woman I thought you were," she said.

"Excuse me?"

"You are weak, Meredith. You are all bluster and no backbone. If you are not willing to fight for the man you love then you have no place being a queen of Kalopsia. We need someone who is strong and will stand up for the people and support the king as he rebuilds us into something great again. Not someone who runs away at the first sign of trouble. Not someone who cowers and hides instead of facing the truth. Go back to Merveille and your country estate where no one will challenge you. Go back and sulk in your misery. We don't need a queen like you."

She turned her back on me again and walked away. I stood looking at her for a moment before my anger got the better of me.

"I am not a coward," I yelled at her. "I am trying to do what is right!"

She swung around to face me. "No, you are doing what is easy. Walking away from King Christophe was the easy thing to do. The hard thing, the courageous thing would have been to stand beside him and maybe even take some of the hits for him. Instead you got your feelings hurt and ran away. That is not love and that is not courage."

"You don't know anything about me," I spat.

"The road ahead won't be easy," Father Felipe had said. "You will need to cling to one another through the storms to come. You will need to be prepared to forgive when necessary and fight for one another and for what you have found together."

The memory of Father Felipe's words came to me unbidden. I had thought he was talking about something else, I thought he had been talking about the battles I would have with my mother. But he had known who Jamie really was that night. He had known that the battles would be bigger than I could have ever imagined.

"I have been watching you for months. I know you better than you think. This," she flicked her hand up and down at me, "this bluster, it is nothing more than a summer squall. It blows up fast but blows away just as quick. There is no substance. Since I've been watching you, all I've seen you do is whine about your circumstances. Poor little privileged girl has to leave the royal guard and take up a title. Boo hoo. Meanwhile, King Christophe had to face his demons and come back to a place that took his entire family away from him. Where were you for him then? You ran away to lick your wounds and whined about how it wasn't fair. When was the last time you thought about anyone other than yourself?"

I flew at her then. All my anger and frustration mixed with the shame of her words being right. I had been a coward. I had run away instead of facing the truth. I was in love with Jamie and instead of fighting for him, I had run in the other direction because I was afraid of getting hurt. I was afraid of him telling me I wasn't good enough. My whole life my mother had looked at me like I was a disappointment to her. I wasn't the proper lady she had wanted and I never lived up to her expectations. Being with Jamie when he was just a guard was easy, there were no expectations. Being with him when he was a king made all my insecurities rise and choke me. What if my mother was right? What if I was a complete failure as a titled lady? I couldn't embarrass Jamie like that, I couldn't burden him with my failings.

Danika took me to the ground again and held me once again in the body triangle. I had shown my weakness to her and now she would exploit it.

"Are you in love with him?" she asked when I finally stopped struggling.

"Yes," I replied. There was no longer any need to lie.

"Then what are you going to do about it?"

CHAPTER 24

Jamie

I slept fitfully. The words I needed to say to Meredith went around and around in my head and I knew I wouldn't get any peace until we actually talked. Managing to get her to talk to me without running off was going to be a problem and I really had no solution, bar locking us both in a room together until she listened to what I had to say.

Giving up on getting any more sleep, I rolled out of bed and pulled on some sweats. It was still early and the palace was quiet as I padded through the halls and down the stairs until I reached the gym. I could hear the thwack of someone using the heavy bag and I paused outside the door. I contemplated turning around and going back to my room, but maybe sparring with someone might just take the edge off what I was feeling.

I stepped through the door and froze. Meredith had her back to me and I watched as she threw punches at the bag. The muscles in her back shifted with each punch and I couldn't help but admire the strength of her body. I loved that she was more concerned about her body strength than how she looked in a dress - not that she didn't look good in a dress. Some of the women I had dated would never work out with such intensity for fear of developing too many muscles, but I found Meredith's muscles attractive.

I cleared my throat and took a step forward, but she didn't turn around. As I got closer I noticed the white earbuds in her ears. With a grin, I tapped her on the shoulder and then ducked as she swung around, throwing a punch in my direction. She saw me and her eyes widened before she pulled the earbuds out of her ears and glared at me.

"You should know better than to sneak up on me," Meredith said with a growl.

"I'm sorry," I replied, "I did try to make my presence known, but you seemed too engrossed in whatever it was you were listening to."

I could hear the music blasting from the earbuds still as they hung around her neck. The music was loud.

"Alter Bridge," she said and then turned it off.

"Pardon?"

"Alter Bridge," she said again. "The band I was listening to."

I nodded.

"What are you doing here?" she asked, walking past me and over to the bench where her gear bag was.

"Couldn't sleep. Thought I could do with a workout."

She grunted a response before taking a long swallow from her water bottle. I watched as her throat moved and had to swallow myself. I looked away. I couldn't let my body derail me. It was the first time she was actually being civil to me, I needed to take advantage of it and finally get her to listen to me.

"Feel like sparring?" I asked.

She lowered the water bottle and looked at me without speaking for so long I thought she was just going to ignore me.

"Okay," she finally said.

I took a deep breath as we walked over to the centre of the mat. I hadn't actually sparred since coming back to Kalopsia. I swung my arms around a few times and rolled my shoulders to warm them up. We faced each other and bowed before beginning to slowly circle one another.

"What do you think of the island?" I asked her.

"It's beautiful," she said and then lunged for me.

I always forgot how quickly she could move. There was something so graceful about watching Meredith when she fought. Her body flowed from one move to another with a fluidity that was mesmerising. I had forgotten. I had forgotten how much I enjoyed the time we spent in the gym.

She became more aggressive as my body warmed up and I couldn't help but smirk. She had been going easy on me but it appeared that now the gloves were coming off. My brain might have forgotten what it was like to spar with Meredith, but my body did not. I relaxed into the muscle memory of what we had done a hundred times before. I was breathing too hard to talk but that was okay. I needed this - *we* needed this. Something familiar. Something to remind us of a simpler time when it was just the two of us and the budding relationship we had been cultivating.

I read her moves and knew I would get to make mine soon. I waited for the right moment and then took her to the mat. I wrapped my leg around her and locked my foot behind my knee, trapping her in the body triangle. She wriggled and tried to worm her way out, but we both knew she couldn't break this hold. She went limp against me, her chest bellowing as she dragged in oxygen. I didn't loosen my hold.

"Now," I said into her ear, "we talk."

Meredith

MY HEART POUNDED IN MY CHEST AND IT WASN'T SOLELY BECAUSE OF the workout I had just had. Jamie's arms were tight around me and his legs kept me immobilised. I knew he wouldn't let me go until he said what he wanted to say. I just hoped that he was willing to listen to me when he was done.

"*Agapoúla mou*," he said softly in my ear and I relaxed back against him.

My love. The endearment rolled over me and I closed my eyes. I hadn't known what the words meant all those times that he had said it to me in the past. After seeing him in the garden the day before, and hearing the words again, I had asked Tonia what they meant. Hearing the words from his mouth again brought tears to my eyes, but I forced them back.

"I have been trying to talk to you for weeks, *agapiméni gynaíka mou*. I know you are angry about my deception but I didn't have a choice. And it doesn't change the way I feel about you."

I squeezed my eyes shut and breathed him in. He surrounded me on all sides - his body was wrapped around mine, his words were in my ears, his scent in my nose. I had longed to be this close to him for weeks and it was my own stubbornness and insecurities that had kept us apart. He thought I was still angry, and I was; I was just angry at myself now, not him.

"And—" I stopped to clear my throat. "And how do you feel about me?" My voice was small and unsure.

His arms tightened around me, bringing me impossibly closer to him. "Meredith," he said, his voice was rough with emotion. "I love you. I have loved you for a long time but was too much of a coward to admit it. I knew how complicated my life was about to become and I didn't want to drag you into it."

"What changed?" I whispered.

"I realised I couldn't live without you," he said.

I wished I could see his eyes. This was a conversation we needed to have face to face. I understood his reasoning for getting me in this hold, I hadn't exactly made things easy on him, but it was time we both behaved like adults and spoke from the heart.

I rolled us to the side and shifted my leg back, breaking the lock of his legs around me before twisting away from him and rolling to my feet. He looked up at me, stunned. I grinned down at him as I stood over him.

"Your head of security showed me a few tricks yesterday," I said.

He smiled as he stood. Then his face turned serious again. "You're not going to run from me again, are you?"

I shook my head and stepped close to him, resting my forehead on his chest. His arms came around me loosely, resting on my waist, and we stood like that for a few heartbeats before I turned my face up to his.

"I need to apologise to you," I said. He began to protest but I lifted my finger to press against his lips. He stopped speaking and waited for me to go on. I took a deep breath. Admitting I was wrong was never an easy thing to do. "I overreacted," I said in a rush. "I got scared and pushed you away because I knew I wouldn't survive if you told me you didn't want me."

"You know that makes no sense, right?" he asked with a small grin.

"I know," I said, "but sometimes I'm a little irrational."

He chuckled and drew me closer. "And prickly, and infuriating at times but also sweet and kind and beautiful. I love you Meredith. I loved you when we went to the chapel and spoke our vows and I loved you when you told me you wanted an annulment, and I love you now. I know I will love you for the rest of my life and I want you with me for that long. I know it's a lot to ask, I know you would be giving up a lot to take on me and this broken down country that I have inherited, but I have to know if you would ever consider staying my wife and being my queen?"

I realised then that I had never told him that I loved him. He had spoken the words to me several times and yet I couldn't remember returning the sentiment. I reached up to cup his face in my hands and looked into his eyes, eyes that were dark and stormy and full of hope that warred with doubt. I had put that doubt there and it made me ashamed of my cowardice.

"I love you, Jamie," I said and then pushed up onto my toes and fit my lips over his. He was frozen for a moment and then his lips responded and he tightened his hold on me. My arms went around his neck and my fingers burrowed into his hair. I couldn't comprehend just how good it felt to be in his arms again. My heart soared and the tension that had been my constant companion over the last months, melted away.

"Is that a yes?" he asked when we came up for air.

I smiled, "It's a yes. *S'agapo. Se latrevo.*" I stumbled over the unfamiliar words but the way his face lit up when I spoke them made it all worth it.

He kissed me again and I melted into him. I knew we would still have obstacles to overcome but I knew that, as clichéd as it sounded, we would face them together.

He broke the kiss and looked down at me, his eyebrows furrowed in concern.

"You do know what this means?" he asked. "You do realise you will have to move here and give up your place as a royal guard and as a member of Alyssa's ladies in waiting? You will need to move away from your family and friends and face the wilds of Kalopsia."

"Kalopsia is hardly 'the wilds,'" I said with a chuckle. "And yes I realise what being your wife means. I am prepared to do it all - anything and everything it takes to have you in my life." He picked me up and spun me around before kissing me soundly. "There is one thing you will need to do for me though," I said when he put me down.

His brow furrowed adorably as he looked down at me. "Anything. Name it."

"You need to tell my mother."

Jamie

I FELT LIKE I WAS TWELVE AND BEING CALLED INTO MY FATHER'S office for a reprimand, not a king in his own right. I had been back to my rooms and showered. It had been hard to leave Meredith when I had finally gotten her to admit her feelings for me, but there was something I needed to do before we could announce our relationship to the world. I took a breath and gave my hands a quick wipe on my trousers before knocking on the door.

"Enter."

I pushed the door open and stepped into the office. Lord Bingham sat behind a desk and when he looked up at me, he smiled.

"Jamie," he said and then chuckled. "Your Royal Highness," he amended and stood before bending his head in a respectful bow.

"Don't," I said, stepping forward. "Just call me Jamie."

"Okay," he said and then walked around the desk and over to the arrangement of couches by the bookcases.

We sat and he looked at me curiously. I swallowed and clasped my hands together, leaning forward.

"I um, well, that is..."

Lord Bingham chuckled again. "Whatever it is, Jamie, just tell me. Is it about you and Meredith?"

My head shot up and my eyes connected with his. "You know?"

He shrugged. "I've seen the way you look at her and the way she looks at you when no one is looking. I figured there might be something between you."

I exhaled roughly and sat back in the chair, raising my eyes to the ceiling. "There is," I said. "Something between us, but it might not be what you think."

"Go on," he said, his voice more serious now.

I sat up straight and looked him in the eye. "I am in love with your daughter, sir," I said, "and although it is a little late, I would like to ask your permission to marry her."

Lord Bingham studied me and I tried not to squirm. "Why is it a little late?" he asked, steel in his voice.

"Because we're already married," I said and dropped my head. "When we were on Le Beau, before all this happened. We were both a little sad and a little reckless. We had been seeing each other in secret and I wanted more. I wanted to shout it from the rooftops that I had fallen in love with her so with a little bit of liquid courage, I proposed. She said yes. Father Felipe has a chapel there and he agreed to marry us."

I hadn't looked away from Lord Bingham and I tried to read his expression, but the man was a vault.

"Why has it taken this long to tell me?" he finally asked.

"Because the next morning, Meredith asked for an annulment. When we went to the registry office, they told us we would have to wait thirty days. Then there was the attempted kidnapping in Barcelona and the whole exiled prince thing came out and frankly Meredith wanted nothing more to do with me. A couple of weeks ago she sent me annulment papers."

"I knew there was something going on with her," he said quietly to himself. "Fool girl. Why didn't she come to me?"

"I'm sorry," I said. "I understand if you don't want to give us your blessing. Meredith wanted to be here but I insisted I needed to speak to you alone. I know I should have spoken to you before this, but it has taken me this long to convince Meredith not to dissolve our marriage. I know it is unconventional and that you may have misgivings about Meredith being here with me but I want you to know that I love her with all my heart and I will take care of her and keep her safe."

Lord Bingham snorted. "Don't let her hear you say that." He stood too and walked over to me. "Jamie," he said, "I couldn't be more thrilled that you and Meredith have found each other. I'm upset that you both felt as though you needed to hide it from me. I couldn't ask for a better man to love my little girl."

Lord Bingham pulled me into a hug and my heart clenched. This man had always been kind to me and had stepped in when my own father couldn't. Having his blessing was an honour and I was so incredibly glad to have it.

"Now," he said, stepping back and looking at me with a glint of mischief in his eyes. "We need to tell Meredith's mother."

I groaned inwardly. Lady Bingham had always been a harder nut to crack. She hadn't known who I really was when I came to live with her as a boy. All she knew was that I had been rescued from a dangerous situation. She hadn't had a problem with me being in her home, but she had had a problem with me playing with her children. I knew she hadn't approved of my relationship with Freddie and that couldn't have been more obvious than when I was a groomsman at his wedding. Things had changed, obviously, but I still wasn't sure that she would be all too pleased that Meredith and I had gotten married.

Lord Bingham chuckled at my obvious discomfit. "It's alright, I won't feed you to the dragon. I'll be right there by your side."

"How did she take the news when she found out who I really am?"

Lord Bingham cleared his throat. "Yes, well, I'm still in the doghouse over that."

"Maybe we should wait—"

"Ah, no. I think it's best if we rip the bandage off and tell her now. Get it out of the way so she can concentrate on the fact that her daughter married a king."

"Right," I said, straightening my jacket and pulling at my cuffs.

Meredith

I SAT ACROSS THE BREAKFAST TABLE FROM MY MOTHER AND PICKED at my food. I knew Jamie had gone to speak to my father and my stomach was a mess of knots, making eating an impossibility. Alyssa breezed into the room, followed by Will, and she smiled at me. I hadn't told her what had transpired between Jamie and me. I wanted to make sure my parents knew first. Freddie and Alex followed the royal couple into the room and my heart sank. Any hope of having a private conversation with my mother had just flown out the window.

"What is with you this morning?" Mother asked.

I looked up at her. "What do you mean?"

She waved her hand at my plate of scrambled eggs. "The eggs have already been tortured enough, don't you think? They don't need any more from you."

I looked down at my plate and saw the mess I had made of my breakfast. I laid my fork down and covered my plate with a napkin. "I'm not hungry, I guess."

"Really Meredith," she admonished. "Why fill your plate if you're just going to play with it?"

"Yes, Mother." I looked down at my lap. I was too nervous about what was going on between Jamie and my father to get too upset with the way my mother spoke to me.

The door opened again and there he was. My Jamie. He sought me out first and my heart gave a little skip when our eyes connected. He smiled and some of my anxiety left me. My father stood behind him and gave me a wink over Jamie's shoulder which made me grin. One down, one to go.

"Your Royal Highness," Mother said, rising from her seat.

"Oh please, no. You don't have to do that," Jamie said. He took a breath and sought my eyes again before speaking. "I was wondering if I could have a word with you Lady Bingham."

"Of course," she said as she shot a look at Daddy, who smiled encouragingly. "Shall we—"

Daddy shook his head. "I think here will be fine."

"But..." Mother looked around at the audience who looked on with rapt attention.

Daddy smiled. "What Jamie has to say can be said in front of everyone." He turned to the others. "Take your seats."

I stood and walked over to Jamie. He took my hand and looked down at me with adoration in his eyes. How could I ever have believed I could live without him?

When everyone had taken their seats, Jamie cleared his throat. "I—"

"We," I said, cutting him off. He looked down and me and smiled.

"We have an announcement to make."

I felt the weight of everyone's eyes on us, but I kept mine on Jamie.

"Meredith has agreed to be my wife," he said with such affection and softness that I felt my heart melt just a little.

"Oh thank goodness," Alyssa said.

"About time," Freddie said at the same time.

I glanced over at them, their faces bright with smiles.

"What?" Mother asked, shooting a look at Daddy. "I, ah, I don't understand."

"It appears young Jamie and Meredith have been seeing each other for a while now," Daddy said.

"Yes, and, um, we may have eloped while we were on Le Beau," Jamie added.

"What?!" Mother jumped to her feet, her eyes darting between Jamie and me. "You're already married?"

I looked up at Jamie and squeezed his hand. "We are," I said. I held out my hand and showed the plain gold band that adorned my ring finger. The same band that I hadn't taken off this whole time. "Wait," I said, looking at Freddie. "You knew?"

He grinned and leaned back in his chair. "I am a close personal friend of the king," he said.

Alyssa threw a napkin at him across the table. "I was the one to tell you, not him."

Jamie blushed. "Yes, well. Meredith didn't exactly make it easy on me."

Mother sank down in her chair. "Oh. This will never do," she said.

"Pardon?" I asked, turning to her. "You can't possibly have an objection to Jamie and me being married."

She looked up at me like I was talking gibberish.

"I love him and I don't care what you think. Jamie and I are married and we intend to stay married."

"What are you on about?' Mother asked, her brows furrowed. "Why would I object? I only ever wanted you to be happy."

Now it was my turn to frown. "You just said, and I quote, 'This will never do.' What did you mean by that other than you don't approve of us being together?"

"I didn't mean that I don't approve," she said, looking stricken. "I just meant that the king can't have eloped. His country needs something special, something that they can celebrate and unite together over. A royal wedding is the perfect thing."

I looked up at Jamie. "What do you think about that?"

"I agree with your mother," he said. "Will you marry me again, Meredith?"

I pushed up on my toes and brushed my lips across his in a chaste kiss. "I would love to."

CHAPTER 25

Meredith

"May I come in?"

I turned at the sound of my father's voice. We had barely had a moment to talk since everything had been revealed and I couldn't help but feel that I had somehow let him down by walking away from the Bellemere title.

"Hi Daddy," I said.

My father swallowed as he looked at me and his eyes went a little glassy. I bit my lip to stop my own tears from falling.

"You look so beautiful," he said coming into the room and closing the door.

My maids made a quiet escape leaving the two of us alone. He was dressed in all his royal regalia. This might be a wedding in a foreign country but it was still the joining of two royal households.

"Daddy," I said with a sniff, turning to lay my head on his chest. "I'm sorry."

"Whatever for, kitten?' he asked, tucking a finger under my chin and tipping my face up to his. His eyebrows were furrowed as he looked down at me with a frown.

"I'm sorry I couldn't be the countess you wanted me to be."

"Oh kitten," he said, his face softening in a sweet smile. "I only ever wanted you to be happy. I wanted you to have a purpose and to see that there was more you could do for your country and your queen than just being in the guard. I knew how seriously you took your job and how it would seem like such a frivolous thing to take up a title. Seeing you with Jamie has made me so happy. Seeing the way you have taken on the role of his wife and queen of Kalopsia has made this old man burst with pride for the daughter of my heart."

I sniffed again, valiantly trying to not let the tears of relief and love overflow and ruin the makeup my maids had spent hours doing.

"But what about the title? What will happen to it now?"

"It's still yours," he said. "And it will go to your daughter or your son - whoever misses out on being the next in line for the throne."

I swallowed. I hadn't thought that far ahead yet. Children. Um, wow.

My father chuckled. "Don't panic," he said. "There's no rush."

"I love you daddy," I said.

"I love you too kitten," he replied and placed a kiss on my forehead. "Are you ready to go down and promise forever to your husband?"

"More than ready," I replied with a teary smile.

IT WASN'T THE SAME POMP AND CEREMONY THAT HAD characterised Alyssa's wedding. It wasn't even as grand as the wedding between Freddie and Alex. But it was beautiful all the same and it was exactly what I wanted.

Jamie asked Father Felipe to come back to Le Beau to perform the rededication ceremony. As far as the people of Kalopsia were concerned, we were getting married for real. We didn't think we needed to publicise the fact that we had eloped.

The ceremony took place in the royal gardens overlooking the Aegean Sea. It was the perfect autumn day with the sun shining and the sky a brilliant cerulean blue. Savannah had made my wedding dress, which was as exquisite as it was simple and elegant. A simple sheath with just a hint of detail on the bust. My father walked me down the aisle and Alex was my matron of honour, with the other ladies in waiting making up the rest of my bridal party. Freddie stood up as best man for Jamie, and Cody and a couple of the other royal guard made up the rest of his groomsman, which included Benjamin. I was shocked to find out that Benjamin had known about Jamie and me all along. The man had one killer poker face.

We repeated our vows surrounded by friends – new and old – and family. It wasn't a big wedding, as neither Jamie nor I wanted a big spectacle, but it was full of love and joy. I was so full of happiness that I felt like I might burst with it. And the way Jamie looked at me just before he kissed me, with those grey eyes all dark and stormy, could not have been more perfect.

In the weeks leading up to the wedding, Jamie had introduced me to his country. For the most part they had welcomed me with open arms. There would always be detractors and people who didn't want to be ruled by a monarchy, but after the decade of tyranny that these people had lived under, most of them were ready to try something new. I was probably not the queen they were expecting, but I felt I was the queen they needed. Kalopsia was in flux and we needed strong women to stand up and help shoulder the burden of rebuilding the nation. I intended to lead by example. I didn't know any other way.

"Are you happy?" Jamie asked, looking down at me as we danced under the stars, surrounded by the people we cared about most.

"I am," I said with a little sigh. I rested my head on his chest and listened to the steady beat of his heart. A heart that beat for me just as mine beat for him.

"You don't regret anything?" he asked.

I tilted my head up so I could look into his eyes. "The only thing I regret is running away when I should have stood by you. Can you forgive me for not having enough faith in us?"

He dropped his head and brushed his lips across mine in a tender kiss. "If you can forgive me for not being totally honest with you."

I grinned at him. "You're already forgiven."

He kissed me again and I heard Freddie whistle followed by a few chuckles. Jamie lifted his head, an adorable blush staining his cheeks.

"May I cut in?" Daddy asked.

Jamie relinquished his hold on me and my father stepped into my embrace.

"Have I told you today how proud I am of you?" he asked.

I smiled up at him. "Only about a dozen or so, but not in the last half an hour at least."

He chuckled. "You are going to make a magnificent queen,' he said, his voice thick. "I always knew you would become someone special."

"Being a queen doesn't make me special," I said.

"I didn't mean it that way, honey," my father said, looking down at me with seriousness. "Anyone can wear a crown. Do you remember when we talked about Louis and Jacques?"

I nodded.

"I have no doubt that Louis would have made a very good king but I think he knew something that no one else knew."

"What was that?"

"That although he would make a good king, Jacques would make an exceptional one. It wasn't the crown, but the man. Louis saw some-thing in Jacques that he knew the people of Merveille would need. And you, my beautiful, sweet, wonderful Meredith have something special inside you that the people of Kalopsia need too. You will make an exceptional queen and it's not because of the crown you will wear; it is because of the woman you are inside."

"Daddy," I breathed as tears streamed down my face. "Thank you daddy for always believing in me."

"I love you kitten."

"I love you too, Daddy."

"Stop making the bride cry, old man," Freddie said, tapping on Daddy's shoulder. "It's time to hand the bride over before she turns into a puddle of tears and snot."

I laughed and wiped under my eyes as my father and my brother hugged. Freddie took me in his arms and began to spin me around the dance floor.

"I love you Mer, you know that, right?"

I looked into his blue eyes that were so much like mine and nodded.

"I'm so happy for you," he continued on.

"I'm happy for me too," I said as I rested my head on his shoulder. "You will come and visit me, won't you?"

He held me a little tighter. "Just try and keep us away."

I was going to miss everyone. I had grown used to having a circle of friends around me. I knew I would need to create my own ladies in waiting here in Kalopsia and Mother was already scouting out the possibilities. She was in her element and she beamed with pride every time she looked at me. It was something I had craved all my life, that look. Now that I had it, I realised that it didn't mean all that much anymore. I was proud of who I was as a person and I didn't need that validation from my mother. Did that mean I was finally a grown up?

"So who do you think will be next?" Freddie asked.

I looked up at him. "What do you mean?"

He grinned. "All of Alyssa's ladies in waiting are dropping like flies. There are only two left. So who will it be? Margaret or Savannah?"

I looked over his shoulder and spotted the two women in question in the crowd. Savannah was hard to read. She always looked impatient or as if she had somewhere else more important to be. Right now she was staring down a waiter with her trademark look of disdain and the poor boy was trembling. Margaret was her polar opposite. The shy wallflower hung back from the crowd, her head down as she tried to make herself invisible. Neither one of them looked like a good candidate for a romance story.

"There's a pool going," Freddie said, winking mischievously. "My money's on the quiet one."

Just to be contrary I said, "Then my money's on Savannah."

Freddie laughed as he swirled me around the dance floor.

"My turn," my husband said, cutting in.

Freddie slapped him on the back as he passed me over into Jamie's waiting arms. "Take care of her," Freddie said as he backed away, "or I'll come for you."

Jamie looked down at me. "I will," he said. "Always."

Jamie

I LOOKED OVER AT MY WIFE, WHO WAS LAYING ON A SUN LOUNGE IN a bright red bikini with a big pair of sunglasses covering her eyes and a hat with a brim so large I was pretty sure you could see it from space. I couldn't help smiling. These last few days with Meredith could not have compared to anything that had come before. I hadn't known it was possible to love someone so much or so hard.

I held up a bottle of sunscreen. "Do you need me to apply some more?" I asked, wiggling the bottle.

She chuckled and adjusted her glasses. "You only put some on not five minutes ago."

"I know, but I wouldn't want that pretty pale skin to get burned."

"I'm sure that's the reason you want to apply my sunscreen. To protect my skin."

I couldn't see her eyes, but I imagined she was rolling them at me. I couldn't help it if I wanted to run my hands over her skin, especially since there was so much of it exposed.

I turned my gaze back to the shore and the softly crashing waves. The beach was private with no access other than from the palace on the cliffs above. It was a long, steep trek, but one we had both braved every day since the wedding. Autumn in the Mediterranean was almost perfect beach weather and I intended to enjoy it as much as I could for as long as I could. Real life would intrude before we knew it and then I didn't know how long it would be before we would have this amount of alone time together again.

"You're not sad that we didn't go somewhere else for our honeymoon?" I asked.

I felt her hand on my shoulder as she sat up and leaned against my back. "No," she said. "This is perfect."

It was a far cry from the Alpine vista of Merveille and I hadn't realised how much I missed being by the sea until coming back here. Merveille was beautiful, but it couldn't compare to the white sandy beaches and aquamarine ocean that was right on our doorstep.

"I love it here," Meredith said, echoing my thoughts.

"I love having you here with me," I said, turning to kiss her.

There was a long road in front of us. Kalopsia was still floundering and it would be many years before we became the nation we once were, but I was ready for the work. I relished it. And I was so happy to know that Meredith would be there, right alongside me as we did this together. She had fallen in love with the island and the people and I couldn't have asked for more. The most amazing thing was watching the country fall in love with her. She was not what they had expected and I had held my breath for more backlash because I married a foreign woman. It hadn't come and I didn't think it would, not with how Meredith had shown the people that she was there for them. Her genuine care and vision for the future spoke volumes. The people of Kalopsia could see that she wanted us to be great again and was willing to roll up her sleeves and help. I'm pretty sure the opinion polls had her ahead of me as preferred leader and I didn't mind in the slightest. She had bloomed under the responsibility of being the queen of a small, struggling country and I couldn't wait to see what the rest of our life might bring.

"I love you, *agapiméni gynaíka mou*," I whispered, turning to kiss her.

"*S'agapo. Se latrevo,*" she replied.

EPILOGUE

Jed

I urged Mistborn into the woods along the narrow path. The horse was a pain in my butt but he was a dream to ride and seeing as though I was the only one he let ride him, I figured I couldn't complain too much.

The morning was cold and snow was thick on the ground. The woods provided a bit of shelter and the ground, although frozen, wasn't covered in the white stuff. I still wasn't quite used to the weather, even though this was my second winter in the Alps. It was a far cry from the horse farm I'd grown up on in Kentucky. Everything about living in this small European country had been an adjustment for me, from working for a royal family to the weather, and the fact that they drove on the wrong damn side of the road. At least Cliff and I spoke the same language - one horseman to another.

There was a high-pitched noise on the wind that could've been a bird or some other small animal and Mistborn tossed his head irritatingly. His ears twitched and he started to dance under me. I held my seat, squeezing my thighs together and holding the reins tight. Mistborn was a wily thing and given half the chance, he would toss me from my seat and take off for parts unknown. Ours was a complicated relationship.

The horse had come to be in my care when it was given to the queen as a coronation gift. A pure-bred Arabian with a bad temper, I had thought at the time that whoever had given the gift to the queen probably had a nefarious purpose for doing so. Turned out I was right. But the queen kept the horse, even after he threw her, and I had to respect someone who wouldn't hold an innocent animal accountable for the misdeeds of the people it was unfortunate enough to be under the care of.

Cliff hadn't been so forgiving. I had taken pity on Mistborn and Cliff - the queen's master of horse - had given me his blessing. No one wanted the cantankerous horse, so I had ended up with him by default. He was a beautiful animal and I had a feeling he had been mistreated prior to coming to live in the queen's stables. A strong-willed horse needed a stronger-willed master, but not someone who would try to break his spirit. I suppose in a way, we suited each other. I was sometimes known as somewhat cantankerous myself.

I took a deep breath of the frigid air. I loved this time of morning, before the palace was awake and the day really started. Mistborn and I rode at this time every morning - rain, hail, or shine. We both needed the escape and the solitude to keep us sane for the rest of the day. We had slowly been exploring the large parcel of land that belonged to the crown and I had to admit that the scenery was growing on me, even if the cold wasn't.

We broke through the trees and caught a glimpse of the lake ahead of us. Now that was something to behold, especially with the snow-capped mountains framing the water and being reflected in it. I urged Mistborn into an easy trot as we crossed the flat expanse of land and then headed back under the cover of the woods. I should be starting back toward the stables but there was a curious row of little cottages that I wanted to check out. I had spied them on another ride and decided to come back and see what they were all about. Cliff said they were hunting cabins and were designed with only the barest of essentials for guests of the queen to stay in while hunting in the woods. There hadn't been a hunting party since the king and crown prince lost their lives during a deer hunt. It happened before I came to the palace so I hadn't had the privilege of seeing just what 'the bare essentials' meant when it came to the royal family.

"Maman! Maman!"

I reined Mistborn to a stop and looked around for the source of the voice. There were no children on the property that I was aware of and definitely none that should be this far into the woods.

"Archer!" A woman's voice echoed through the stillness. "Come back!"

"Come and watch me Maman," the little boy's voice replied. "Come and see!"

"Slow down!" the woman called again.

Her voice sounded familiar, but I didn't know who it was. Before I could slide from Mistborn's back, the brush in front of us parted and a little tow-headed boy burst through the woods and into the clearing. He pulled a bright red kite behind him as he ran, not looking where he was going.

Mistborn danced under me and snorted before wheeling around. He reared, his front hooves kicking out at the boy and the fluttering kite. I fought with him, trying to calm him, but when the little boy cried out in alarm, the battle was lost. Mistborn reared again before bucking and kicking out with his back legs. I held on as long as I could, but Mistborn was too strong. I landed with a thump, my head hitting the ground. I experienced a blinding flash of pain before blackness claimed me.

Savannah

I CHASED ARCHER THROUGH THE THICK UNDERGROWTH. I SHOULD never have bought him that kite, but when I had seen it in the toy shop I couldn't resist. The poor child had barely anything to his name and I felt so guilty for having to leave him and Papa alone so much. I thought maybe he and Papa could take it down to the lakeshore and play with it during the day while I worked. The last thing I had expected was for Archer to take off into the woods with it as soon as he saw it.

I heard the unmistakable sound of a horse's neigh – although it sounded more like an outraged cry of indignation. But it was Archer's answering cry that made me move faster. It was one thing to be caught trespassing by the game keeper and another thing entirely for Archer to be trampled by his horse. I broke through the brush and came to a stop at the sight of the big grey horse, who stood stamping his foot and snorting big puffs of steam into the cold air. Archer stood in front of him, looking up at him in wonder.

"Archer," I called softly. "Come here baby."

"Look *maman*," Archer replied without moving. "Isn't he beautiful?"

I looked at the horse again. I recognised the big brute. He was one of Alyssa's horses, but not one that she rode. He had been a gift from that traitor Jordan Wicks. I would never understand why she hadn't gotten rid of the horse after what that man put her through.

But none of that was relevant right now. I kept one eye on Archer and the other on the temperamental horse as I slowly inched forward.

"Don't touch him, Archer," I said calmly, trying not to spook either horse or child. "Just come back here to maman."

"What about the man?" Archer asked, pointing to the slumped bundle on the ground that I had failed to notice.

"What happened?"

"He fell when the horse went up on his back legs," Archer explained patiently. "Do you think he's dead?"

I certainly hoped he wasn't dead. I didn't even know who he was, but if he was riding Mistborn then he must be one of the stablehands. The last thing I wanted to do was to explain how I stumbled upon a dead stablehand in the middle of the woods at dawn.

"Archer, *mon cœur*, I need you to go and get *pépé*. Quickly now."

"Yes *maman*," Archer replied with a sigh.

I waited until he had cleared the horse and the man before approaching the big grey beastie with caution. "You're not going to hurt me, are you?" I asked the horse who snorted at me. At least he had stopped rolling his eyes around and now seemed calm, if annoyed.

I approached gingerly until I could crouch down and see to the man. I pulled back the collar of his coat and gasped. Jed.

His dark lashes brushed the pale skin of his cheeks - skin that was paler than I had ever seen it. I gently brushed my hand through his hair and my hand came away sticky with blood.

"Oh god," I breathed. "Please don't be dead."

I leaned down to see whether I could hear his heartbeat or feel his breath on my cheeks. He moaned lightly and I pulled back, looking down at his face, but his eyes were still closed.

"Jed," I whispered as I ran a finger over his eyebrow, smoothing away his frown.

His eyelids fluttered open and he stared up at me with deep green eyes before they fell closed once again.

"Jed," I whispered again, leaning close enough that his cheek brushed mine. "Please wake up."

He turned his head and his lips brushed mine. I felt a shock of electricity course through me at the touch of his lips on mine and jumped back in shock.

"Mmm," he murmured.

My heart was racing and I didn't know what to do or where to look. I felt my cheeks burn with embarrassment - at what, I wasn't quite sure. Maybe at the inappropriateness of my reaction.

"Come on *pépé,*" I heard Archer say and took a deep breath to calm my racing heart.

"I'm coming, I'm coming," my father replied.

I scooted back from Jed, keeping a careful eye on the horse, who snorted and stamped his foot again at the intrusion, as Papa and Archer came back into the clearing.

"What do we have here?" Papa asked.

"It's Jed," I replied, standing to my feet. "His head is bleeding and he seems to be unconscious. We need to get him into the cabin."

"Do you think that is a good idea, *mon amour?* Shouldn't we just leave him so that we are not discovered?"

"*Non père,*" I replied forcefully. "I will not leave an injured man here to freeze to death. Now help me get him into the cabin."

"But what about us? What if we are found?"

I stood and stared down my father. I loved him, I did, but I didn't particularly like him sometimes. "We will cross that bridge when we come to it," I replied.

Papa threw his hands in the air and then crossed the clearing to help me. We dragged Jed through the snow and back to the cabin where I had hidden my son and my father. Mistborn followed along behind us without any direction. Archer chattered away happily to the horse as if they were best friends. The horse didn't seem to mind.

Want to be the first to know when the next Young Royals book is available?

Sign up on my website (www.emmaleaauthor.com) to get an alert email.

JAMIE'S LETTER

To my dear Christophe,

If you are reading this then all hope is not lost.

I have thought a lot over the last few months about what I would say
to you if everything came tumbling down around our ears. I am
ashamed to say that I was too afraid to voice my fears or to even warn
you what might be headed our way. In that, I failed not only you, but
your mother and sisters too. I am truly sorry that I didn't make sure
you were all away safely before calamity hit.

I wrote this letter after I knew Father Felipe had managed to get
you off Kalopsia safely. My heart is heavy with grief but my hope is
that one day you will return and take your place on the throne that you
were born to sit on.

I loved you from the moment your mother told me she was expecting. The first time I held you in my arms, you stole my breath and my
heart. My son. My heir. But most importantly, the manifestation of
the love I had for your mother.

I have always been so proud of you, Christophe. You always
showed such a fierce love and loyalty and I knew, as I watched you

grow, that you were destined for great things. The mantle of authority hung on your shoulders from a young age and you carried it well. I had no doubt that one day you would become a king for the ages and surpass the deeds of even the greats that came before us. I am only sorry that I will not live to see that triumphant day.

Don't make the same mistakes that I did. Be vigilant and watchful. Never take your position for granted and never forget that as a member of the royal family, you are first and foremost a servant to the people.

Above all else, Christophe, love. Love with all your heart. Don't let the cares of the world harden your heart. I would give everything up to spend one more day with you and your mother and sisters. I would trade my life for theirs and for yours if it meant more time with you.

I regret many things in my life, but the one thing I have never regretted is allowing myself to love and I implore you to do the same. At times the world will try to pull you away from those that hold your heart, but don't let it. Time is finite; use it well. The problems will always be there, but those you love may not be.

And now, my dearest Christophe, son of my heart, let me leave you with these words that my father spoke to me. Be bold and strong. Rule with your head and your heart in tandem. Stride confidently forward but never forget from where you came. And love. Always love.

Your father,

Alesandro Ferdinand Christophe Kostopolous

GLOSSARY

Kalopsia is a fictional place, but I borrowed heavily from the Greek islands for inspiration. In my imagination, Kalopsia's national language is a somewhat augmented version of Greek, which is why Jamie uses some Greek phrases as terms of endearment for Meredith. Below are those phrases (including the Greek letter translation) and the English interpretation.

agapiméni gynaíka mou - αγαπημένη γυναίκα μου - my darling wife
s'agapo, se latrevo - Σ'αγαπώ, Σε λατρευω - I love you, I adore you
agapoúla mou - αγαπημένη μου - my sweetheart/my love

THE YOUNG ROYALS

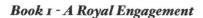

HAVE YOU READ THE OTHER BOOKS IN THE SERIES?

Book 1 - A Royal Engagement

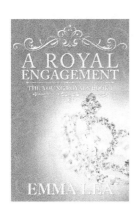

Despite being the second child of the King and Queen of Merveille, Alyssabeth thought that if she kept a low profile she could stay out of the media's glaring spotlight and live a relatively normal life. That was until her father, the King, and her brother, the Crown Prince, was both killed in a hunting accident.

Her dream of joining the UN was no more and instead she needed to return to the small European country of her birth to pick up where her father and brother left off. Her Harvard degree in International Relations is forfeit and in it's place she must become Queen, that was if the misogynistic Parliament can see past their prejudices.

Not much had changed in the small country in her four year

absence, but there are two noticeable differences. Her brother's two best friends Will Darkly and Jordan Wicks have grown up into two very intriguing men. Jordan practically swept her off her feet from the moment she stepped off the plane, but Will's more reserved, darkly intense interest in her gave her tingles.

Alyssa wasn't sure she was cut out to be Queen, but she knew that she wanted to do her father and brother proud, so she was willing to give it her best shot, even if it meant going toe to toe with Parliament. And then there was the small matter of her needing to be married in order to fulfil her birthright and take her place as the Head of State.

Book 1.5 - Lord Darkly
There are always two sides to the story...

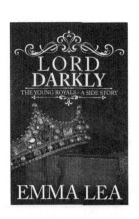

A Royal Engagement was told exclusively from Princess Alyssa's point of view...now see Will's side of the story.

The last few years have been hell for Will Darkly, Duke of Camphrey, Lord of Pemberton. First his mother died, then his father, leaving the estate destitute and we won't even go into how he and his sister were betrayed by someone they trusted. Now, just when he has finally landed on his feet, his best friend, the Crown Prince Jacob St. Benét, is killed in a hunting accident.

Jacob's death brings Will face to face with his childhood crush, the prince's sister, Alyssa, now the crown princess and heir apparent and she's even more beautiful than he remembered. She's also involved with the one man who could cause Will to commit murder.

Grieving for his friend, trying to keep his business moving forward, and avoiding the attraction he feels for his best friend's sister leaves him short tempered and irritable and something has to give before he loses his mind.

Book 2 - *A Royal Entanglement*

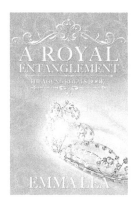

On the day of the new Queen's coronation, a man from Lady Alexandra's past turns up unannounced in Merveille. Lord Frédéric intercepts him and discovers that Alex had left this man at the altar six months ago and now he was here to claim her.

Alex hasn't told anyone the real reason she left everything she had worked so hard for in the States to move to Merveille and take up the position of Queen Alyssa's personal assistant. But now the main reason for her flight from the US has turned up on the palace's doorstep and she is backed into a corner. The only person that she can think of to help her is Freddie, but she's worried that getting too close to him might just do more harm than good.

The last thing Freddie wants is to get entangled with a woman. He liked to keep his options open, but now that he has returned to Merveille for good, his mother is trying her damnedest to get him married off and producing the next Bingham heir. When Alex asks for his help, he is only too eager to help her and maybe get his mother off his back in the process. He never expected to fall for her.

Book 3 - *A Royal Entrapment*

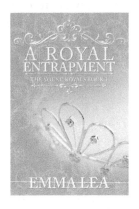

The Queen is getting married and Priscilla is required to work alongside the Lord Chancellor, Dominique, to ensure that the whole affair goes off without a hitch and that they don't, unwittingly, start World War Three. The only problem is that Priscilla finds Dominique insufferable and Dom isn't all that enamoured with Priscilla either.

When Priscilla's sister, Bianca, falls for Dominique's brother, Louis, the two young lovers hatch a plot to ensure that they can spend time together, but it means that Dom has to pretend to be interested in Priscilla and get her to date him.

The more time they spend together, the more Dom and Priscilla start to like each other, except that now Dom is caught in a difficult spot...should he tell Priscilla that he only asked her out because his brother wanted to date her sister, or should he keep quiet and hope she doesn't find out?

Book 4 - A Royal Expectation

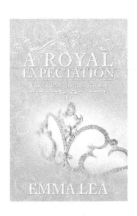

Lady Jeanette Bower had always known what her life was going to look like. It had been drummed into her since she was a little girl. She would marry a titled gentleman and make him a splendid wife who was above reproach. It was what her mother had always wanted for her and Lady Jeanette always did what her mother wanted her to do. She was a good girl. The only problem was, Lady Jeanette didn't expect a six foot four Australian with sparkling tawny coloured eyes and a mischievous grin to walk into her life and show her that there was perhaps another path for her to take.

Drew Taylor had just landed his dream job and the fact that it was half way around the world from his meddling mother was just icing on the cake. He never expected to be swept off his feet by a woman on a hot pink Ducati. A woman who also happened to be one of the queen's ladies in waiting. And then there was the complication of the viscount she was supposed to marry. How could a cane farmer's son from tropical Queensland compete with a man who could give Lady Jeanette the title she had always wanted? He couldn't, but that wouldn't stop him from trying.

ACKNOWLEDGMENTS

I love Meredith's and Jamie's story but it wasn't without its challenges. Jamie was a dream to write but Meredith was quite a bit harder to nail down. She was a complex character who had these two conflicting ideals inside her that I sometimes had trouble articulating. What I loved most about her was that she was so strong but had this hidden sweet side that only came out around her father and Jamie. And Jamie? Well, I fell in love with him right from the first book in the series and was looking forward to writing his story. I'm already thinking of ways to write a spin-off series with him in it, maybe 'The Young Royals - The mediterranean Edition.'

None of this would be possible without the love and support of my family. I am so very thankful for my husband and the encouragement he gives me daily. He is willing to sit down and listen to me prattle on about my imaginary friends and how they are misbehaving and will even offer solutions to plot holes all the while pretending his wife hasn't lost her mind. I love you dearly, my sun and moon.

Thanks also to Kathryn who continues to support me with her words of encouragement and her eagerness to read my very rough first drafts - spelling and grammar mistakes and all.

And I can't mention spelling or grammar without also mentioning Brooke who takes my simple clay pot and polishes it to a high shine.

I am so grateful to these two wonderful women and what they bring into my life. Without them, I would be lost.

ABOUT THE AUTHOR

Emma Lea is a barista, artist, cook, mother and wife. She lives on the beautiful Sunshine Coast in Queensland, Australia with her wonderful husband, two beautiful sons, her dog and cat (both of which are female because, hey, we needed to balance all that testosterone!)

She is a ferocious reader with eclectic tastes and has always wanted to write, but never had the opportunity due to one reason or another (excuses, really) until finally taking the bullet between her teeth in 2014 and just making herself do it.

She loves to write stories with heart and a message and believes in strong female characters who do not necessarily have to be aggressive to show their strength.

If you enjoyed reading this book, please share the love by leaving a review and telling your friends!

To connect with Emma Lea
www.emmaleaauthor.com

THANKS

Thank you for reviewing this book and recommending it to your
friends and family.
Honest reviews are important for authors and I appreciate the time
you have taken to share your thoughts.

Would you like to receive an Advanced Review Copy (ARC) of my next
book? If so, please contact me via my website
(www.emmaleaauthor.com) or my Facebook
(www.facebook.com/emmaleaauthor) page

OTHER BOOKS BY EMMA LEA

This is Emma Lea's complete book library at time of publication, but more books are coming out all the time. Find out every time Emma releases something by going to her website (www.emmaleaauthor.com) and signing up for her New Release Alerts.

SWEET ROMANCES

These are romantic tales without the bedroom scenes and the swearing, but that doesn't mean they're boring!

The Young Royals

A Royal Engagement

Lord Darkly

A Royal Entanglement

A Royal Entrapment

A Royal Expectation

A Royal Elopement

Bookish Book Club Novellas

Meeting Prince Charming

Broken Arrow Trilogy

Broken

Cursed

Eternal

SWEET & SEXY ROMANCES

In my Sweet & Sexy Romances I turn up the heat with a little bit of sexy. No swearing, or very minimal swearing, and brief, tasteful and not too graphic bedroom scenes.

Love, Money & Shoes Series

Walk of Shame

Strictly Business

Skin Deep

In The Money

All At Sea

Love, Money & Shoes Novellas

The Five Year Plan

Summer Fling

Standalone Novels

Amnesia

HOT & SEXY ROMANCES

Hot & Spicy Romances turn the heat way up. They contain swearing and sexy scenes and the characters get hot under the collar.

Recommended for 18+ readers

TGIF Series

Girl Friday

Black Friday

Good Friday

Twelve Days

Twelve Days of Christmas - Her Side of the Story

Twelve Days of Christmas - His Side of the Story

Quickies (Collins Bay Novellas)

Last Call

Standalone Novels

Learning to Breathe

TOO HOT TO HANDLE ROMANCES

These are definitely 18+ reads and contain graphic sex scenes and high level swearing – not for the faint of heart

The Young Billionaires

The Billionaire Stepbrother

The Billionaire Daddy

The Billionaire Muse

The Billionaire Replacement

The Billionaire Trap - coming soon

The Playbook

In Like Flynn

Music & Lyrics

Rock Star

Songbird

Strings

Made in the USA
Las Vegas, NV
10 April 2025

20782652R00154